THE
DOWAGER

THE
DOWAGER

Elise Sanguinetti

CHARLES SCRIBNER'S SONS · NEW YORK

Library of Congress Catalog Card Number 68–25420

10 9 8 7 6 5 4 3 2 1

ISBN 978-1-5011-8409-3

DEDICATED
TO
Edel Ytterboe Ayers

"Why Art Thou Cast Down, O My Soul?"

Part One ～～～

Chapter 1 ❧

The autumn winds came early to Charleston. They cried across the sea and whipped the trees so that the gray moss lashed back like hair on an aging and half-crazed woman.

September was the month for storms. They came with the names of simple girls and threw their hammers like giant gods. This year was no exception. The palms bent double; a television repairman, as he was later identified, was hurled from his second-floor window and dashed dead upon the cobblestone street below. At a private school for girls a middle-aged headmistress summoned an emergency chapel and thanked the Almighty for the preservation of other people's children.

It was not a great matter, really, not as human affairs go; only two killed. There was some attention in other city newspapers, but mostly quickly forgotten. Charleston, as a whole, took it in its stride. The city, "Old Dowager Woman," as the Gullahs once had called it, was accustomed to storms, human and otherwise. Besides, it was good, another season. The sultry summer heat had lifted, another season gone, another come. The gates were unlocked, people returned; there was a newness, freshness in the city. Things would be doing. Charleston things.

Behind the gates, behind the walls, doors, summer slip covers were removed, the straw rugs rolled back, the silver replaced, and a lady sitting at a Hepplewhite desk planned a party for two hundred.

Clearly, then, that year's storm was finished; nineteen hundred and sixty-six; damage slight. The high thick walls had borne well, holding fast, as they always had, against intruders, storms, the uninvited. These were the outside walls, gray and worn, surrounding the gardens and the tall pristine gallery houses. Still, and it is so, there were other walls, too, secret, crumbling, unwanted walls. Human walls, one might say, laboring inside a few of the people who on a blue crisp October day received a finely engraved invitation to a party on South Battery Street.

For these few, it was the inside walls that truly mattered:

They called her Winky, though the origin of the name and the time when it seemed more fitting had long since been forgotten. Only to some of the older families in Charleston, her Aunt Pett's friends, was she Antoinette, Antoinette Lagare Carr. For to besmirch those fine old names by something as "well, really silly" as Winky was ridiculous. Aunt Pett's friends had long memories, and where memory failed invention took its place. Memory and invention. Winky was surrounded by both.

Now, at twenty-five and "home again," she was what the city had once made her, the daughter of Ann and Petrie Carr, the tall blond young woman whose "fine grained" Lagare features were marred only by the two front teeth which crossed slightly, a reminder of the dentistless years when Petrie, her father, had had his "set-back," when they first came to live in the tall antique house with Aunt Pett.

Yet what did Charleston know of her really? Only that she was "likeable," as they say, that she, of course, had made her debut at the St. Cecilia (no divorces in the family, not as far as anyone readily recalled), that she was graduated from

Wellesley—with honors, they thought—and now she was back after a summer at one of those foreign universities, Norway or Denmark, someplace like that. It didn't really matter. Now, tanned and unchanged, she was often seen about the city, at the yacht club, sailing, walking along East Bay, a rather lonely figure really, a gray cardigan around her shoulders. Winky. The American girl, a nice *Charleston* "gehl," as the accent went.

Naturally, there was speculation as to just whom and most of all *when* Winky would marry. It was sad to turn out an old maid in Charleston, hugging to the memory of the long dead and the haunting, aging "receipt" for Peach Leather, a candy. Indeed, it was time for Winky to marry. All her friends were, of course. There was talk, wasn't there, about that Tom Gearhart? Here the smile always appeared, the smile almost benign in quality. Secretly, it would have pleased not-so-accepted Charleston, "likeable" as Winky herself was, should something develop there. It always pleased not-so-accepted Charleston to see one of the old families fail in these matters. For the Gearharts, midwesterners or something, had not passed the rules set down by inner Charleston, the "real" Charleston. Of course they had money. But money, said Charleston, was no passport. Mrs. Gearhart—well, she just wouldn't "do," a certain manner, kept mentioning, hinting actually, the St. Cecilia Ball; one never mentioned the St. Cecilia—bad taste. Mrs. Gearhart was "presuming," as one of Aunt Pett's friends explained it, trying to get "in," you know, buying every antique she could get her hands on and working with the church just for an excuse. ". . . Probably never heard of the Episcopal Church until she became a member of St. Philip's . . ." Oh, there were many tell-tale signs. Pity. The young man seemed pleasant enough, in a kind of over-fed, jolly way. The young people seemed to take to him. "Tom's so funnn-eee . . . I mean the way he . . ." It was obvious his mother was pushing him. Tom was her ticket.

Through all of this Winky kept her silence. For that had been her way these weeks since she had returned. Only inwardly did the fierce emotions ebb and break. The loneliness, the longing was sometimes more than she could bear and once late in the night she waked, startled herself calling the other name: "Walter?" The plea had been such a silent thing heretofore.

Chapter 2 ～

"Bring the mountain to Mohammed!" said Aunt Pett in her command voice, the sherry voice. "Winky shouldn't have to go chasing after somebody like that. He's probably one of those funny people up there anyway."

"Funny people up there" had become a favorite expression with Aunt Pett lately. In her mind's eye she had taken to lumping all "notherners" into one single horrible newspaper vision of the bearded, bejeaned young people she saw working with the Civil Rights movement in the South or else marching down streets in Boston, Philadelphia or New York for whatever cause Aunt Pett never read too closely. "Some *non*sense!" the latter was usually explained away.

Winky started into the drawing room, but at the pronouncement of the words "up there" she hesitated in the hall. Aunt Pett and her mother were having their nightly sherry and discussing— What else? Not the storm that had recently passed, not Tom Gearhart (a sometime conversation, never private), but Winky's planned trip to New York and "that young man up there, Walter whatever his name is." Winky had heard the same talk over and over since she had been home, her mother usually whispering and Aunt Pett forthright as usual. Poor Walter, how amused he would be to be identified as merely someone "up there." Everything she had told him about Charleston had amused him anyway. It angered her at first, the amusement, and rather amazed her to discover her own loyalty.

"I don't know," said her mother with the same touch

of weariness in her voice that appeared whenever the subject of Walter or New York came up. It was not really so much Walter, or even New York, that brought on the tone, Winky had considered. Rather it was the crisis they were in: an only daughter, twenty-five and not married. It was this, the crisis, exaggerated or not, that took precedence now over all her mother's worries. Of course her mother never came right out and said anything, but the sighing and the nervous twisting of the ring were there all the same, a kind of minor, silent panic.

Winky had not yet begun to take the crisis too seriously.

She started to go back to her room. But she stood there, listening, fascinated.

"You don't even know anything about him," came Aunt Pett's voice. "Winky probably doesn't either. You meet somebody in a place like that, a foreign country away from his own surroundings, and you never know *what* they are."

"Everett is his name, Walter Everett. The family's from Pittsburgh, but he's living in New York now. A writer," sighed her mother. "Winky says he writes."

"Writes *what?*" said Aunt Pett. "I wouldn't trust anybody like that. Probably has colored blood in him. You don't know." The second sigh was audible even from the hall. "I'd rather see her married to that—that German around here."

"Tom Gearhart?" her mother asked. "He's not German, Pett. Only the name."

"There's no difference, no difference at all."

"Oh, I don't know. I just don't know. I think Winky has more—"

"Winky has what?" asked Winky, now entering the room.

Both women looked up at her. Aunt Pett was holding

her knitting, one of the seemingly endless white washcloths whose finished products no one ever saw. Once Winky's younger cousin, Felicia Whitfield, had said Aunt Pett looked exactly like Franklin Roosevelt. The remark had always amused Winky, the thought of Franklin Roosevelt sipping sherry and knitting away on an endless white washcloth.

"Oh, hello, dear," said her mother, her blue eyes startled in her increasingly tired face. "You look lovely. The dress is becoming."

Winky was wearing a tweed dinner dress, one her mother had seen for two years now. "Thank you," was all she said.

"Are you going out?" her mother asked brightly, too brightly, Winky thought, like a patch quilt covering a lie.

"Uh, Tom Gearhart's," Winky said. "It's his birthday. He's giving a do for himself."

"Oh?" said her mother not without a tinge of disapproval. "Ask him in then, so we can congratulate him." Her mother's lips pinched into a smile, the forced effort to be pleasant. It always occurred to Winky that her mother knew others were aware of the effort.

"He's not coming by for me, I'm just—"

"Chasing after the young men, I say," said Aunt Pett. "Why can't he call for you here? No manners. No manners at all."

"Because he thinks I'm perfectly capable of driving three blocks to his apartment." Winky hadn't meant to sound abrupt, not with Aunt Pett. Even with it all she really loved the older woman, her father's aunt, who years ago had taken her father as a child and whose strength unwittingly had made him what he was, the gentle, soft-spoken man he appeared, scholarly in mind, weak of purpose, the silent brooder now in his ill health, drinking away his own lost will.

"Piff," said Aunt Pett. "Young men should call for the young ladies! I don't like this new way they're all talking about, young girls going about wearing practically nothing and talking and acting like crazy people." She sipped her sherry, a generous sip. "Where are the parents? Trash!"

Winky's mother began twisting her ring again. Winky looked at her, sitting in the old Adam chair (one of the Petries' pride, as were the Adam mantle, the Hepplewhite, the Chippendale, the carved molding, and the dark portraits hanging on the walls, looking down upon them like masters from their sunless graves.) Her mother's face was strained, her own portrait above her—the dark, short hair, the full blue eyes, thin upper lip, smiling wistfully in her youth as if she knew somehow the years would gray her hair, swell her body, and with imaginary fingers, press the lines into her gentle face.

The lines were well marked now as she sat in the chair, the nearby lamp making a gray halo over her worried face. For a moment Winky wanted to go to her, tell her everything would be all right, and for the time, at least, make her whole again. There were these pulls between her mother and herself, to go or to stay.

"Well," Winky said instead. "On with the sherry! I really have to go. Tom's been acting like a nervous housewife about this whole thing."

"Never heard of a young man giving a party for himself," said Aunt Pett. "Is he a sis?"

For the first time Winky wanted to laugh. She had even asked herself the same thing once or twice, not seriously, just questioned. "No, just anything for a party."

"He sounds like it," said Aunt Pett. "A German sis. All the men are dead, all the *good* men."

"You won't be too late, will you?" asked her mother, ignoring Aunt Pett's latest bit of theory.

"Not too." Winky turned to go.

"Oh, and yes, Winky," said her mother.

Winky turned back to her abruptly. Her mother had never learned the art of farewells. There was always the final message, the final question.

Her mother put her hand over her left breast, a gesture Winky detested. "Pett seems to think—" she dropped her hand into her lap. Her hands were lovely. They were still lovely. "Pett seems to think you really shouldn't go to New York just now. We think— Why don't you invite this Walter down to see *you?* He'd probably like to see Charleston, don't you think? He could stay here, with us." Her voice seemed to trail away.

Winky wanted to smile. Charleston was the last place on earth Walter would want to see, Walter with his passionate love for Scandinavia, the early morning hunts and the fishing trips when the air was cool and the sun warm on the face. "No one said I was actually *going*, did they? I said I *might*, that's all. Maybe look around for a job or something."

"You haven't heard from him then, not since you've written?"

Winky knew she should never have told her mother about Walter. But the anguish of silence had made her blurt out everything in one agonizing night: *She wanted to leave Charleston. No, she couldn't work on the newspaper again. She was suffocating here. With everything. The house tours, the little supper clubs—everyone trying to get in the right one. They're like tribes, jungle rites. And the Junior League . . . Why hasn't he written? Telephoned? What do you think? What DO you think? . . .*

There was something about the transfer of pain, and the pain then had been well marked on her mother's face.

"*You were discreet, Winky? This summer?*"

"*Discreet?*" The word hung between them, awkward, almost obscene. It was the only time talk of sex, even the hint of it, had ever brushed between her mother and herself.

How different that talk than the first night she had returned home. Everything was Walter, Walter: "*. . . Yes, I met this Walter Everett. Uh huh, I went to Pittsburgh right after we got to New York. His family, oh yes, so nice—I think maybe we're going—*"

"He's been terribly busy," Winky said now to Aunt Pett. She pretended to yawn.

"Busy doing what?" demanded Aunt Pett.

"Pett dear," said Winky. "You don't know anything about him. Not one single thing."

Aunt Pett lifted her chin.

"He works. He's writing, every day, very hard."

"You call *that* work? Play; that's all it is. Just play." Pett looked away. "He *is* one of those funny people, probably a Communist." She turned her gaze to Winky's mother. "Those kind of people, you know, nothing but trash, they ought to be put in prison instead of being allowed to roam about the streets."

Winky looked at her, started to say something, thought better of it. She waved at them. "Cheerio, have a nice evening, you two."

"Now, *try* not to be too late, Winky," said her mother. "I think I'll have to go over to the Reveneaux party—just make an appearance." She looked at Aunt Pett. "I really don't want to go, I'm so tired. She's having two hundred people. *Two* hundred!"

"I didn't know Beverly had that many friends," said Aunt Pett.

"It'll be good for you, Mother, to get out, see some people," Winky said.

"I suppose I'll have to go . . ." Her mother put her hand to her right eyelid. ". . . since none of you are going. Petrie said he just wasn't up to it."

Just wasn't up to it, Winky thought. She wondered how long her mother could give the same excuse.

"I should go with you," Winky said. "Please tell them why I'm not there, that it's Tom's birthday."

Her mother said nothing and then with what looked like studied difficulty rose from the chair. "I guess I'll just wear the black dress again."

"It's nice on you," Winky said.

The forced smile appeared once more.

"Tell Miss Boggs to come in to see me, Winky," said Aunt Pett. "She's been worrying about her kidneys again. Speak to her, please."

"Yes, yes I will," Winky said and left the room.

Miss Boggs was Aunt Pett's trained nurse, or Aunt Pett was hers; Winky had never quite decided the order of things. Miss Boggs lived in the house with them and was continuously underfoot, giving little silent, starched messages that her kidneys, too, were forever with them.

Winky hurried down the back stairway. Miss Boggs' room, the former nursery, was behind the downstairs drawing room. Through the closed door Winky could hear the muffled voices of television actors:

"But, Peetah, *dah*ling, don't you seeee? Won't you seeee?"

Male voice (rich and narcissistic): "No, Janice. I've tried.

No man on earth could go through what I've gone through these last four years. *No* man."

"Oh, Peeetah—"

"I'm sorry, Janice."

"But what am I going to dooooo?"

"I . . ."

Winky rapped on the door anyway. Poor Miss Boggs. Winky had always had a certain amount of sympathy for the woman, living in the house with them, neither servant nor equal. She had no living relatives and this over-heated room with the television, the magazines and her African violet was her world, cut off as it was from trays, stairs, Aunt Pett's commands and her own silent wars with Leuvenia, the Negro cook.

Once her mother had said: "I tell you, Winky, it isn't easy being Miss Boggs, living alone like that. You see?" The statement had mildly startled Winky. Did her mother actually see her in the role of this sad woman?

Now, still in her uniform, Miss Boggs was sitting in the one armchair in the room, her nurse's cap lying on the bed like an abandoned head. The gray roots of her hennaed hair had begun to show.

"Sorry to interrupt you, Boggsie." Boggsie! But the name pleased Miss Boggs, and Winky always used it on sensitive occasions such as interrupting one of her television "stories," as she called them. "Aunt Pett wants to see you. I think she's ready to go to bed or something."

Miss Boggs looked at her watch and then back at the television, an almost longing look.

"Any time, actually," said Winky.

Miss Boggs rose from the chair and snapped off the television. "She's not having one of her attacks or anything, your aunt?"

"No, nothing like that—unless you'd call lecturing to me an attack." She grinned at the woman.

Miss Boggs smiled slightly, a twitch, actually, and began putting on her cap again.

"True Secrets of Beauty" proclaimed the title on the cover of a woman's fashion magazine. In there, Winky thought, Miss Boggs had discovered about hennas and lanolites and creams, all the works and pomp of the cosmeticians. What a foul trick.

With her cap on, though, Miss Boggs was her official self again. "Are you going out?" she asked, inspecting Winky from toe to head.

"Tom Gearhart's. It's his birthday."

Miss Boggs smiled benignly, knowingly. "How nize. You need to have a nize time."

Winky looked away. "Oh, we will." She shrugged. "Sort of."

"You're still young, you know. Now is the time to have nize times with your friends."

"I guess so." Winky turned to the door. "Well, good night, Miss Boggs."

"Oh, Winky."

"Yes?"

Miss Boggs put a finger to her lips, a sure sign of intrigue. "Now you know how I am and everything. I mean I don't like to tell on people or anything. I always say 'you mind your business and I'll mind mine.' "

"Of course," Winky agreed.

"But the cook's been at it again."

"Leuvenia?"

Miss Boggs nodded her head. "You know the roast beef we had yesterday. There's not a piece of it left—a *six*-pound roast and it's just vanished." Miss Boggs nodded gravely. "I *saw* her, with my own eyes, put at least six eggs in a sack and walk off with them. Lord knows what else."

"Ohhh me," groaned Winky.

"Now, of course, I don't want to say anything to Miss Ann about it. Poor thing, she's just got more than the Lord should allow—with your—well, your mother's just bowed down, that's all."

The innuendo was a clear reference to her father, Winky knew, but, as usual, she ignored the intention of the error.

Miss Boggs sighed and shook her head, but the excitement was in her eyes anyway. "You just can't get good coloreds nowadays. They're just sitting around waiting for handouts from the government, doing nothing."

"The Navy Yard's employed a lot of them," Winky said. "I guess we just can't compete with the salaries."

"If they aren't getting handouts from the government, they're all marching around trying to be white—singing love songs to us every night over the television!"

It was no secret, of course, Miss Boggs' antipathy for the Negro race. She regaled the entire family about hospital "experiences" she had had, from Chicago to Alabama, terrible stories about young white girls who had been victims of Negro rapes and beatings: ". . . ruined, you know. One of the girls never spoke a word again, just savagely torn apart, you know."

She always told these stories in whispers, her face contorted at the very memory of the scene. Mostly she told them to Winky and her mother, only hinting to Aunt Pett about her terrible "experiences":

"What I've seen in my time wouldn't do to tell in polite society."

"Of course *not*," Aunt Pett always answered. Aunt Pett's own experiences with Negroes had been long, and if not always, occasionally rewarding.

Miss Boggs had become a Republican. That occurred when Lyndon Johnson, she said, declared from his throne that all nurses were required to bathe Negro men. "I'll never enter a hospital again—not even when I'm dying."

"Well, that's too bad about Leuvenia," Winky said.

"I think it's her granddaughter again," said Miss Boggs. "Your mother doesn't know it, but she had the girl out there in her room with her, taking food to her from the kitchen."

Winky started to say that if it didn't bother Leuvenia having the child there, it certainly shouldn't bother anyone else. Besides, that had always been the price for having "help" —brown paper sacks marching out of the kitchen with two eggs here, slices of bread there, a cup of lard. A kind of tradition, one might say.

"We'll talk about it tomorrow. All right?"

Miss Boggs jerked her right shoulder. "Have a nize time with your friends."

Winky closed the door softly. "Lectures, lectures, lectures," she said to herself and walked out into the main hall. The heavily panelled door to the left was closed. She started to open it, to tell her father good night. Each night Petrie Carr went to the library under the pretext of "working on the book." Ever since Winky could remember her father had been writing the book, *Historic Churches of Charleston*. She had actually read three chapters in manuscript, but as the years went on she was never asked to read anything else. Gentleman that he still was, Petrie Carr did his drinking behind closed doors. There were never any scenes or boisterous tempers or high spirits; only silence. They all knew, even Aunt Pett, though the subject was never approached in front of her.

"It's killing him." Winky could hear her mother's voice, the desperate whispering slashing at her own heart.

Why these things? Why to us?

Outside the night was still with a chill brought from the aftermath of the storm. Winky glanced back at the house. How fine it looked now in the night with the light from the carriage lamps thinly veiling its morning scars. The wooden balconies above shone pristine, plain, the work of a singular craftsman. The house was like her father, really, still wearing its pride yet inwardly dying a little. When he was young, when she was younger, her father was tall and good and full of grace. "The Petrie charm—yes, your father has the Petrie charm . . ."

The familiar ache was closed inside her. "It's everything," she said to herself. "Everything." She walked slowly along the walk to the outer wall. Out there, through the tall wrought iron gates, were the streets of Charleston, waiting.

Chapter 3

Tom Gearhart loved food.

His obviously well-fed body was a kind of monument to the fact. Yet, as Winky once said, Tom was the only person she knew who was not offensive in his abundance. Some people even thought he was handsome in a blue-eyed, boyish kind of way. He was tall, fleshly "firm," with dark hair, and he did have a style, picked up at Princeton and sustained through the decade since. Tom was also proud of Princeton. He had a Princeton chair, a Princeton tie, Princeton glasses and pictures—one, he always pointed out, of himself and six of his club members all holding beer steins. Only Tom was holding a small statue of The Three Graces. People always laughed at that one (even if the laughter was forced).

Alas, poor Tom was a school snob, and though he studiedly referred to his own institution as "college," there was never any doubt just where he had gone. Those four short years at "college" had given Tom Gearhart confidence.

Still, his greatest love was food. When he called Winky the night before about the dinner he was giving, he went into rich detail: "Yes, daughter, She-Crab soup—strictly my own. And I've got *the most* sensational cauliflower simply crying for your Hollandaise. It'll be *gorgeous*, angel. Who's coming? The same. No comment."

Tom did not always share the Charlestonians' esteem for themselves, at least not openly. He preferred his own native Cleveland, and it had been a luckless day, indeed, when his parents decided to move nearer the Charleston plant (Gearhart Machine Parts, Inc.). Yet, as a bachelor, Tom was invited and in turn invited back, playing the game, loving the game. Bachelors were at a premium in Charleston, and, besides, the city was pleased to have the Gearhart plant swell their already burgeoning industry. It was only in private that Mrs. Gearhart became the target for the stings of "inner" Charleston. But she knew.

Still, Winky liked Tom. In a way he, with his alternating midwestern R and broad A, was a kind of link with the past and Winky's own college days, a refuge, one could say. They both liked the same things—records, books, wines, "fixing things." They had spent two entire Saturdays re-doing the patio outside Tom's apartment. They had gone to practically every antique store in Charleston looking for old wrought-iron chairs that Tom himself had painted black to go with the small statue Winky had brought back from Oslo (a trip Tom had considered inane, "considering everything").

They knew many of the same people from college days. Tom knew Winky's roommate, a girl with Scandinavian ancestry, who, in much the same loose-end situation as Winky, had talked her into the trip to Norway. The roommate was the reason for Tom's and Winky's meeting in the first place. ("Yes, Ardys told me you were down here in this quaint old city.") Tom also knew Walter Everett. Walter couldn't remember Tom.

So it was that Winky and Tom were declared a couple. Wherever Winky was, Tom was not far behind—all very neatly and rosily platonic, save for one horribly awkward night when Tom, on the precipice of passing out, a not too infrequent occurrence, had attempted in a fumbling, young boy's way to make passionate love, and Winky, half-pitying and half-repulsed, fled the apartment. Neither of them ever mentioned the incident again, though Tom, in a rather jocular way, sometime referred to "when we are married . . ." Once, they had made a proposition. They decided that if by the time they reached forty and were still unmarried they would marry, a kind of planned propinquity.

"By that time you'll probably be the greatest car salesman in South Carolina," Winky had said and wished she hadn't. Tom's "job" was a sore subject, not so much from his own way of thinking but from his parents'.

"Nothing but a car salesman, just a common ordinary car salesman," Tom's mother, after a third scotch and soda, had said to Tom one night when Winky was having dinner with the Gearharts.

"But, Dragon dear," Tom had said. "At least they're *foreign* cars. Isn't that somewhat better?" Tom sold Mercedes. Both Tom's mother and father owned Mercedes.

Winky seldom saw the Gearharts. Most of Tom's "entertaining" was done in his own apartment, a move that had occurred one heated night when his mother had had a particular heyday with Tom's over-abundance and lack of ambition.

"Just look at your father! Look at him! And then see yourself!"

"Those who have the gold make the rule," Tom had said and fled the house, with baggage and a can of mushroom soup.

Winky and Tom together had found the apartment, and Winky was in on most of Tom's "entertaining," helping him shop, straightening up the place, dumping his unwashed shirts into a pile in the closet, leaning out the back door to take a drag on a cigarette—Tom's idea; he didn't want the rooms to be cluttered with smoke before the guests arrived.

Tonight, however, Tom was on his own.

Winky gave a fleeting glance at the cars outside the apartment before she went in. They were all there: Lollie and Dick Pringney (Dick with his droning legal mind extolling in his Charleston accent endlessly on land-line disputes); Suzan and Bob Ribaut; and "oh, my God"—Bill Ashe was back again—Bill, another bachelor, with his lofty wandering eye meant only for Suzan Ribaut, married and mother of one. The eye was reciprocated. No secret.

It would be quite a night.

Winky opened the gate and walked the short distance to Tom's door. The apartment was in "Old Town," as the Charlestonians called it, a house really. An industrial engineer, his wife and "nine thousand children" lived in the other side of the house. The children continuously harassed Tom with their squeals, runny noses and unguided energy. They called him "Uncle Tom," which, with no racial overtures, infuriated Tom. He had told the nine-year-old boy once: "I am in *no* way related to you, Jonathan; now get that straight. Okay?" The remark had amused Winky. The industrial engineer had fathered unattractive children.

The outside of Tom's apartment did not go with the inside. The outside was strictly Charleston with the wall, the gate, the old brick, the Georgian door. Inside, the rooms were chock-full of fading status symbols: pop art, op art, no art and one huge canvas portraying a hideous bloated face of a child-like woman sucking a lollipop.

"Madonna with a Lollipop," Tom had labeled it.

Nevertheless, the apartment managed to bar the outside world, Charleston, which no doubt was the intent. Tom's world was a place of books (few and relics of college days), records, German wines, Princeton, bastard Swedish modern and a roll of dust beneath a Bahamian bar—cozy, careless and completely absorbed. It was Tom's place out of the sun, sprung from ordinary soil, perhaps, but cultivated and trained so that at last the ordinary remained but was hidden with a casualness that belied the cultivation.

His mother, resigned after a full month of pouting after Tom's departure, had tried in her way to remedy some of Tom's taste. She had placed a new, thick, harshly-colored Persian rug on the floor and had had her maid Viola lug in a large reproduction, highly-carved "Chippendale" chair. "Dragon's Throne," Tom had dedicated it, and promptly moved it under "The Madonna."

Winky entered the apartment without knocking.

"Here she is, my paramour!" said Tom from behind the bar. He was wearing a cook's apron with "Come and Get It" embroidered with red thread across the left breast pocket. Tom's aunt in Cleveland had made the apron. "Poor, unfortunate Aunt Mavis," as Tom referred to her once. "She knocks away on a sewing machine all day and eats wieners and sauerkraut at night." Tom never mentioned any of his other relatives.

"It's stuffy in here," Winky said, quickly turning from Tom.

"The room or the people, Winky?" asked Bill Ashe in his tired, new (English) accent, a *tour de force* combined as it was with his normally Charlestonian A's: *leyut* for late; *deyut* for date; *peyupuh* for paper.

"Both," said Winky and laughed. She went over to Bill. "The return of the native."

Bill Ashe kissed her on the cheek. Only recently had he learned that bit of grace.

"When did you get back, William?"

Bill Ashe had a minor job with the State Department,

which kept him travelled and weary and "informed." He was tall and slender with a bow tie, a crew cut and that eye. Whenever Winky thought of Bill Ashe, which was not often, he was always standing in a room, glass in hand, with his right foot slightly resting on the ball of his foot so that he looked incongruously as if any minute he might fling out into some complicated ballet step. Yet one knew he would not because he was so travelled and weary and "informed."

Sometimes Winky thought it was that, the world-weariness, that attracted Suzan Ribaut; Suzan's own husband Bob sold insurance: ". . . But have you evah thought aboot what might happen to little Lulie Rhett after you're gawwwwwne?"

Bob Ribaut was a charmer, a real charmer. But he was a Ribaut after all.

"Yesterday," said Bill Ashe tiredly. "Last night, as a mattah of fa-act. I got back last night."

"How nice," said Winky. "Just for a visit?" She turned to see Bob Ribaut and Dick Pringney rise to their feet.

Suzan Ribaut giggled. She always giggled when attention was pointed elsewhere.

Suzan was sitting on the sofa next to Dick Pringney, and Winky went over to her. She always did. She didn't know why. Suzan was the one person in Charleston Winky had a distinct disliking for. Yet whenever she was in a room Winky went straight to her first.

Even so, one had to admit Suzan was a stunning-looking young woman, in a conscientious sort of way. She wore no make-up and this with her long dark hair, brushed-back bangs and high voice gave her, though slightly irritating, a kind of spoiled untouched young girl's quality. Suzan liked the image and played it to the hilt.

Tom's apartment had a way of seeming to unclothe these people. In their own surroundings they were someone else. The large old rooms, high ceilings, portraits, rugs—all—gave them a kind of additional aura. At home, "Cumberland Place," Suzan was everything she had been born to, breeding, grace and life-long inclusion, as were they all. But here they stood alone, with their personalities in their hands, and the mind saw them uncloaked. They were better with the portraits and ceilings and chandeliers, and Winky often thought it was this, the additional aura, which always brought departed Charlestonians back to their city. They always came back, most of them, those who had the aura. And those who did not built their lives around it anyway, lying to their friends in other cities about "cousins," more often than not the wrong branch, according to standards.

"How are *you*, Suzan?" Winky said. Winky always emphasized *you* when she spoke to Suzan. Somehow she always managed to greet Suzan with more enthusiasm than anyone else. The effort was rarely returned.

"Why're you so late?" Suzan asked in her thin little girl's voice.

"Lectures!" was all Winky said and sat down in the chair nearest the sofa.

Suzan turned to Dick Pringney again. "Well, like I say, I *knew* something was going on. Those planes—all day—nearly drove me crazeeee—worse than the jets taking off all day."

"They'll get him," said Dick Pringney. His horn-rimmed glasses reflected from the lamp above his head.

"Get *who?*" Winky asked.

Suzan turned to Winky, almost surprised to see her sitting there. "Didn't you hear?"

"Hear what?"

Suzan put her hand to her neck and leaned toward Winky. "It just horrifies me. This *Nigrah*." She raised her hands in a gesture of emphasis and touched her right hand to her throat. "Carolyn Forzier. Raped her." She studied Winky's face for a moment. "Yes! One of the twins. *You* know."

"My god," Winky said.

"Uh huh." Suzan nodded solemnly.

"How *old* are those girls? They couldn't be more than thirteen or fourteen."

"No, they're in college now. Seventeen, I think. They graduated from Ashley Hall last year."

"Ye gods!" Winky leaned back in the chair. "Where *was* she?"

"She was taking some sort of nurses' aid course or something, and you know that parking lot, across from the hospital?"

"At night?"

"Late afternoon, broad daylight—"

Winky just looked at her.

"Uh huh."

"How do they know it was a Negro?"

"I don't know. Maybe she told them or something. She's in shock. I don't know."

"They'll get him," Dick Pringney said again. "I saw the sheriff at the courthouse this morning. He's got his dogs out—"

"And those planes *all* day long," said Suzan. "It gave me the willies. But just think of the poor Forziers. Her father's in the hospital, you know—Angus. I guess they won't tell him anything." Suzan looked at Winky. "Didn't you hear those planes?" She giggled. "I called up Chesie this morning, and she said she was so nervous she was just sitting there drinking two martinis at once."

Winky kept looking at her. "I didn't know what the planes were for."

"They've got the woods covered," said Dick Pringney.

Winky looked at Dick then. There was hatred in his eyes behind the glasses. People were always saying it was only the "red-neck" of the South who truly hated the Negro. Most of the people she knew here in Charleston didn't "hate" Negroes; they were merely indifferent or thought of them as kindly servants whom they loved while they lived, mourned when they died and occasionally memorialized with old "receipts" in the Junior League Cookbook; more totally they thought of Negroes as a "problem," an intellectual problem—somewhere else. Still, should the test come, should anyone in this room, or any of the people Winky knew in the city, should they see a Negro being treated unfairly or harmed, these very people would be the first to his defense. It was the individual they loved; in mass there was indifference.

There had been little racial trouble in the city and when there was no one paid much attention to it. The city government was integrated, the police force, public schools, restaurants. "Everybody's too busy going and giving parties to pay any attention to people marching around," said elderly Mr. Reveneaux one night to a visitor from Savannah. "Colored and white. Charlestonians have always got along with each other. Some of our friends live next door to colored people. No fuss."

It was a fact. A puzzle, perhaps, to the outsider. Judge Mawry and his northern wife, who years ago had "entertained Negroes" in their Charleston house and suffered ostracism, were only a myth now to most of Winky's friends. They listened to the story of the poor judge and thought of him as, well, "peculiar" and there was mild pity, of course, that he had to live in the North now. But there wasn't hatred. Even Dick Pringney would never admit to actual hatred of any kind, yet it was there, now, in his eyes.

Winky had often tried to analyze her own feelings. It was difficult to be truly honest. She had rarely known a Negro in a social way, not since college and not really then. To be honest she didn't know whether she wanted to or not. She had loved, truly and sincerely, as other Charlestonians had, many of the nurses and cooks who had worked in her parents' and friends' houses through the years. But that, as many of her more "liberal" friends told her, was not a test of anything. She had felt pity, and impatience on numerous occasions, a feeling she hated as much for the Negro as she did for herself. Once she had discussed all this with Walter, Walter with his arrogant liberalism and outrage. The term had infuriated him; he said it was she who was arrogant. Perhaps. But what she really thought was that they *both* were arrogant.

Still, now, she thought of the Negro in the South Carolina woods, the autumn leaves falling into deathlike rain, the gray moss, the dogs, the fear. The terrible fear, panic, hunted down like a field rat.

But the young girl? She shuddered slightly.

". . . I mean, I mean," Suzan was saying. "I mean somebody you *know* and everything. Nothing like this has ever happened in Charleston. You read about Washington and all, but not *here*."

No, not in Charleston, Winky was thinking. Most of the "rapings" never crossed color barriers, and most of the time the actual rape wasn't necessary anyway. The stories written in the North by Northerners about leering white men raping poor innocent Negro girls were mainly stories told by the Negroes themselves for what release or prize Winky was never sure. For it was an unfortunate fact: many Southern Negroes, educated or illiterate, could be notorious liars, charmingly so on occasion, giggling wonderfully behind the naive writers' backs. And there they rested, the lies, in good, gray, time-honored print.

"Well, things are changing," said Dick Pringney with his air of Pringney authority. "People everywhere're getting tired of this Nigrah business. It's Asia now. 'Asia for the Asians!'"

"Drink, love?" Tom called from behind the bar.

Winky looked over at him, slightly dazed.

"Drink?" He lifted a glass.

Winky glanced back at Suzan and Dick, and then slowly got up from the chair.

Lollie Pringney, with her blond adenoidal face some called "pretty," was sitting at the bar facing Tom.

"You're how old now?" Lollie was asking Tom.

"Twenty-seven," said Tom.

"Lying will get you exactly nowhere," Winky said.

Lollie laughed. "Every time I ask him he gets a year younger."

"Thirty-three," said Tom. "The Dragon always says I'm twenty-five. She likes to diminish herself that way."

"Tom!" said Lollie. "You ought not to call your mother that!"

"Affection, dear girl. A kind of affection."

". . . Good-bye, good-bye, good-bye," warbled the Italian singer from the record player.

Winky put her hand to her forehead.

"Suffering?" asked Tom.

Winky shook her head. "Suzan and Dick were just telling me about the Forzier twin." She sat down next to Lollie.

"Isn't that horr-i-ble?" said Lollie. She looked at Tom. "Did you hear about it?"

Tom nodded. "Pi-*ty*," he said and dropped one large ice cube in his glass.

"*Really*, Tom!" said Winky.

Tom laughed. He had an infectious laugh.

"Such sympathy," said Lollie, but she was smiling.

"But the dogs and everything," Winky said. "It's like something out of Faulkner."

"Well?" said Tom.

"No, we're *not* Mississippi," Winky said. "And Mississippi isn't Faulkner either. Go back to Ohio, then."

"Why, no," Tom cocked his head, "I think Mississippi's sort of cheery. I bet if you took the brain out of one of those lily-white deputies down there, or *here*—do forgive me—all you'd see would be niggers, comic books and sex."

"And they're always having children and things—people like that," said Lollie Pringney. "Thousands of them."

"Poverty plans and taxes," Tom said. "Why should I have to pay for some other bastard's pleasure?"

"The subject has just changed," Winky said.

Tom bowed in mock graciousness to Winky. "Tall glass or short?"

"Tall," said Winky and watched as Tom took up a glass. His hands were pale with short fingers. She looked from the hands to his eyes—deep, deep blue. The contrast had always perplexed Winky. She detested Tom's hands, but she was drawn to his eyes. There was something sad about his eyes.

"Where's my birthday present?" he asked Winky.

"A dust mop," Winky said, and Lollie Pringney laughed.

"But I've got something for *you*."

"What for?"

"Because I'm always thinking of you, queen, never of myself. Do you know I'm the same age Jesus was when he died?"

"There the similarity ends," said Winky.

" 'My Kingdom for a grave—a lit-tle, lit-tle grave. Somewhere on the King's Highway, where . . .' "

"You're not Shakespeare either," said Winky.

"*Good-bye, good-bye, to Rome . . .*" The singer was still groaning his farewell.

"Tom Gearhart!" came Suzan Ribaut's voice in back of Winky. "You've got *green* john peyupuh!" She brushed back her long hair with her right hand, slowly, a bid for instant poise.

Tom laughed.

"That's the cutest thing I ever heard of. Anybody'd have green john peyupuh in their bathroom."

"But it was for *you*, Suzan. I saw it at the grocery store and right away I thought of you. 'That's Suzan Ribaut,' I said to myself."

Winky turned. "Tom's discovered a new personality, Suzan. Charity. He's already been comparing himself to Jesus."

Tom grinned and placed a cigarette in his holder, a short black one. "Yes, the late J.C. and I have much in common. You know?" He was looking at Suzan.

"That's the most sacrilegious thing I ever . . ." Suzan stopped short. "Oh, hello, Bill," she said in a much more child-like voice than she had used when talking to Winky and Tom.

Tom looked at Winky. Suzan and Bill Ashe's attraction for each other amused Tom highly. He liked to have the two of them, he said, because he had always wanted to be in on aiding and abetting a sordid affair.

"Another scotch, Thomas," said Bill Ashe tiredly. Bill Ashe always avoided Suzan at the beginning of an evening.

"Why don't you *ever* use a jigger, Tom?" Winky said, watching as Tom re-filled Bill's glass and then added to his own from the open bottle. "Your trough runneth over."

"Because my hours are numberless."

"Numb would be more like it," Winky said. "How many does that make?"

Tom leaned forward on the bar. "Why, how *kind* of you to be concerned."

"I'm not."

"But it's better than pot, isn't it, love?"

"Who knows?"

Tom lifted his glass. "Pot and Trotsky and bed-ins! I'm a Socialist! Hail to thee, dear old Trot!" He grinned. "Wasn't it old Trot who got the trots in . . ."

"Terribly amusing," said Winky, knowing that the act was a clear reference to Walter Everett. Walter was known as Princeton's greatest contribution to Socialism, according to Tom, who repeated the statement as a weekly purge.

"No offense, Antoinette. None at all."

"A bore, Tom. *Vous êtes un bore!*"

"*Peut-être.*" Tom glanced at his watch. "The Hollandaise, pet. The Hollandaise."

"Oh, me," groaned Winky. "Why do I always end up in the kitchen?"

"Can I help anybody?" Lollie Pringney asked. Lollie Pringney always asked if she could "help." She never did.

By ten o'clock Tom was still in the small kitchen. Pans were steaming on the ancient gas stove, and Tom had added a tall cook's hat to his uniform. Sweat was pouring down his face. (Scotch, Winky identified it.) On the bare wall, over the stove, someone had painted a reproduction of Botticelli's *Birth of Venus*, but Venus was holding a martini glass. Tom had asked a Charleston "artist" to do the picture and was furious when the artist drank up all his whisky during the days of creation. Now, even Venus was sweating.

Winky had escaped the kitchen in a bid for oxygen. Outside, in the living room, the party had progressed to its fourth-scotch stage. Bill Ashe and Suzan Ribaut were sitting on the sofa, safely ignored, and Dick Pringney and Bob Ribaut were fascinating each other with tales of land-line disputes and life insurance.

"But I want you to be happy, Winky," Lollie Pringney was saying to Winky. "I mean like Dick and I are. You know, Dick and I'll have been married five years this December, and I just don't know any other couple that're happ-ier'n we are."

"That's nice, Lollie," Winky said. She was thinking she just wasn't in the mood, not now, to listen to the marital bliss of Lollie and Dick Pringney.

"No, really. I mean just a little thing. The other day after Dick went to work I saw one of his socks—you know—on the floor? And I just picked it up and kiyissed it." She shook her head, smiling in remembrance of the act. "I don't know —I just missed him, that's all."

"Really?" Winky looked away. The idea of kissing Dick Pringney's sock did something to her stomach.

Lollie took hold of Winky's arm. Lollie was always touching people. "No, really. I *do* want you to be happy. You were my maid-of-honor and everything."

Winky smiled at her. "Thank you, Lollie."

"I *do*. Really." Lollie looked down at her hands, and

then back at Winky. "I don't see why you and Tom don't marry. I mean you really do like the same things and all that."

"One reason only," Winky said.

"What?"

"I'm just not in love with him, never will be."

"But he's in love with *you*."

Winky looked at her sharply.

"I know he is."

"How?"

"Everybody knows."

"Lollie, for godsakes!"

Lollie sipped from her glass. "You're still thinking about the one in New York, aren't you?"

"And how did you know about him?"

"Tom told me."

"Oh."

Lollie nodded. Her eyes were twinkling as if they were playing a game, and she had known the correct answer all along. "What's he like?"

"Walter?" Winky leaned back in the armchair. "Oh, I don't know. He grew up in Pittsburgh of all places. His family's in steel, have been practically since the Wise Men. Walter hates it—wants to be a writer. One of those things. He's divine." She glanced at Lollie. "Tom knew him at school, I guess. I . . ."

"The feasht is on the table, ladies and ginellmens . . ."

Tom had staggered out from the kitchen, and when he bowed his cook's hat fell to the floor.

"Our birthday boy," said Winky.

Behind the bar, in a darkened alcove, Tom had set his birthday table. Winky could see Tom's mother's touch: the ornate silver, the huge florist's chrysanthemums, yellow and white with the petal tips frizzed, florist's fern, green candles. How she hated colored candles. Somehow, though, with Tom, they were more touching than revealing.

"The table's kinda nifty, Tom," Winky said. She pictured the mother and son busy with their preparations.

"I mean, for a *bachelor* and everything," said Suzan Ribaut.

"Did you get the candles to go with the john peyupuh?" asked Dick Pringney and laughed loudly into the candlelight.

Tom didn't answer. Even in his slightly swaying stance, he was smiling, blatantly, proudly.

Wine glasses were set by each place, and by the glasses were gay red and white striped cardboard tubes, one end of which was a tassle to pull, revealing in the popping clamour a red tissue child's cap.

"This is so much fu-un," said Suzan Ribaut, placing the cap cock-wise on her head. In the candlelight she looked even more like a young girl.

Tom, still standing, popped his and giggled drunkenly. "Here's to me!" he said. "Thomas William Gearhart, the turd!"

"Dear Jesus," said Dick Pringney, "you mean there're *three* of you?"

"Three!" said Tom.

Lollie Pringney punched Winky. "The cake," she whispered.

Winky had forgotten. Lollie had carefully instructed Winky to place the candles on the cake Lollie had hidden earlier. A bore. Birthday cakes were always a bore, especially having to eat the thing afterward.

"Oh, Tom!" Winky said. "You forgot the wine. Shall I fetch?"

Tom swayed and flopped into his chair, a kind of feat. "By all means," he said. His eyes were half closed.

"Because we all so desperately need it," Winky said, getting up from the table.

In the kitchen she found Lollie's candles for the cake.

"Hurry up, Step-'n-Fetch-It," came Tom's voice, followed by unanimous laughter.

Winky jabbed three candles into the cake and jerked open the refrigerator door. She stood fast, staring inside. Then she looked away and slowly back again. "*Lagrima di Cristo*," read the label on the wine bottle. The words struck her crazily, the words, the picture, the script and, far away it seemed, the drunken laughter in the other room. "Tears of Christ." It was sweetly horrible somehow, as if Christ Himself were sitting weeping inside the refrigerator.

She thought of the Negro running in the woods, and she turned from the bottle, for a moment.

⤬

"Dick Pring-ney spewed on my birthday cake." Tom's words came with difficulty.

"You *asked* us to blow out your candles," Winky said.

"Not like that."

"Tom, stand up."

"But Dick Pringney spewed on it."

"For godsakes, Tom."

"Why're you so *mean* to me?"

"Stand up."

"But I've got this—" He touched Winky's shoulder. "Wait—right—chere. I've got this—"

"Where are you going?"

Tom glanced back slowly. "Wait right there."

Winky sat in the armchair. "Just where do you think I could go?"

She leaned back. She was tired and, now, oddly depressed. Bob Ribaut was lying on the floor balancing a brandy glass on his forehead. Winky wondered if this was a bid for cleverness or an attempt to ignore Suzan and Bill Ashe, who were dancing on the other side of the room.

From the record player came the voice of Charles Trenet, an old record, warped. He was singing, *La Mer*, and Winky thought of Walter and the time in Paris when the two of them got stuck in that crazy elevator and Walter kept shouting down to Madame de Tiere and Madame couldn't or wouldn't hear him, and they stayed in the elevator for an hour.

Her throat ached and she wanted to cry. She, like the song, *La Mer*.

Tom looked pale when he returned to the room. "Let's go outside," he said.

"You look like Mr. Green," said Winky, getting up from the chair. She wanted to get out of the room. She wanted to go home, but she knew if she did she wouldn't sleep. She would only—

"Hey, where're you two going?" shouted Dick Pringney from the sofa. "To neck?"

"You're a cheery one, Richard. You *are*," said Winky. She still wanted to cry.

The small courtyard was filled with fallen leaves and the gnarled trunk of the Lady Banksias looked gray and ghostly. Winky shivered. "I should have brought my coat."

"Here," Tom said. "Take my coat."

"Chivalry?"

"No, just alcohol."

They sat down on two of the wrought-iron chairs, and Winky leaned her head back. The two lamps from the back doorway reflected on the bare branches of the one tree and from inside came the muted sounds from the record player. Winky breathed deeply. "This reminds me of Paris. One afternoon I stayed in that little park, you know? By the Seine, where those benches are? It was gorgeous and the leaves kept falling. Sad."

"Were you by yourself?"

"Uh huh."

"Nobody picked you up?"

"Nobody."

"Pity."

"Yes, yes it was."

"Want a drink?"

"You jest. Surely, you jest."

"I'll go get us two glasses."

"That is exactly what we don't need, two glasses." Winky sat up. "Tom, why *do* you drink so much?"

"Nothing else to do."

"No, seriously. You don't need to drink like you do."

"But, I *do*."

"Why?"

"Because I'm fat and middle-class and I've got this——"

"Stupid."

Tom didn't say anything for a while, and then he said: "In my pocket, reach inside."

Winky looked at him.

"In the side pocket of my coat. It's a present."

"Honestly, Tom," Winky sighed. She removed the coat from her shoulders, fully expecting to find a flask. "If you don't watch . . ." Her fingers found a small box. "Tom! What in the world?"

"I don't know."

The small box was wrapped in gray and white striped paper.

"What have you been up to?" Winky quickly unwrapped the paper, and before she even lifted the lid, she put her hand to her mouth. "Tom?" she said softly.

The ring, a solitary diamond, shone back at her from the small velvet cushion. Panic took hold of her. "Tom!"

"Uh huh," was all he said. She could almost feel him smiling.

She quickly closed the lid. "What is this? A joke? Tom Gearhart, what do you mean?" And then for no reason she could possibly imagine, she laughed.

"No joke," Tom mumbled.

Winky looked at him. He was sitting hunched over in his white shirt, his mouth hung slightly open. He looked fat, fatter somehow than he ever had and so very vulnerable.

"Oh, Tom. Why did you have to go and . . ." She put her hand on his but instantly wanted to take it away.

He turned to her then. "Why not?" he said weakly and shrugged his shoulders. "It's a long road to forty."

The embarrassment was almost worse than the tone of his voice. "I don't know," Winky said quietly.

"I know," Tom said. "Because we're *nouveau* and nobody in our family ever signed the Declaration of Independence, and all I've got is a poor aunt who knocks away on a sewing machine all day."

The intended humor didn't come off. "Don't be silly," Winky said, forcing the anger in her voice. She jerked her hand away.

"You want to marry an old *Charleston* family, so you can dust off your ancestors until the day you die."

"I said don't be silly."

"Or that Communist, Walter Everett. Spend your nights in cozy little cell meetings and your days marching around with hand-made signs."

Winky was glad for the sarcasm. She looked down at the box again and slowly handed it to Tom. "Let's go inside."

Tom shrugged his shoulders again. "But you didn't have to laugh," he said, almost like a young boy. "The Dragon helped me pick it out."

"But Tom. Whatever on God's green earth ever gave you—"

"You could have said it was pretty." Tom shoved the ring in his pants pocket. "You didn't have to laugh." His voice was whining.

"It was pretty. It is. I—" Winky was suddenly very cold and she got up and fairly ran to the door of the apartment. At the door she put her hand to her throat. *Walter! Walter! What's happening to me? What's* . . .

By two-thirty that morning Tom had passed out or rather gone to sleep. He was sitting on the floor in the living room, his chin touching his chest. He had on his cook's apron once more with "Come and Get It" written across the pocket.

"I've had it! I've had it! I've had it!" said Suzan Ribaut. "Let's get out of here!"

"Well, what're we gonna do with the birthday boy?" asked Dick Pringney.

"He's all right," said Bob Ribaut. "I've left him here like that a thousand times. He wakes up eventually and goes to bed."

Bill Ashe laughed. "Jesus, he looks like a great white whale sitting there."

Winky said nothing. She started toward the door.

". . . When my lover has gone," sang Dick Pringney drunkenly. "Hey, Winky. Don't go yet. Let's leave some notes at least."

Suzan Ribaut giggled. "We can sort of *pin* them on him."

It was a good idea, they all declared, and after Lollie found the pins in Tom's bedroom, they wrote the notes:

Lollie Pringney wrote: "There's Bromo in the john. I checked." And Suzan Ribaut wrote: "Near the *green* john paper."

Dick Pringney wrote: "Happy days, man!" And Bill Ashe's was rather clever, they all thought. He wrote: "A jug of booze, a loaf of bread and Thou, alone, screaming in the wilderness."

Winky didn't write anything, but no one noticed. She glanced about the apartment, saw the ashtrays filled with cigarette ends, ashes, dirty glasses, crumbs on the floor, and she thought of Tom waking up to it all. She was remembering that he had invited the Walkers, a new couple, in for drinks tomorrow afternoon.

"I just thought it'd be kind of cheery to have a couple of mint juleps on a fine old October Charleston afternoon," Tom had said.

"Poor clown," Winky thought and walked out the door into the black morning.

Chapter 4 ~∾

Once years ago someone had told Winky that a Chinese symbol for trouble was two women under one rooftop. The statement had intrigued her, and it came back now as she returned home after the evening with Tom. She could see the reading lamp in her mother's bedroom still on, hazed like a sickness in the darkened house, one blight in the night, and she was hoping somehow to escape the acute ears of her mother. She looked at her watch. Three-twenty. She was tired, exhausted. And if there were any reproaches to be made "let it wait till morning, please; let everything wait."

But the voice in the upper hall came anyway, like a whine: "Is that you, Winky?"

Winky paused for a moment, closing her eyes in resignation. She entered the bedroom.

"You *know* I can't sleep until I know you're home."

Her mother was lying in bed, her horn-rimmed glasses resting on the finely printed pages of Jane Austen's *Pride and Prejudice.* The book, after years of appearing with each successive crisis in their lives, was tattered now at the binding.

The room was hushed, darkened, like a sick room where pain and anguish had struggled too long. How different this than the room she had just left. The very sickness of it, almost planned it seemed, irritated her now with her own temple throbbing with tiny thrusts of pain.

"It's thoughtless. Truly thoughtless." Her mother's face, cold-creamed of color and line, seemed incongruous with the pink bed jacket and Tester bed. Sixty-three, her mother.

"*. . . Yes, Winky was a late child, you know . . .*" The voice so assured, so veiling, long ago . . .

"You just can't go out alone like this anymore, driving at night." The two marks on her forehead deepened. "All night I kept thinking about that Forzier child." She placed the book aside. "It's just asking for trouble."

"Mother, now look!" Winky touched her burning eyes with the tips of her fingers. "Here I am, standing in front of you like a naughty child. See." She put her hand to the top of her head. "I refuse to ruin my life with every silly fear that comes to my head. I'm not you." She regretted the remark as soon as it was said.

"Oh, *Win*-ky." The tone called for the usual tears that came so freely now. They did not come.

"I couldn't *bear* anything happening to you. You know that."

"I know. I'm sorry."

Her mother looked beyond Winky. "Your father fell tonight."

Winky didn't move. "Fell?" She put her hand to her mouth.

Her mother's expression did not change. "He—" She breathed deeply, looking at Winky then. "He must have been halfway up the stairway, and when I reached him he was just lying in the hall—just—" The tears did come, gathering in her eyes, resting there.

Winky moved closer to her. "Is he—is he—hurt?"

"No, no, I don't think so." Her mother reached for a kleenex at her bedside.

"Did he make any sense? I mean was he—?" Winky had never been able to use the word "drunk" in connection with her father, not even in thought.

"I don't think so. Actually I don't think he had had very much to drink. He seemed quite clear—afterward." Her mother sat up straighter, the two pillows with Aunt Pett's lace edged on the pillow cases at her back. "There's something— I—I think it's his . . ." She put the kleenex aside and with an odd kind of dignity said: "Winky, I think there is something wrong with your father's mind."

Winky stood rigid, looking down at her mother, kept looking at her eyes, free of tears now, puffed and red-rimmed. She couldn't look away. "With his mind?" She heard her own voice like a whimper.

Her mother averted her eyes.

"What do you *mean?* What on earth are you talking about?"

Her mother did not look at her.

"Mother?" Winky's voice was loud in the closed room.

"For sometime I've noticed. Little things. It began while you were away, earlier, I see now." She looked at Winky. "I thought he was merely confused or it was his—"

"His what?" Winky said.

"His drinking." Her mother nodded, her lips pinched— their collusive secret out.

"But what? What began?" Winky studied her mother's face, trying to see something there. Her mother sometimes was given to exaggeration, dramatization. It was a social gift which oftentimes charmed, but in connection with her father the gift came poorly.

"I'm afraid we must face this, not be cowardly, you know." Her blue eyes widened, darting like a crazed person.

Winky sat down on the foot of the bed. Fear came to her, and she felt the small, rapid beating of her heart. "But what have you *noticed?* I mean what does he *do?* Say?" She brushed back her hair impatiently. "What does he . . . ?"

"Forgetfulness. That sort of thing. Once this summer when you were away, once or twice, he called you 'Leigh.' " The tears gathered in her eyes again. "We would just be sitting and talking, and he would ask me, just out of the blue, 'Why did Leigh leave us? Go away on that trip?' "

Leigh was her father's dead sister. "So?" Winky said. Her heart was beating faster. She put her hand over her chest. "*You* do that sometimes. Confuse things. *I* do. We all do."

"But that's not like Petrie. Don't you *see?* He actually thought you *were* Leigh. He thought Leigh was in Norway. I said, 'Why, Petrie, Leigh is dead,' and he said, 'Is she?' Then he was seemingly all right again. There have been many other things."

"Oh, *Mother.*"

"Yes, I know."

"Why didn't you tell me before?"

"I couldn't. You seemed so worried—about other things."

"But—" Winky let her hand drop to her lap, and she looked down at it, tracing the small veins gently with her left fingers. Her mind was darting to and fro, remembering little things, her father coming home from his office when she was small—his laughter, his wonderful laughing, his majesty at Sunday dinners, sitting commandingly at the head of the table. His gentleness. "No," she said aloud and then looked up almost shyly at her mother.

"I didn't want to tell you now."

"But—" Winky shook her head. "He hasn't said anything to me, I mean anything different or strange. He does look thin, so terribly thin." She thought she might cry.

"You haven't seen him very much since you've been home."

"I know, but—" Winky fumbled with a loose thread on

the bedspread. "He's either gone, or—in the library."

"Once while you were away, at breakfast—he looked at me so curiously and asked where we were and when were we going home. Leuvenia was serving breakfast just as she always does."

Winky kept looking at her.

"I was so taken aback I couldn't answer, and then he seemed all right again—just a moment of incoherence."

Winky pulled the thread loose.

"My own father went that way, you know."

Winky gazed at her mother.

"Atherosclerosis, I think they call it, a series of tiny strokes in the brain. It isn't insanity, just tiny—" Her eyes seemed empty of life. "My father remembered things that happened years ago, but he couldn't remember what happened only a few days ago. That's the way it started. He became very foolish; no one understood. They laughed at him eventually." She said this matter-of-factly as if she were a spinner of tales, speaking of some unknown person she had heard of once. "It killed my mother. She tried to cover up, you know." She put the kleenex to her nose. "I really don't think I could bear to see Petrie become foolish. He has always been so—*proud*." Her voice broke.

Winky stood up, anger rocketing inside her. "Mother, quit this! Quit!" She brought her doubled fists to her mouth.

They looked at each other, mother and daughter, and then the tears came full, streaming down her mother's face. Winky stared at her. She dropped her hand to her side. "Cry! Go ahead and cry!" The anger trembled in her voice. She kept staring, her eyes fixed on the convulsions of the body but not seeing really, and then it came to her, as true sight returned, how frail her mother looked, lying there, her body too small to hold such emotion. "It's good for you to cry," she said quietly then.

The crying did not stop. It was as if all the weeks and months of bottled fear and loneliness had been let free and, now free, must be total. Winky reached to touch her, but did not. She could touch other people in their grief, try with the touch of her fingers to ease their pain, but not her mother. She didn't know why. She merely stood watching, hearing the child-like sobs uncontrolled.

"Mother?" she said finally, quietly.

Her mother only looked at her, her face swollen and red, her eyes startled like a frightened doe's eyes.

"Please don't."

"Oh, Winky," her mother said in a strange, frightened, half-apologetic voice.

"You said we had to have courage."

Her mother put the wadded kleenex to her nose. "I know. It's—" She wiped her eyes with the tissue. "Sometimes his mind is so clear—for days—and then— But it seems to be getting worse."

Winky closed her eyes. For a moment a picture formed in her mind of her father, aging, unkempt, senile, a giggling old man, foolish. In college once she had visited a home for the old as a course of study. There had been such a man there. Winky had never forgotten his face. He seemed to want to please. "Oh," she said aloud and rubbed her forehead, turning her head from left to right, as if she could erase the picture. She bent toward her mother. "What can we do?"

"Nothing."

"Have you talked to a doctor?"

"Yes, I talked to Williams. Of course, Petrie refuses to see Williams—as a patient."

"What did Williams say?"

"Oh, he's known, he said. He sees Petrie—playing golf, you know."

"But what is it? What did *Williams* say?"

"Just that it's this thing—hardening of the arteries, and there's nothing that can be done. If it gets worse there are pills to quiet him, make him feel easier. The drinking, so much of it, is bad, of course." She paused, her breath coming in small jerks. "But there is nothing anyone can do."

"Nothing?"

"Nothing. I asked him about Mayo's. Everywhere."

Winky took hold of the bedpost lightly. All her remaining energy seemed to have left her. "Does he—suffer?"

"I don't know."

Winky said nothing.

"I'm so sorry. I'm so very sorry to have to tell you." ·

Her mother reached for another kleenex and knocked over a small glass vase holding a cutting of blooming tea olive. The flowers were a custom with her mother. Each day, each season, the vase was filled and re-filled with something from the garden. It had been a long habit, since childhood. Now, soon, there would be chrysanthemums and after the chrysanthemums, holly, the camellia, the Christmas rose and after the rose, the jasmine and after the jasmine, the Lady Banksia and after the Banksia— Whenever Winky thought of the seasons, she thought of her mother, whose nature, too, turned with the winters and the springs and the long torrid Sunday summers.

Winky wiped the spilled water with a handkerchief she held wadded in her hand. "You must try to rest," she said. "You've worried too long, alone." She placed the spent blossoms back into the vase, dawdling with them, arranging and re-arranging. "Before too long frost will be here and the tea olive will be gone, so will all the chrysanthemums." Her voice had a sore, hoarse timbre to it.

"Yes." Her mother seemed to relax with her sigh. "Time goes so quickly. When I was your age I thought the world lay before me forever. I kept worrying what I would *be*, what I would become. Imagine." A smile lingered on her lips. "I'm sorry, Winky dear, truly sorry, to have worried you with all this. So young— But there *are* these things for the living." The words came with difficulty. "I refused to believe it, too, at first—about your father."

"That's all right. It's just that—I don't know. As I said, I haven't noticed anything. He seems just as he's always been to me."

Her mother nodded. "In your mind he must always be."

Winky looked away.

"I think, you know, I was a little afraid to tell you."

"You shouldn't have been."

"You've always been such a sensitive girl. I wanted to spare you this, at least for a little while longer."

"You're—you're very good." Winky fought back the tears. "But now you need sleep."

Her mother felt for the book by her side, like a blind person, fumblingly, and with it before her began smoothing the pages tenderly.

"I said, sleep."

Her mother smiled again. "Jane Austen will do that for me. Really, she's so soothing, better than any sleeping pill."

Winky could say nothing. She watched as her mother put her glasses back on, an almost efficient gesture. With the glasses she seemed more herself, more alert, her morning self. Yet there were the queer shadows in the room, the hazed bed lamp, the silence as if her morning mother had suddenly come to this ephemeral darkness. Winky stood gazing down at her. She thought of a painting she had seen once in the Louvre, two women huddled together, one older and one younger. There was fear in their faces, and it was night. Winky had always tried to imagine what the fear was, invading armies, fierce weathers, the night, death?

"Where do we go?" she whispered, not knowing herself exactly what she asked. But her mother didn't answer . . .

Morning. And Charleston awakening. This bird-cage of a city, queen of the South, with its sea air and haughty pride had always sounded different to Winky than any other city in the world. Nothing seemed to change here, not really, not the sounds, the smells, nor the way the seasons came; only the seas and the rivers changed, now fierce, now calm. True, there was the sound of jets screeching across the sky nowadays. And somewhere, far, there was the hammering of restoration, preservation, as the city preferred to call it. But in early morning there was still the distant fog horns giving way to occasional Gullah tongues. Winky could hear two fish peddlers arguing on a back street nearby. This was her city, her corner of it, and wherever she went, in whatever remote city or village, it haunted her, following her, living with her like the blood she bore inside. "The most beautiful city in the world," a scholar-scientist was reported as saying in the newspaper yesterday. It was.

The first thing Winky saw, or looked for, when she awakened in the morning was the chipped angel which rose above the mantel at the molding along the ceiling. The angel came free from a round, full-bloomed rose like a pistil in a tiger lily, holding fiercely to a horn at the mouth, warning of the Lord knows what—day's doom or heraldry. It was the wing of the angel that was chipped, but the horn was perfect as well as the grace of feature, forehead, cheekbone, nose, chin, eyes hollow and round without iris or pupil, a small child's eyes long ago.

The artist had given the angel humours. Or so it seemed to Winky. Some mornings the angel seemed happy, like a young Puck or sprite, other times weeping or mourning. This day there was nothing at first. And then as she looked, as indeed it had been each morning since September, gradually the slow hands of anguish settled upon her. Her first thought, routinely, was of Walter:

"*Do you write letters?*"

"*Every day. I'll write every day—to you and for you.*"

Vague whisperings. Like a game it was. She would choose. One day she would go over their first meeting or maybe the time at Lillehammer: *Skal vi drikke?* Laughter. Or Paris. Or Copenhagen. Copenhagen had become old; she had been over that too much. She saw Walter's mouth, the firm lips, and the dark, almost middle-eastern eyes that so seldom smiled, and now she turned over, away from the angel. She lay there staring at the bedroom door and after a while the distant hammering and the Gullah arguing had quit—only silence—and the clear sound of her mother's voice last night came back to her:

"I think there is something wrong with your father's mind."

She kept looking at the door, but the hideous picture of the senile man long ago tried to come to her again, and she turned from the door in a plunge of despair. "Oh." She sat up in the bed, putting her hands to her face, her hair falling over her hands. *Think of something else! Think!*

Yes, Tom. She looked at her finger where the ring would have gone. "I wonder if it would have fit?" she asked herself, idly stretching her fingers out before her. "I wonder if . . ."

"Exposing yourself like that! On a stage!" Aunt Pett's voice came from the sewing room across the way.

"Just because I'm finally doing what I want to do! You've never wanted me to do one thing I've wanted to do—ever! You and Mother!"

The latter, a rather high-cracked voice, though now edged with fury, was the voice of Aunt Etoile, Aunt Pett's sister. The two sisters genuinely and sincerely hated each other. Everyone in Charleston knew of the feud, which had come to be as much a part of the city as Fort Sumter itself. They took sides, the people, and as teams in school lined up either to the right or the left, perhaps slightly extended to the left, Aunt Etoile's side. Aunt Etoile, poor and living in the garçonnière behind the Pringney house, was no competition for anybody; therefore, the charity was easier come by.

Aunt Etoile had never married, and though no one in the family had ever satisfactorily explained the precise germ of the sisterly war, Winky had always thought it was Aunt Pett's marriage and subsequent inheritance that caused the germ to finally develop into mobilized war. Aunt Pett had brought "standing" once more to the Petrie name through her marriage, but "poor Etoile," as she was everlastingly referred to, still orbited in genteel poverty.

It always seemed an unfair battle to Winky, for whereas Aunt Pett had her Rooseveltian looks, was tall and large-boned, Aunt Etoile was petite, small-boned, like a proud and tattered sparrow, dressed in brown and filled with terrier-like energy. Small means now, or the energy, may have caused the sunken cheeks and the hollows under her amber eyes, yet she still bore the good Petrie chin and lift of the head.

Aunt Pett brought out all the unused bite in Aunt Etoile, and she would stand before her sister, her words spat out in a melee of confusion and anger, all the while Aunt Pett, who dreamed dignity more than life, sitting regally with her hands folded in her lap, looking as if she were witnessing the antics of a demented clown.

Still, should the test come, if it would come, Winky believed there was some spark left for peace, if only attachment, mainly because of the past and the memories when they were both young and there was still hope somehow for all who bore the name of Petrie. Winky thought that; she wasn't sure. But the battles amused Winky now, gave relief somehow, and she smiled as she listened:

"You aren't an actress, Etoile," Pett's deeper voice broke through the other's angry words. "If you were you wouldn't have been turned down all these years. Making a fool of yourself. The Dock Street Theatre isn't Broadway—as you claim it is."

"Selfish!" snarled Aunt Etoile. "Jealous!"

"No," said Aunt Pett calmly. "I've merely considered you a Bohemian type. The Lord knows where you inherited it."

Winky almost laughed aloud. Aunt Etoile, a Bohemian? The only association Aunt Pett could possibly have had with anything vaguely connected with the word was the opera.

"You're just angry because you were left out of the Pringney party the other Sunday!" said Aunt Etoile. "Don't try to give any excuses—you were just plain left *out!*"

There was a short silence and Winky could imagine Aunt Pett gathering all her resources together, growing tall in her chair as she always seemed to do at the height of crisis:

"Etoile, you know perfectly well the Pringneys have always been *my* friends. It has been a long and satisfying relationship—through the years. I've heard all about last Sunday, a very funny group of people. Frankly, I was shocked at Faye Pringney and should I have been invited I think I would have been forced to refuse."

"That's not so, and you know it!"

"I'm no urchin, you know, living in the back of somebody's house like—like a servant or something."

Tears, chaos, thunderbolts. And then Winky heard the rather soothing voice of her mother: "Etoile, dear, now control yourself. You two mustn't carry on this way. We're such a small family. We need all the loyalty we can command."

"Just because I got a part in the play," sobbed Aunt Etoile.

"Why, Etoile, how simply lovely," said her mother. "What is the play?"

"*Arsenic and Old Lace*," came the whimpering voice.

"And who are *you* to be, Etoile?" asked Aunt Pett.

"Did you hear her? Did you hear her, Ann?"

"Oh, you two!" came her mother's voice. "There're just the two of you now—it seems to me—"

"Our *moth*-ah," interrupted Aunt Pett, "would never have stood for such a thing—mixing with Bohemians, exposing herself in public like a common chorus person."

"But, Pett, your mother loved the Dock Street Theatre. She went to it frequently, and so did your father."

"Yes, and so do I. But do you think for a moment *Moth*-ah would have been up there on the *stage?*"

"No one thinks of it that way, Pett, not nowadays."

"Of course," said Aunt Etoile. "Pett's just not up with the times. Just sitting there, not up with the times at all!"

"Yes, thank you. I am *not*."

"My ability for acting," said Aunt Etoile, "is straight down from Mother's line."

"Ridiculous. Perfectly ridiculous. When I think how Mother worried over you, courting sailors and people like that."

"They weren't sailors!" The voice turned oddly shy. "Mr. Cutter was a leftenant, a very fine man."

"From some peculiar place up . . ."

Winky got out of bed. She had heard the story of Mr. Cutter over and over, from Aunt Etoile, Aunt Pett, her mother. There were different versions of the story, depending upon the teller, and by now the tale had grown worn, all three versions.

"He talked through his nose," said Aunt Pett.

"He most certainly did *not*," spat back Aunt Etoile. "He was a very cultivated gentleman."

"Hah!" said Aunt Pett. "Everybody knew, though Mother tried to be discreet. Out West for your health! Really, Etoile. You didn't fool anybody—not for a moment."

"Pett, please." Winky heard her mother's tired voice. "Etoile has always been frail."

"Not too frail to live with a man she wasn't married to!"

"Now, Pett, I'm not going to—"

"That's all right, Ann," came Aunt Etoile's voice. "They've always been that way, Mother and Pett. Lies every bit of it. Pett knows it. She wanted to ruin my life, break it off with Mr. Cutter and myself. I was the younger one, a nothing, a nobody. They hated me because I was prettier, talented. Even asked me to mow the lawn once! Just think of *that!*"

"Talented!" said Aunt Pett. "You should be on your knees instead of parading around on a stage."

"All right. All right," came Aunt Etoile's voice. "This is the last. You'll never have to see me again. I'll—I'll never enter this house again as long as I live—my *own* grandmother's house. It has been desecrated!"

The threat had been heard before, bi-annually.

"Of course you'll come again and often," said her mother.

"Good-bye, Ann. Should you want me for anything you must come to *me* now. I shall be at the shop or in my little room."

Her "little room" was actually a small house, five rooms, built with old brick by slave hands a century and more ago, now surrounded by Mr. Pringney's carefully groomed garden, camellias, azaleas, loquat, Japanese plum, pittosporum and the Pringneys' majestic house rising across the garden half-hidden by live oaks and Spanish moss.

"Now, Etoile," said her mother.

"Call me at the shop during the day."

Aunt Etoile, along with the spinster Miss Reveneaux, operated a small shop where they sold candies, Peach Leather and Benne Seed cookies along with assorted gift cards, prints and china. During the tourist season Peach Leather was the going commodity, finding its way into houses in Detroit, St. Louis, Cleveland, Pittsburgh, New York.

Winky went to the balcony outside her room and watched as Aunt Etoile and her mother walked through the garden to the gate, Aunt Etoile talking constantly, moving her head in the fury of her terrier anger.

Winky sighed. It was not a day for anger. Above, the sky was blue as far as she could see, and the sun on her face was hot with the barest of chill in the air. Below, the dogwood leaves were scarlet against the green bays and cherry laurels. Over by the fountain she saw her father and Beauvoir, the

Negro gardener. Beside them was a balled camellia, ready to be planted in the corner near the house. Winky stood there watching her father's tall, stooped body as he spoke with Beauvoir. He was wearing a tan cardigan and the old brown hat, the latter always with him, as much a part of him now as the iron-gray hair, the ruddy, bony face and the piercing gray eyes that so often tried to smile. At the distance he seemed as he always had, not the man her mother had spoken of last night, the dying man, the man whose creative mind was clouding from brittle arteries. With the sun, the sky, the air, the leaves, last night was some half-forgotten shadow, a tale told by a woman in an old night.

Winky turned quickly from the scene. Inside, her room had a Saturday feel, colder than the sun with the distant sounds of a busy traffic ending a week, readying for the night and the long quiet of Sunday. Saturday! The last day for the delivery of mail and then there was all Saturday afternoon, the night, Sunday. How to fill the time? She could read, sleep, she could— What could she do? Play golf. How many hours? The weekends were the worst with her nerves taut and the long emptiness of the rooms. She dressed hurriedly.

Before she went downstairs Winky glanced once into the sewing room, but Aunt Pett didn't see her. She was sitting looking down at her hands and with all her eighty-two years she seemed in absolute control, her odd dignity even in hidden repose defying the years. Winky started to enter the room but didn't. She was in no mood to face the aftermath of crisis, not now. In the downstairs hall she met Miss Boggs who was carrying a tray on which rested one glass of water and one yellow pill, the pill resting pristinely on a white paper napkin.

Winky smiled at her. "Good morning, Miss Boggs."

Miss Boggs twitched her own smile. "Did you have a nize time with your friends?"

Winky put her hand to her forehead. "Too nice, I fear. Any pills for that?"

"I've never had time to take to drink." Miss Boggs gave her genuine smile, a sour one. "They say Bromo Seltzer helps."

And you should know, Winky was thinking. The sherry decanter in the upstairs drawing room had an odd way of diminishing throughout the day. Winky glanced up the stairway. "You'd better hurry with the pill. Aunt Etoile's been here."

"I know. I heard them all the way down here."

"I'm sure you did."

"You know when you get old like that sometimes you act like children."

Winky barely nodded.

The sour smile appeared again, a dismissal.

Leuvenia, queen of the disappearing beefs and eggs and brown paper sacks, was reigning in the kitchen talking to herself; rather, one could say, she was giving a concert, a play, taking all the parts:

". . . you say you gone git *me*, man—I'll knock you *flat* 'fore you evah knowed youze a *man* . . ."

"You ain't no woman, gal!"

"I'ze nuff woman t'know you ain't no *man!* Stealin' money under folkses' pillahs. I seen ya black hand creepin' underneath theah. I weren't sleep."

"I ain' fooled with yo money."

"Do it agin heah, and I mean what I say—I'll knock you outta this heah world so flat you won't come near me agin goin' to *glowry!* You heah?"

No doubt about it. Leuvenia was a born actress, playing the roles to the hilt. Leuvenia's overheard dialogues, accurate or inaccurate, were the only glimpse the rest of the household had into her true self. Otherwise, she was someone else, another actress, a dark face in a white kitchen. A lie.

Still, she lied to herself, too; for in her play she always triumphed, the heroine, the goddess, the clean, truthful, the upright:

". . . Checkerboard, you ought not to done that. He daid."

"I'm sorry, Miss Leuvenia, I jist got tiiiid seein' that man treatin' you like that—hittin' a po' defenseless woman that ain't got no man to protect her or nothin'."

"But he daid, man."

"Yes'm, I done it for you counta you such a *fiiiine* woman."

"And a good morning to *you*, Leuvenia," Winky said as she entered the kitchen. "And are we bright and cheerful on this blue, good day?"

Leuvenia turned quickly from the sink, dropped a butter knife from her hand. "Lord, Miss Wanky, you half scared me to death!" She put both hands under her heavy breasts. "Lord, Jeeeeezus!"

Winky laughed and put her hand on one of her sloping shoulders. "I'm sorry, Vinnie."

"Whhuh," she puffed. "I'm just gone have to set down for a spell." She sat in the high-backed rocker, her stockings rolled down beneath her kneecaps, a sure indication of some mysterious ache somewhere. Leuvenia believed in "signs." The signs were in a book she read daily and had something to do with blood and the moon. If the signs weren't right, that is if there was "too much blood in your head" one day, you weren't supposed to have a tooth pulled. Another sign meant rolled down stockings. Winky had never fully understood it all but believed it might have its merits just as boiled bark from the north side of a red oak tree, which Leuvenia swore by for colds and other medicinal purposes. During pregnancies she ate baked red clay, a kind of pie. No more nausea. An old remedy, a tradition in her family. It worked, she said.

Usually Leuvenia was very neat in her crisp white uniform and apron, a good-looking woman in spite of her weight and years which, even so, seemed much younger than the forty-nine she claimed. She smiled now at Winky, a sweet smile that gave a flowerlike quality to her face.

"Mighty jumpy this morning," Winky said. "What've you been up to?"

The smile vanished. "I don't know what's the mattah'th me. Thank I'm gone have to go gack to the doctah. I got this pullin', and everytime I turns over in the bed looks like somethin' down in mah stomach just wants to drop out."

"It won't, though," Winky said.

Laughter, giggles.

"I always thought doctor talk came on Mondays."

More giggles. Leuvenia leaned forward in the chair clasping her slat hands prayer-like over her nose and mouth. Mondays were sheer unadulterated all-day gloom to Leuvenia, who saw the days of the week travel ahead like some slow, meandering snail, carrying its burdensome shell like dozens of baskets of washing, pans and dirty dishes. The "signs" were always wrong on Monday.

"Now about breakfast—" Winky opened the refrigerator door. Eggs, orange juice, all the regulars sat neatly waiting.

"You been out courtin' with Mr. Tawm again?" More

laughter. Leuvenia thought hangovers enormously funny, to say nothing of Tom, whom she had glimpsed on various occasions, once in Bermuda shorts, a scene which never seemed to erase from her mind.

"Uhhh," groaned Winky.

"You better watch out. 'Fore long we gone be halfta callin' you Mizz Tawm."

"Uh huh. But you'll have to shackle me first."

"Lord, Miss Wanky, you just kiyills me."

"I kill myself." Winky took out a grapefruit, sliced it and sat on the small stepladder near the kitchen table.

"That all you gone eat?" Leuvenia watched the procedure, fascinated. "No wonder you looks so po' around heah. Men folks don't like no po'-lookin' gull."

The grapefruit was sour. "Never fear," Winky said. "Miss Boggs and I shall grow African Violets together."

"Miss *Bawgs!*" Hilarity. Leuvenia crouched to the side of the chair and brought a handkerchief to her eyes. "Talkin' 'bout African—" She twisted to the other side.

Winky had never been able to see the great humor in Miss Boggs, but Leuvenia saw something there, some mystery that brought forth mirth and camaraderie between herself and Winky, a kind of collusion, a private joke.

"This is about the worse grapefruit I have ever tasted in my entire life. Where did Mother find it?"

"How come you don't put salt on it?" Leuvenia stood up. "Now, you just go in the breakfast room and let me fix you a good breakfast? Heah?"

"Why so kind?"

"I don't know. Just feels like being kinda smart about myself this morning."

"I thought you were dying of illness."

Leuvenia opened the refrigerator door.

"No, this is enough. Sit back down." Winky's eye caught sight of the morning's newspaper apparently set aside earlier by Leuvenia. "Did they ever catch the man who was supposed to have raped the Forzier twin?"

Silence.

Winky looked at her. "You heard about that, didn't you?"

Leuvenia eased herself back down in the chair, her arms crossed. "Yes'm."

"What happened?"

"Faber Ruffin you talkin' 'bout?"

"I guess. Nobody said what his name was."

"It was all over the newspaper and television this morning."

Winky paused, her spoon in mid-air. "They caught him then?"

"Yes'm." There was a look in Leuvenia's eyes Winky had not seen before, an aloof, even arrogant look. The actress had disappeared.

"How old is he?"

Leuvenia yawned. "He's Sister's oldest boy, you know my friend Sister that lives next door to my mama?"

"Oh, yes, Sister."

"Known him all my life. He ain't no older'n John, Jr. 'Bout twenty-seven, you might say." John, Jr. was Leuvenia's son, a young man of dubious character. Some years ago he had taken a job as chauffeur for the Ethiopian ambassador in Washington and wrecked the ambassador. John, Jr. had made headlines, yellowed now, which Leuvenia still carried in her billfold.

"He isn't related to *the* Faber, is he? The one who died, you know, who always helped at the St. Cecilia ball?"

"Aw, no'm. I thank he just kinda took on the name."

"Do you think he did it?"

Leuvenia looked toward the garden outside the kitchen door. "No'm. Faber's a good boy. He ain't never been mixed up in nothin'. He's even been to college."

Winky looked at her profile, the curved forehead, the widespread nose, the full mouth, high cheekbones. "College?" she said.

Leuvenia continued looking toward the garden. "Sure has. That boy ain't *nevah* done nothin' bad."

Winky kept looking at her profile. As far as Leuvenia was concerned, at least whenever she talked here, no colored person had ever been guilty of anything when a white person was involved. Understandable, perhaps. Yet it was strange. When Winky had covered the courts for the newspaper, and a Negro defendant, involved in a crime against one of his own color, came into the courtroom, a beaten, frightened, torn figure of a man, all the Negro spectators would roar with laughter. It was the same when he tried to speak for his defense. It worked the other way, too. Should a Negro rise above his own, become distinguished in one way or another, there was jealousy, not pride, unless of course the man was remote, one who had distinguished himself as a fighter, television personality or baseball player. Odd, it seemed they would stick together, a unit against what they deemed a hostile world. But perhaps the Negro knew what the white man would never know, no matter how intense the white man's probings.

"I just don't understand it," Winky said aloud.

"What's that?"

"I mean why they would arrest somebody like that?"

Leuvenia yawned again. "I tell you just right frankly,

Miss Wanky, the po-lice they don't care whether our color's guilty or not."

"Not even the colored police?"

"Colored's sometimes worse'n the white. Sorry thangs."

"Aw, Vinnie, I think they do. I mean they just can't go around arresting somebody for absolutely nothing. I mean, why did they arrest him in the first place? There must have been some evidence."

"They don't need no ev-idence. They gone burn him, thas all." Her thick lips curled downward and for a moment there was truth, and the truth was hatred. "Well, I gotta get mah vaccumin' done. I ain't gettin' nowhere settin' here talkin' to you."

Winky speared the grapefruit. "Well, you'd better just put the shoulder to the wheel then." She lifted the spoon of grapefruit, looked at it, put the spoon back on the saucer. "Hey, what're Daddy and Beauvoir putting out *another* camellia for?"

Leuvenia giggled. "Po' thang."

"What d' you mean?"

Leuvenia yawned again.

"Huh?"

"Nothin'. Just yo daddy sure like them thangs, don't he?"

"Uh huh." Winky stood up. "I think I'll go out and see what they're doing. Happy vacuuming. Don't let Miss Boggs get you."

"Now, Miss Wanky, go own now." Giggles. "You gone git me in trouble with that woman." She put her left foot round her right ankle as a child would do who has waited too long after the call of nature.

"Why, I wouldn't think of it. After all, Miss Boggs and I've got a lot of African Violets to grow before we're done."

Laughter throughout the dining room, into the hall, and finally the purr of the vacuum.

Winky looked at her watch. Eleven-fifteen. The mail usually arrived between twelve and twelve-thirty. She went outside to the garden. Beauvoir had already dug the hole for the camellia, and her father was bending over the plant, straightening it for planting, an *Alba plena*, her father's favorite with its white purity and fragile life.

Both of the men looked up at her. The aging Beauvoir with his strong hands, massive feet enclosed now in thick-soled boots, removed his hat. "G'morning, Miss Wanky."

Her father said nothing.

"It's a bit early to be planting camellias, isn't it?"

"No, it's all right," her father said. "We'll soon be getting the autumn rains." He stood up. "Good morning, Leigh."

Winky looked at Beauvoir, who instantly lowered his eyes.

"Leigh?" she said softly. "This is Winky." She tried to laugh. "Winky." She searched his face.

His smile faded. "Winky, yes. I guess I've been thinking about Leigh too much lately. She went on that trip, you know. I don't know why she wanted to go." He shook his head. "I worry about autumn crossings. A bad season."

"But, Daddy, Leigh is—" Winky turned away. She pulled a sasanqua leaf and crushed it in her left hand.

"Now, plenty of peatmoss, Beauvoir, and we'll need some leaf mold—from the compost in the back. Would you bring it, please?"

Winky slowly opened her hand and saw the crushed leaf. Behind her she could hear the trickling from the water hose. She turned. Beauvoir was shuffling toward the back of the house, and her father was bent over the newly dug earth filling it with water. There were bubbles in the muddy water, and the smell of the dirt was pungent, cleansing somehow. But it was like last night with the tightness in her chest and the aching in her throat. Was she going to cry *here?* She put both hands to her neck, watching her father's curved back as he knelt. She kept gazing at the back, the old tan sweater, the gray hair showing beneath his soiled hat.

"Now that should be enough until Beauvoir gets back." He stood up slowly. "Why were you so late last night, young lady?"

"Last night?" she said thinly, then she smiled broadly. *You do remember! You do remember!* She brushed her hair from her face. "I don't know. But I guess I shouldn't have gone anywhere. I mean, after what Mother told me when I came in."

"Was she angry?"

"Not very. But she did tell me about your falling."

"Oh that. Foolish. I must have slipped somehow." He seemed embarrassed. For the first time in his life her father seemed embarrassed.

"You may be foolish," Winky said teasingly. "But you're not very old."

"Ah now, wait until you're sixty-five."

"Look at somebody like Mr. Archibald—in his eighties or something and looks and acts younger than I do."

"You never did say why you were so late?"

"Tom's. It was his birthday, and he had a bunch of people —and well, *you* know."

"I see." Her father tilted his hat back and leaned against the trunk of the oak tree. His eyes looked almost blue. "You're not getting overly fond of Mr. Gearhart, are you?"

"Let's not talk about it. Later, not now."

"Is it that painful?"

"Fairly. He slipped a huge, gaudy diamond on my finger."

"I see."

"No, you don't."

"Do you have the ring?" He glanced at her hand.

"It went right back into its little velvet casket. As a matter of fact, it was never taken out of there."

"Ah, Winky," he lightly touched the top of the young camellia, "sometimes I think you must be very much like your great grandmother."

"Why?"

"I never knew her well, of course—my own grandmother. But they say she was a charming woman—married three times, a bit of a scandal in those days, I suppose."

"No similarity there," Winky said.

"She was lost somehow, they said. Never seemed to find her world, if anyone does really." He straightened his hat. "You must find yours. I want that for you."

The blueness of his eyes and his simple words deepened the ache in her. She went over to the oak and stretched her hands up along the gnarled trunk. "I think I've found mine, my world. But I don't think my world wants me."

"Then you haven't found it."

"Yes, yes I have."

"Everett. Everett is his name, isn't it?"

"Yes. Walter Everett."

He leaned down and pulled a blade of grass. "Strange, we all long for those things far away, don't we, something we think we want. We long and look all our lives. Power, success, the perfect God, glory, the perfect love."

Winky said nothing, but between them there were the unsaid things, the things she wanted to pour from her soul, the terrible struggle to hold on, to everything, it seemed, even courage.

"It's especially that way when you're young. I remember my own *Wanderjahre*, the confusion and then coming back here."

"At Oxford? That was a kind of perfect time—for you, wasn't it? Did you ever really plan to come back to Charleston?"

"Oh, once or twice I thought of other places. I even thought of staying on in England. But Charleston is my home. And then—there was your mother."

"Was there ever anyone else?—except Mother?"

He smiled. "Not seriously."

"How good. How truly good." She looked down at her hand. "I guess I really wasn't the epitome of tact with Tom. I'll call him or something." She put her hand to her neck. "I'm so tired. Honestly. Exhausted."

"No sleep."

"Not much. You didn't hear Aunt Pett and Etoile's performance at dawn this morning, did you?" Strange, she still wanted to cry.

"No, I've been too busy with Beauvoir." He bent then, over the place where the camellia was to go.

"It was horrendous, Etoile and Pett." Her voice was unusually loud, forcing gaiety.

"Yes?"

"Wouldn't you think now, in this bomb-dropping, black-yellow-white age we live in—wouldn't you think it wouldn't hurt anything for Etoile to prance around on a stage a bit?"

Her father chuckled.

"But, honestly." The ache was easing now, lessening. "You should have *heard* them. Aunt Pett was mad because the Pringneys left her out of some 'do' they gave, and Etoile's still mad because of the Lord knows what." Winky sighed. "The poor harmless beautiful Dock Street Theatre."

Her father stood up, brushing the dirt from his hands. "Pett and Etoile are the last of an age."

"Yes, I guess so." In the distance Winky could see Beauvoir coming toward them, pushing the wheelbarrow filled with peatmoss, pine straw and rotted leaves.

"But then we're all the last of this age," her father said. "Charleston is changing, no matter what anybody says. Most of the people here are too close to it to see." He seemed to be looking about him, at his garden readying itself for its winter sleep. "Changing gradually. The people, old customs are dying out. But then the whole South is changing. Not just this Negro-white thing. There's something new, hard—whispers. I don't like it." He looked at Winky. "When Pett goes, when Etoile, and even—I do wonder."

"You?" she meant to say to herself, but she said it aloud. She quickly turned to Beauvoir. "Why talk of dying, Beauvoir, when, look, we have a new young camellia, to grow and grow and—"

"My daughter doesn't like to talk about dying, Beauvoir. What do you think of that?"

Beauvoir shook his head. "Me neither. That's bad luck. We all gotta go, though, when our time comes."

"True," Winky said. "But not today. Not on a blue day. People never die on a blue day."

"Yes'm, they do."

"Why, Beauvoir, you're just as morbid as Daddy."

The water had partially drained from the hole, and Beauvoir began mixing the peatmoss with top soil. "Just like last night," Beauvoir said. "I didn't get me a minute's sleep."

"With all the work you do, it seems you'd sleep like a lad," her father said.

"Train Man was at it agin."

The Negro "Train Man," as he was known in certain Charleston circles, was one of the city's more renowned personalities. He thought he was a train and ran down the sidewalks whistling his whistle and making noises like a train gathering speed.

"Backin' up *all* night, and chuggin' forward. My wife she got so nuhvous she slammed up the window and said—said: 'Hey, Train Man, you runnin' late, better go on now to the next station. Folks's is waitin'. But it didn't do no good. Allll night, chuggalug, chuggalug, CHUGGALUG, whee, wheeee! Backin' up, runnin' forward— Lawd God—"

Both Winky and her father laughed.

"Doesn't he have family here?" her father asked.

"He's got an awntee, but the rest of 'em don't pay him no mind."

"Other people are good to him, aren't they?" her father asked. "They wouldn't be cruel to him?"

"Aw, no sir, they teases him some, 'cept this one man lives down the street a piece—sorry thang, lays up drunk half the time—he throws rocks at him sometimes."

"How mean," Winky said.

"Yes'm," Beauvoir said. "He's one of them what gets *meeeen* when he dranks. Don't drank nothin' 'cept white stuff and wine. They say wine'll run you crazy."

Winky laughed. "I'm awfully glad I didn't know that when I was in Europe this summer."

"It'll do it," Beauvoir said authoritatively.

Winky realized her father was looking at her, and there was a slight bewilderment in his eyes, only slight and only for a moment. Was it the talk of drinking? Or the mention of Europe that caused the look? Whatever, the look was there, a hurt, eyes that seemed to plead for an answer. They both looked away.

"Well, Beauvoir," he said after a while. "Let's plant our youngling."

The young camellia stood upright and green in the mulched ground, packed by Beauvoir's strong hands and surrounded by pine straw. Perhaps there would be one or two blooms by January and then the next year and the next . . .

"You'll fertilize the rest of the things I spoke of, won't you, Beauvoir?" her father asked.

Beauvoir nodded, and her father watched as he walked back toward the carriage house. "You see, Beauvoir's one of the last, too."

"Yes, yes he is," Winky said. "And a lot of people will be glad he is, I guess. They want it all to go—the accent, the Uncle Tomish bit, even the gentleness and manners it sometimes seems to me."

They began walking toward the house. "Situational ethics, I think they call it now," her father said. "But we never know the Negro. He won't let us know him."

"Don't you think you know Beauvoir—after all, he's been here thirty years or more."

"No, not really. But if I could paint, and I wish that I could, I would paint Beauvoir a strong man, a real man, with honor and divinity in his soul." He hesitated for a moment.

"That is the way I see him. And underneath I would write as they did of Job: 'And so he died, being old and full of days.' " He turned to Winky. "Would it be honest?"

"I think so."

"I am Beauvoir's friend, and I hope he is mine."

Winky looked up at him. How thin he was with his eyes, only the eyes, smiling plaintively.

There was the sound of the mailman outside the entrance gate, a clanking noise as the lid of the mailbox shut. Winky listened as the lid banged once—twice. She knew the mailman's habits by heart: first, the magazines and newspapers; then, the bills, circulars, letters.

"Mailman's early today," her father said. "Let's see if there's any word from Leigh."

"Leigh?" Winky barely whispered the name; all the while they had been talking he had seemed so right. She watched his stooped figure as he walked with quicker steps to the gate.

She continued to watch as he collected the assortment. Newspapers. A magazine. Bills. A letter. He carefully examined the content. "Here's something for you, Winky."

She could feel her face scarlet. It was a postcard; the address was typewritten. Walter typed everything, even postcards. She remembered how he—

Her father handed her the card.

". . . Junior League Meeting, Wednesday, October 31. BE PROMPT. Spring House Tour to be dis— . . ."

The words blurred before her.

"Why, Winky, you're— What's the matter?"

She tried to laugh, but the tears were streaming down her face.

Chapter 5

So it was final. Winky would stay in Charleston. She could not leave her father, nor her mother for that matter. All her plans made so carefully during the summer were off, done, finished. The expectancy of New York had been the one, solid thing that had made the recent weeks bearable.

Winky left her father in the garden and went straight to her bedroom. The telephone rested there beside her bed like a human thing. All she had to do was lift the receiver and in a matter of minutes there would be Walter's voice. Surely, if he heard her voice again everything would be different.

Why hadn't she heard from him? Her thoughts came crazed: Perhaps he's ill, dying. Silly girl. Somebody would have written. No one had written. It was as if she had died, going down, down, down into darkness and wilderness, while they, the silent who had not written, they were with the witty, the intelligent, the believing, the alive. Forgotten.

"The reason a person doesn't write, Winky, is simply because he doesn't want to; no other reason," someone had told her once when she was seventeen and "madly in love" with a young boy at Episcopal High in Virginia. Strange, she couldn't even remember his name.

The telephone drew her to it, and she rested her hand on it. She tried to put herself in his mind, receiving her call, perhaps a nuisance, a bore, but worse, pitying her, imagining her down here, isolated in what he continuously referred to as "a small Southern town," a dreary wilderness, while his own life, his city, sprang with vitality, people who were doing things, important things, the beautiful business of people involved.

No, she would not call.

She glanced at the desk in the corner of the room. "I'll write him, tell him about Daddy. A natural thing. Then he'll answer."

"But, Daddy!" She whimpered and fell across her bed, sobbing.

When the tears and the heavy gulps of breathing had at last quit themselves she slowly got up from the bed and went over to the desk. The stationery box rested dumbly in the second drawer. She took out the box, opened it. There had been so many letters these past weeks, all torn and destroyed finally, night after night. It had been comforting somehow to unburden her thoughts on the thin gray pages. Then, when she had finished, purged herself, she would put the pages in the envelope, address it, then open the envelope again and re-read the letter, pretending she were Walter and how he should receive such words.

"Walter darling," she wrote now and scratched out the words. "Walter dear." And finally: "Dear Walter."

She drove to the post office, and with no hesitation dropped the letter in the "Out-Of-Town" mail.

"And who has the greatest hangover of them all?"

She turned. It was Bill Ashe, looking world-weary even in the post office. For a moment Winky had thought it was Tom, a certain similarity in the intonation of voice.

"Hello, Bill."

Bill Ashe put his long fingers to his forehead. "Do you *know* what I had to do this *morn*ing?"

"No idea."

"I actually had to *fling* myself out of bed and take Mrs. Bradford and three of her friends who are all about one thousand years old out for a drive! Way out to Lagare Plantation, of all places." He lifted his eyes ceilingward.

"Whatever for?"

"Because her ancient car had broken down—at last, and, my god, she called up at dawn!"

"Oh, Bill. How killing." Winky glanced back once at the slot where she had dropped her letter.

"You're going to be at the supper club tonight, aren't you?"

"What supper club?"

"You belong, you should know."

"Oh. Saturday. I'd forgotten."

"I presume Thomas will be able to make it."

"He may, but I won't."

Bill Ashe touched his forehead again. "I really can't say I blame you, but Suzan and Bob invited me, so I guess I'll have to go." Sigh. "I have to be in Nairobi, of all places, by next Wednesday."

"How exciting. For how long?" Winky felt suddenly dizzy. She wanted to get back to her car.

"Oh, only for a couple of days actually."

"And when will we be seeing you again?"

"Soon. Soon—two or three weekends from now you might say."

"Good!" Winky waved at him and started to walk away.

"You better check with your boy friend and come along tonight."

"What boy friend?"

"Why, our boy wonder. Tom, of course."

"Friend. Only friend."

"Oh, really?" The question was almost a yawn. "I thought we'd be hearing wedding bells soon."

"Sorry." She turned to him. "Bye now." She left the building.

In the car Winky turned the ignition key irritably. "Supper clubs!" *Suppahclubs,* as it was pronounced. There must have been five or more such affairs in the city, the people all carefully chosen, depending on the club, and each Saturday couples took turns hosting. There were better and lesser clubs; each knew his place. Winky and two others were the only unmarried members, treated with a certain secure benevolence afforded in view of their rather sad status. The clubs had become a part of the ritual of Charleston's social life, the latter an unending, unceasing, nightly round of parties, a rite certain Charlestonians entered in their teens and practiced to the grave, a gay, graceful life hosted with taste and subdued elegance.

Winky drove down Meeting Street. She half noticed remnants of the September storm, old trees uprooted here and there, fallen bricks, some debris still cluttering the streets. She had liked the storm. It was the one thing (with the exception of one long arduous hour with the dentist) that had eased her thoughts since she had been home. Everyone else had sat in rigid silence during the storm as the latched shutters trembled about the house and the winds howled like a wounded beast. She, alone, was exhilarated.

When she neared East Battery she parked her car on a side street and walked the distance to High Battery, the sea wall that ran along the eastern side of the peninsula city. The iron railing was hot to the touch as she leaned against it, but the winds blew cold through her hair. The sea was choppy, the glare blinding. She lifted her face to the wind. How many times she had sailed in weather just like this. With her father, friends. The seas and winds were different in Norway. But Walter had liked them as they sailed the fjords.

She glanced at her watch. Ten minutes until two. Leuvenia would have dinner ready. Since coming home Winky had had a rather difficult time readjusting to Charleston's two o'clock dinners. It was the only city she knew that still practiced the early English custom. But Aunt Pett clung to the hour as she did everything else peculiarly Charlestonian. No one, save her father, could be late; the hour could not be changed, not by one inch of the clock's long hand.

She walked back to the house, and along the side piazza she saw Leuvenia hurrying into the kitchen, her apron ties flying in the wind behind her like ghostly hands. Leuvenia's timing, much to the everlasting exasperation of Aunt Pett, was always off.

"Better hurry," Winky called to her.

Leuvenia shoved the air with her hands, a gesture that somehow signalled the awesome, sitting, waiting Aunt Pett. Winky laughed and sat in one of the black wrought-iron chairs on the piazza. The white columns and railing made odd designs on the floor. She traced them with her foot, partially toeing the growing signs of coming afternoon.

"And what will you do this afternoon?" she asked herself. Read. Sleep. She thought of calling Williams, the doctor (her mother's cousin). Perhaps Williams would give her some sleeping pills. Sometimes it seemed she hadn't slept in months, reading far into the night, finally trying to sleep, then turning on the bed lamp again, smoking, thinking, remembering, turning, wide-eyed, listening to the steady, terrible beat of her own heart.

She would call Williams. Or maybe . . . .

"Hit's ready!" Leuvenia's face peeked out from the long dining-room doors.

Her father was not at dinner. His chair, with its smoothly worn Sheraton arms, sat solitary at the end of the table. Her mother sat at the other end with the Hester Bateman tea set behind her, its velvet patina wearing well in contrast to her own tired face.

"You know what I think? Do you know what I really

think?" asked Aunt Pett as she ladled the Mock Terrapin soup. "I think Frances Chesney's child is a Communist!"

Both Winky and her mother looked up at her.

"Whatever gave you *that* idea, Pett?" asked her mother.

"I've been on the telephone all morning, talking to Faye Pringney and—"

"Faye Pringney?" asked Winky. She started to say that was odd, considering Faye Pringney had left her out of last week's party and invited Aunt Etoile instead. But she continued with her soup.

"Yes," said Aunt Pett. "Faye was telling me all about her—a nineteen-year-old girl quitting college and going somewhere to work with Negroes." She said the last word with discretion, glancing toward the kitchen.

"Oh, she's just young, Pett," her mother said. "It's probably the Peace Corps or something."

"No. It's somewhere up there. Frances ought never to have sent her to that school."

"I went to the same school," Winky said. "And I'm not a Communist."

"You should have stayed right here," said Aunt Pett. "The College of Charleston is one of the best institutions in the country. Dr. Laird was telling me just the other day that the young people can scarcely get into it any more."

"I think it's good for a young girl to be in a different atmosphere sometimes, just to find out how the others do." Her mother was defending her own decision made some years ago.

"What for?" asked Pett.

"As I said—to learn what others think and do."

"Silly," said Aunt Pett. "They learn it and always come back here. Charlestonians don't like other ways."

Winky sighed, one calculated to be heard. "But that's

why I'm going to Frances Chesney's party tonight," said Aunt Pett. "I feel sorry for her, having a child going that way." She rang the small silver bell at her side. "Leuvenia never puts mace in this soup. It's supposed to have mace."

"You're going with us tonight, aren't you, Winky—to Frances Chesney's party?"

"No, I don't think so."

"Why not, child?" asked Aunt Pett.

"I don't know," said Winky.

"Why, *Winky?*" her mother said, looking at her curiously.

"You ought to be seen more," said Aunt Pett. "Young unwed girls should be seen every chance they get."

"With a scarlet U, I suppose," Winky said.

Her mother frowned at Winky and shook her head, a coded message Winky knew by heart: "Don't be flip with Aunt Pett, dear," said the message. "She's quite old, you know . . ."

"Did you want me, Mizz Pett?" asked Leuvenia.

"Mace," said Aunt Pett, looking from Winky up at Leuvenia's dark face now trimmed, since this morning, with a lace cap. "You have forgotten the mace."

"We ain't got none."

"Oh, haven't we?" asked her mother. "I'm sorry, Pett. I'll get some Monday."

"Very well," said Aunt Pett. "We don't want to forget the old receipts, do we?"

"No'm!" said Leuvenia, straining enthusiasm, and vanished.

"Will you be with Tom Gearhart tonight?" her mother asked Winky.

"No."

"Winky, I declare," said Aunt Pett, "you act like you're

having a nuuuuvous breakdown."

"Pett!" said her mother. Her voice sounded like a muted scream.

Aunt Pett blinked at Winky, her amber eyes considering her recent statement.

"Don't worry. I won't disgrace you, Aunt Pett. If I have one I'll have it discreetly."

"Everybody's going crazy nowadays," said Aunt Pett.

The remark remained, hovering over the table.

"'*Cheeeez*us luuuves me, this I knows,'" sang Leuvenia from the kitchen. The singing was mixed with the rattling of pans.

Leuvenia's sudden outbursts of song were daily, usually when she was bored. No one remarked on the burst.

"I wonder if the Forziers will be there tonight?" asked Aunt Pett. "You wouldn't think so, would you, after what happened to their daughter."

"Surely not," said her mother. "That poor young girl, a nightmare. Poor, poor people."

"She's out!" said Aunt Pett. "Faye Pringney told me all about it. The girl didn't even stay overnight in the hospital. They're trying to say it wasn't really you-know-what now. Trying to protect the child, you know."

"Poor people," her mother said again. "How are they taking it? Did Faye say?"

"It's the child's twin they're worrying about. *She's* the one who is so upset. Faye took a dish of something over for them. Just curious if you ask me. They caught the boy who did it." Aunt Pett glanced toward the kitchen. "Colored," she whispered.

"Dear me, let's not speak of it at the table," her mother said, turning to Winky again. "I do wish you would go with us tonight. Don't you feel well?"

"No, just tired, I think."

"They're going to have a trial," said Aunt Pett.

"What?" Her mother looked confusedly from Winky to Aunt Pett.

"A *public* trial, Faye Pringney told me. They have to try the boy, you know."

"Oh, dear. How perfectly terrible for them," said her mother.

"I'm not going to it," said Aunt Pett.

"I should think not," said her mother.

"Everybody else, trash, will be there, though."

"It seems the child has suffered enough," her mother said.

"You don't look well, Winky," Aunt Pett said, ringing her small bell again. "Thinking about that young man up there."

Winky said nothing.

"You're not going to get any better, just sitting around mooning," said Aunt Pett. "Go out—go out with your funny man if necessary."

"What funny man?"

"That German, Gearhart or whatever his name is."

"He's too funny," Winky said.

"Well, you'd better just get up some gumption then. No Petrie, or Carr, sits around and moons just because things don't go the way they want them to. Pitying yourself! The most selfish thing I know of. Mooning and whining."

Winky pushed her chair back and rose from the table. "You will forgive me, I'm sure."

"Oh, Win-ky," her mother said.

"Let her go," said Aunt Pett. "It's very bad for the health to dine when one is—"

Winky didn't hear the finish of the remark. In the hall she took hold of the newel, rested her head on her hand.

Perhaps Aunt Pett was correct. Perhaps she was "pitying" herself. But—was there to be no release? Ever? She climbed the stairs slowly.

She tried to read, a long rambling story in *The New Yorker* about a sensitive young English girl's adolescence in India. The young sensitive girl's mother was trying to cling to the past when her own family had riches and titles, and the sensitive young adolescent was just awakening to sexual . . . Winky couldn't concentrate. She got up, went downstairs and sat on the sofa in the downstairs drawing room. The house was silent, the three o'clock silence, with Leuvenia gone, the rattling and the singing quit. Everyone else was taking a nap. She picked up an old copy of *Newsweek*. Inside was a feature story on George Wallace, Governor of Alabama. She rested the magazine in her lap and closing her eyes became aware of the ticking of the mantel clock.

The ticking was stubbornly even—on, on, on. As she listened the ticking seemed to grow louder as it had when she was a child and sat on this very same sofa, staring at the clock, fascinated by its spider hands and half-hour gongs. She looked at it, a beautiful work really, by Eli Terry. Should one have to be reminded of the tick of time it might as well be done by beauty. Tourists, especially New Englanders, always noticed the clock.

Tourists. Twice Aunt Pett had permitted the house to be opened during the spring season. The concession came mainly because of Aunt Pett's undying loyalty for the Historic Charleston Foundation. Winky, along with many of her friends, had been a guide through many of the houses, and Winky had been appointed her own house to show.

The tourists, mostly middle-aged with Florida tans, would gather in the hallway as Winky, hearing her own

Charleston A's and O's, quietly and methodically would begin:

"... This is the Archibald Petrie Town House. Archibald Petrie was a planter and the son of Amos Petrie, one of the first Church of England bishops of South Carolina. The house was built in 1732. We in Charleston call it a double house because it has two rooms, instead of one, facing the street entrance."

The people, then, sheep-like, would glance back at the entrance door. "... the architecture is Georgian and is especially noted for its arched doorways and oval walls in the various rooms. Here in the hallway you may be interested in the French *vernis Martin* chairs ..."

"As you can see the library is panelled in South Carolina cypress. All the paint has been stripped in this particular room ..."

And she would go throughout the house, explaining the special craft of the stairway, pointing out furniture, porcelains, old silver, paintings, chandeliers, the Aubusson rug and the Adam mantel in the upstairs drawing room, then Aunt Pett's bedroom, her mother's room, her father's, then out into the garden where the yellow Banksia roses peeked over the wall and the wisteria hung in lush glory over the arch toward the carriage house.

Most of the tourists were really quite nice, only occasionally asking what seemed inane questions: "Why do so many Charleston houses have Chinese porcelains? Why don't *gulls* wear the full hoop skirts like they do down home in Mississippi and places like thayat?"

Winky wanted to say "because we think it is tacky" in reference to the skirts, but she would merely smile and say, "I really don't know."

One tourist, a particularly curious Texan, broke one of

Aunt Pett's Rockingham figurines in the upstairs drawing room and after that the house was closed forever, Historic Charleston Foundation or not. There had been a bit of a rift with a certain Mr. Stoney over the closing, but Aunt Pett held fast, consenting only to leave her gates open for garden glimpses.

Winky, her head resting on the sofa back, half smiled at the memory. It had all seemed so long ago. She did adore the house. How different it was from Walter's family's house in Pittsburgh in spite of the Everett money—a monstrous Victorian horror overcrowded with furniture and pictures the Everetts had picked up in Europe sometime in the early nineties when the family had had its first heyday with money. At least war and poverty had saved Charleston that; the Victorian era just didn't exist here, one blessing, if the only one, from Reconstruction days.

She became conscious of the ticking of the clock again, and her arms and fingers began to tingle as if they cried for use. She began to roam the rooms, sitting in chairs, mashing out half-smoked cigarettes. She went into the library, searched the titles in the book cases, sat in her father's red leather chair with the smell of tobacco, worn leather and brittle pages from ancient books. The tingling in her arms had not stopped. And then in a flash of blind tide she picked up the telephone, dialed a number:

"Richard Cummings, please."

A buzzing noise and then, "Cummings here." The voice was weary, almost impatient.

"Dick?"

"Yes."

"Dick, it's Winky."

"Winky? I thought you were travelling the high seas."

"No, I'm back. At least I think I am."

"Yes? Good time?"

"I guess so. Dick, look. Is my old desk still there?"

"It's here, but filled up. I thought you said you were quitting the glorious Fourth Estate."

"I know. But I've just re-joined it, mentally at least. Have you got anything for me?"

A pause, too long. "We're pretty tight right now." Another pause. "But let me talk to upstairs. Come in to see me Monday. Okay?"

"Put me on obits. I don't care."

"You sound desperate. What's the matter?"

"I don't know. I'll tell you about it."

"See you Monday. I'll do what I can."

"Thanks, Dick."

"Okay."

Winky was sure Dick could work out something. She had done a fairly good job before, at least they all said so. If he could, would— Well, she was here. She was definitely here. And here she would remain. "Charleston's Brenda Starr!" She laughed hollowly, and the loneliness of the sound almost frightened her.

"I do wish you were going with us, Winky. I hate to leave you here alone."

Winky was watching her mother as she sat before her dresser, securing one of the long jade earrings she always wore to parties. "You look lovely. *La belle.*"

"This old dress still seems to do, doesn't it? But before too long I guess I'll have to get another."

She was wearing her long black dress with the rounded neck and three-quarter-length sleeves.

"A dress like that is always good. Black tie, too, I suppose. Is Daddy going?"

"Yes. I'll watch for him, of course."

"It's tiring, isn't it? I mean, not letting him make a—*you know.*"

Her mother closed her eyes. "Yes, yes it is."

"I should go, really, if just to help you out."

Her mother rose from the dresser. She did look lovely, not so tired. The black brought out the blueness of her eyes and the blush of skin. Winky said so.

"I just don't feel like going."

"I know."

"Leuvenia fixed a salad and a few things for you."

"I'm not very hungry."

"Now you must eat properly, Winky."

"Oh! I forgot to tell you." Winky put out her cigarette in the ashtray before her. "Did I tell you? I called Dick Cummings. He may give me my old job back on the paper."

Her mother snapped closed her evening bag and looked at Winky. "I'm so sorry."

"Sorry? I'm delighted."

"Yes, but you did want to try New York, didn't you?"

"Only halfway. Not really."

"You know, you can still go. I don't want anything to hold you here. I—I would regret that all my days."

"You're not holding me here. It's my own choice."

Her mother sat beside her on the settee. "It may be a long time—Petrie's illness."

"Let's not talk about it just now." Winky stood up. "You just go to the Chesneys'. Try to have a good evening. People are more understanding than you think. Really."

"I don't think many people have noticed," her mother said.

"No, I'm—"

"Ann!" Her father's voice came from the outer hall.

Her mother quickly gathered her coat and evening bag, making quick little nervous steps. "Now, do try to eat a little something, Winky. You're getting awfully thin."

"I will." She followed her out into the hall. Her father stood there, and seeing him she smiled. He looked quite elegant, even proud of himself, though the tuxedo hung loosely on his tall, thin body and the cut was a bit old-fashioned.

Winky laughed. "You do look like the proud peacock, sir."

"I think I look pretty handsome myself," he said almost cockily.

He took her mother's arm, and the two slowly and gracefully descended the stairway. How many times Winky had seen them leave just so. She looked after them until they reached the hall below, tears finally veiling her sight. *Don't change. Don't change. Don't change.*

At eight-fifteen the telephone rang.

"Heard any mermaids lately?"

It was Tom.

"No, just like T. S. Eliot—they don't sing for me."

"Why, Antoinette, I just *don't* understand you. There you are, living in a beautiful house, have absolutely everything in the world, three *fine* children and—"

"What do you want, Tom?"

"I've just gotten rid of the Walkers."

"The new couple?"

"Uh hu*uuh*."

"How were the juleps?"

"The juleps were excellent, but the Walkers were a drag."

"What's the matter?"

"She's got sowyuth in the mowyuth, talks constantly, and he sits there like a petrified owl."

"Can't blame him, I suppose."

"Let's have dinner."

"What for?"

"Because I'm starved and I had some ungrateful people over last night who ate me out of house and bar."

"I wonder who that could have been?"

"How about? We can go to a quick and dirty if you want to."

"I don't know, Tom."

"Why aren't you at the supper club? Didn't you have anybody to go with?"

"Shall I hang up?"

"No, I want to have dialogue with you over a bit of dinner and bourbon."

"We've already done that."

"My wounds are healed."

Winky glanced at her desk; the stationery box was still open. She wouldn't be able to sleep anyway.

"All right. Where do you want to go?"

"Yacht Club?"

"No, we'll get the overflow from the Chesney party."

"Henry's, then? Perdita's? Everybody's supping at the supper club. Nobody'll be there."

"All right—but home afterward."

"Naturally. I shall be by for you in my little peoples' car."

"See you about that time."

Winky placed the receiver down.

She glanced at her desk once more, and a weariness coiled her body.

Part Two ∼∼∼∼

Winky had heard of Walter Everett before she ever really met him. By the time she reached Wellesley his career at Princeton was already legend.

Later, when she thought of him, when she went over and over their time together, she sometimes wondered what he had actually been like in college, and, for that matter, what she herself was like.

As for herself, she could readily recall: an outwardly assured and inwardly tangled freshman, trying to find some smattering of identity among the myriad bicycles, strident-voiced females and a certain "let's get it organized NOW" attitude.

Those first few weeks were her first encounter with what seemed the frantic machinery of the North, and it was much like an infant's awakening to starched uniforms, fretted howls and huge swollen faces looking down from glaring white ceilings. The womb of Charleston, and, later, the sad rolling land of Virginia, had soothed her, rocked her and tuned her senses. Wellesley was a wilderness, busy, harsh.

Winky never met Walter Everett the entire time she was in Massachusetts. But she followed his career. It was unavoidable since one of the more active "cliques" at college, in which Winky at one point found herself on the periphery, was studiedly interested in his career, especially a girl from New York who for four long years carried his torch to no avail.

As an undergraduate he had fallen deeply in love with a Eurasian girl. That, "they" said, occurred on one of his various summer trips to the Far East. No one Winky knew ever actually saw the girl, but one of his "closest friends in life" had met her, said she was the most "beautiful, intriguing creature I've ever met." One summer there was to be a marriage; next fall Walter Everett was back in graduate school, unmarried, and there was something about a Vassar girl and an hilarious, though eyebrow-raising, trip on a march through the South.

During Winky's junior year Walter Everett was studying for his Ph.D., closeted, oddly aloof, and escapades in Asia, the South and elsewhere unrumored. He disappeared. Through channels she later learned he was an assistant professor of English at Williams, was dismissed, had written an unsuccessful play, and, later still, had volunteered "of all things" for the war in Vietnam. None of it made any sense.

But by that time Winky didn't care. She was back in Charleston and all the names that had once seemed so important quite soon became very unimportant; they faded and gave way to the old familiar names—Rhett, Ravenel, Pinckney, Pringney . . .

It was her father who encouraged Winky to take the summer course at Oslo, though at twenty-five she thought she could scarcely be classified a "student." A friend had written her, asking her to go, and she promptly dismissed the letter, bringing it up one day at dinner merely as a bit of conversation to interrupt one of Aunt Pett's and Aunt Etoile's tirades.

Her father was enthusiastic with the idea, speaking in a nostalgic way of his own years at Oxford, insisting a study abroad was a "civilizing force" for any young American.

Time had passed all too significantly since her father's years at Oxford, however. Winky realized just how much as one hot, humid June day she found herself in New York standing alone at Pier 45 in a crowd of every shape, size and form of human creature imaginable. Charleston, South Carolina, with its rivers and hanging moss was one billion light years away.

Here again, then, were the sounds and sights of the American North. Since leaving college Winky's ears had become so attuned to the soft, though quickened, accent of Charleston that the mingling of broad A's, harsh R's and breathy D's and T's struck her instantly as something once so familiar she could recite it as one might a foreign tongue:

". . . But, Mummy, Jamie sai*t* he was coming. I mean, I mean . . ."

"Now, do you have your passport, Heatherrr?"

"Yes, but Jamie sai*t* . . ."

"Stop pulling at your fingernails, Heatherrrr . . ."

. . . And where was Ardys? Winky had roomed with Ardys Langenberry throughout school and college and not once, even when she used to visit her in St. Louis, had Ardys ever, once, been on time for anything.

Ardys did arrive in a cloud of nerves, chatter, black summer suit and one frail bespectacled associate editor in the trade department of the same publishing house where Ardys herself held a position in the children's department.

The associate editor had given Ardys an orchid, a huge purple one, and Winky wanted to laugh, knowing Ardys's fetish for anything she deemed overdone.

Diet as she would, Ardys was still on the right side of plump. But she was tall, carried her weight well, and was actually what one might call a "good-looking" young woman.

She wore her brown hair rather long and she had the kind of understated style St. Louisans strove for.

Nevertheless, she seemed to overpower the associate editor, who said very little and merely stood grinning at Ardys and her huge orchid. The grin, Winky considered was his way of fitting into the occasion. It was a festive grin.

Passengers were boarding.

"D'you want to come aboard, Henry? Have a drink for old *bon voyage's* sake?"

The associate editor didn't believe he would; not just now.

"Well, good-bye, then," whined Ardys in mock timidity, something she had obviously learned in recent months.

The associate editor then shed his former self and planted a small kiss on Ardys's forehead.

"Well," Winky said as Ardys and the associate editor finally parted, finger tip from finger tip.

"Oh, God," Ardys said, her breath coming shortly. "I've got to think, get away. What do you think of him? He's not at all the way he looks."

"He looks all right."

"You didn't like him, did you?" Ardys had been asking the same question for the ten years Winky had known her.

"How could I tell?"

"I don't know. I just don't know. I've got to *think*."

The associate editor was waving timidly as the ship left the pier. Winky was waving to him in newly found friendship; Ardys was below arguing with somebody about luggage.

The piece of luggage was recovered, but the purser, or whoever, had not guessed well as to dinner companions.

They were male, which at first glance gave a renewed bounce to Ardys, who had already sized up the passengers and given a tirade about how everybody had money nowadays and there wasn't "a decent place left for anybody, really decent, to go anymore." But as the shorelines dimmed, table twenty-two soon became cell twenty-two, for four.

Across from Winky sat Arthur Bailey, a chemist, divorced, from Whittier, California. Art, as he said "everybody" called him, was a fortyish-age man, with a blank face, thinning blond hair, one lock of which was carefully combed over his bald top. He had curiosity. By the time dinner was served the first night he had explored the ship from top to bottom, fore and aft. He knew everything, a statistics man. He knew how many crossings the ship had made, he knew how many engines moved below. He even knew how the ship was wired, which he explained to nobody at some length. On the less technical side he had counted the number of passengers, knew their names. There were celebrities aboard, he said, a movie star, an English historian, a Negro quartet, the Ofay Brothers, who were booked to sing in Stockholm.

The second night out it was learned Art had had a tragedy. But he was recovering ("Life goes on. . . .")—recovering from a divorce, a job he loathed, a psychiatrist who had bungled his case. A "cruise," he thought, would help him "get away from it all."

Even his tragedy invoked no compassion. All Winky's sympathy went to his wife Nadine, whose picture Art had shown them, a plumpish brunette with a pompadour, smiling for all the world as she stood before an unspectacular bush in an unspectacular California backyard, clutching the hand of a thin, frowning, small replica of Art himself.

Across from Ardys sat Harry Tosdale Flemming III, a

different act altogether. A recent graduate of Harvard, Harry Tosdale Flemming III was more declaratory in his disappointment of his seating arrangement. But for different reasons. He kept eyeing the captain's table. He sniffed at the food, the ship, the service, and poor Art might as well have been a porthole as far as he was concerned.

After all, his father had been Ambassador to Finland once, and he had been a guest of King Olav of Norway on many occasions, both at his hunting lodge and at Skaugum. Crown Prince Harold was an "awfully good friend of mine." Why shouldn't *he*, friend of kings and no common touch, be seated at the captain's table?

Harry Tosdale Flemming III was rather good-looking in spite of his cell of self-aggrandizement. A tall brunette, his profile was finely etched, his nose straight with all his features balancing to give a study in a kind of distinction. He was a guarded man. His head moved slowly, and his eyes surveyed. Winky had seen him on deck one morning, his chinos just right, his dark shirt neatly buttoned. He surveyed, even then. Remarkable. Even his hair was neatly planted.

At the table his few remarks were usually addressed to Winky, but that was only after his second martini and the third night out. The first night he merely acknowledged the other three with a nod: "Harry Tosdale Flemming III," said he, finished his dinner and fled. Winky had no idea why he had chosen her to receive his remarks. Ardys said, "Because you have a way of sort of frightening people. It's something about the way you look. I've never seen anyone be really rude to you; they wouldn't dare. He probably thinks you're titled or something."

Winky had never seen herself that way and wasn't sure it was a compliment. Whatever, she did not care for Harry

Flemming. He, too, was to spend the summer in Oslo, "a kind of amusement" before entering investment banking—"father's," he said.

It was Harry Flemming who first pointed out Walter Everett. This occurred one night about mid-Atlantic, and it was the first and last bit of enthusiasm Winky was ever to see from Harry.

"MY GOD!" he said, suddenly jolting the table and spilling his brandy on Art's pants leg. "There's Walter Everett!" He actually laughed, a surprisingly high-pitched one. "What is *he* doing on this tub? My God! Of all people." He grinned broadly, bending forward. "Wouldn't you know *he'd* be at the captain's table?"

"Walter Everett!" said Ardys. "*The* Walter Everett?"

"Do you know him?" asked Harry Flemming incredulously.

"Not exactly. Which one is he?"

"There." He pointed. "Next to the woman in black." His eyes were glowing.

Winky's first glance was one of hollow disappointment. She saw a thin face, dark eyes, dark hair, a bit too long for her own taste. There was nothing particularly distinctive about his face save its thinness, which emphasized his eyes; sad eyes, old eyes. Yet when he smiled— Later, much later, Winky often thought his smile had the charm of the first born, the favorite, the unspoiled, teasing. He could get away with anything because of a smile. He was also a listener, Winky saw as he listened with intense eyes to the woman in black, a woman older than himself, ignoring the captain, the other guests.

"How old is he?" Ardys asked Harry.

Harry was still grinning. "Hell, Everett must be in his thirties by now."

"Not married?"

"Not that I know of. He was *going* to be, I know, three or four times." He laughed.

"Where did *you* know him?" Ardys asked.

"In Maine. His family and mine have houses near each other. The Everetts have summered there for years!" Harry smacked the top of his head with his open palm. "Wouldn't you just know old Everett would be somewhere around?" He considered his question. "That guy's everywhere."

"What does he do?" asked Art, also looking, actually bending forward, carried away with the whole thing, though earlier he had remarked he had never heard of anybody by that name.

"Everything," said Harry, not even glancing at Art. "Pardon me, this is one guy I've *got* to speak to." He almost gulped with anticipation and sprang from the table, his tall figure weaving among the diners at a slight slant.

Table twenty-two watched.

Harry planted one large hand on the thin shoulder of the other. Walter Everett started slightly, glanced behind him, looked blank and then the smile— He stood up. He was tall, taller than Harry Flemming, but he was leaning on something. It was then Winky saw he held a cane.

"Wonder what's the matter with him?" Ardys asked.

The table continued to watch. The two shook hands, and then Harry, flushed and grinning, began straightening his tie, trying to stand taller. He said something and Walter Everett laughed, then leaned against the back side of his chair, listening. Harry was the talker, making up for what he may have deemed intrusion, or perhaps relief there had been recognition, then he made a gesture toward table twenty-two. For a fleeting instant before she looked away Winky saw Walter Everett full-face. It was a kind face. When she glanced up again he was still looking her way. She took up her brandy, sipped it.

Walter Everett was now introducing Harry to the others at his table.

"Who is he? Who is he?" Art kept asking.

"Walter Everett," said Winky.

"Yes, but who is he?"

"Just a person."

"Uh huh," said Ardys, "and here he comes."

Something quickened inside Winky, something almost kin to fear. She rested her fingers at her throat.

The lady in black stopped Walter, said something; they both laughed. Then Walter and Harry continued toward the table, Walter using his cane and Harry, the large child, grinning, returning triumphantly.

". . . This is Ardys Langenberry, Winky Carr and Art uh, uh—" Harry tried his introductions.

"Art. Art Bailey." Art stood up, stretched his hand out. "Whittier, California."

"Whittier. Yes, of course," said Walter Everett. He had a good voice. Deep, clipped, quick. "I've been invited for a drink; would you mind?"

"No, of course not. Of course not. Let me get you a chair," said Art, eyeing the cane.

"No, please. I can still walk, at any rate."

It was Harry who got the chair, taking one from an adjoining table without asking the family who sat there.

"What happened to you?" Ardys asked as soon as Walter was seated.

"Had an accident."

"Car?"

"No, ran into a bullet."

"Into a *bul*let?" Ardys had an unhappy habit of cocking her head and contorting her face whenever she asked a question, a holdover from adolescence, a habit which, then, had been greatly admired and imitated, but which, now, did not wear well.

"A small gift from the Viet Cong."

"When?"

"About six months ago." He looked over his shoulder for a steward.

"Pretty rough over there, huh?" asked Art.

He ignored the question and leaned forward slightly. "But tell me," he said, addressing the table at large, "where are you headed?"

"Oslo," said Harry. "We're going to the summer session there. A bore probably. Say, why aren't you sailing those Maine waters? Is your family there yet?"

"Yes, they're all there." He looked over his shoulder again. No steward in sight. "Every single one of them."

"What in the hell are you doing on *this* tub?" Harry had overworked the word "tub," but then it was new to Walter Everett.

"Friends. I have some friends in Oslo, they wanted me to come over, the doctor said it was all right and so did Uncle Sam—graciously, I might add."

"Norwegians? Are your friends Norwegian?" asked Harry.

"She is, he isn't. They have a house. You'll have to come to see it. They have a very fine art collection."

"I'm just taking the cruise," said Art sadly.

"You don't seem too happy about the whole thing," said Walter, smiling.

"Oh, I will in time, I guess. Personal, you know. Personal things."

"Well, all this will cure you," said Walter. "This is a beautiful trip. The fjords will heal you if nothing else. We'll see to that." He turned to Winky.

The look caught her unaware.

"And where are you from?"

"Charleston," said Winky. She felt suddenly timid.

"South Carolina?" He pronounced it Caah-ro-*ly*nah.

"Yes." It rarely occurred to Winky there was another.

Walter put his hand to his chin and rested his elbow on the table. "Say something." His eyes were smiling.

Winky laughed. "Why?"

"I roomed with a boy from Charleston, South Carolina, once. One whole year, and I never understood one word he said."

"Oh, where?"

"That's it! *Wheyah?* You sound exactly like him."

"You roomed with somebody from Charleston?" Winky tried to regain composure.

"At St. Mark's. I can't remember his name. The only thing I remember: he never could get up in the morning. He kept saying: 'Waaaaltah, we're leyet agin.' I wish I could think of his name."

"Chesney?" Winky asked.

"Yes, Jim Chesney!" Walter leaned back. "That was a long time ago. What ever happened to him?"

"He's still in Charleston, banking."

"Still leyut getting up in the morning?"

"I don't know."

He kept smiling at Winky, the fine lines creased about his eyes. When he wasn't smiling, however, his eyes tended to brood, and the line marked from his nose to his lips suggested smiling actually did not come easily to him. He kept tapping his fingers.

"I haven't been South very often," he said, "once to Aiken, South Carolina, when I was ten and, God help us, to Alabama once. 'Munt-gumry.' Actually, a very beautiful city—parts of it."

"I think I've heard of that trip," said Ardys.

Walter turned to her, a quick movement of the head.

"You and a certain Vassar girl? The march on Montgomery?"

"Where did you hear about that?"

"I listened."

He studied Ardys's face for a moment.

Harry Flemming placed his hand on Walter's shoulder. "What about that Vassar chippy, Everett? Hadn't heard that one."

"Long time ago—a *long* time ago." He glanced backward. "Where *is* that brandy? I ordered one, didn't I?"

"I'll get it for you," said Harry. "I know one steward on this tub who isn't . . ."

"No, sit down, Harry, please. He'll be here in a . . ."

A young woman with straight blond hair, brown eyes and instant assurance appeared seemingly from nowhere. She put her arms about Walter's neck.

"All right, Julie," Walter said without turning around. "If you're hanky-pankying around again I'll be forced to tell your good, solemn husband."

The girl scanned the table, then, perhaps recognizing some slight rapport, she winked at Harry, who immediately jumped to his feet and began adjusting his tie again.

Walter did not stand up. The girl was Julie Perkins, he said. "Long Island's contribution to the wicked." She and her husband also were headed to visit Walter's friends in Oslo. "They invited themselves, of course."

"Rise!" said Julie. She took up Walter's cane. "And don't forget your big stick."

Walter stood up slowly. "She nags her husband, too." He shook hands with Harry. "Thanks, Harry. See you later. Give your family my regards."

"I will! I guess they know we've run across each other."

"Sure," said Walter. He gave a fleeting glance at the table. "See all of you later, I hope."

Winky watched them as they left the dining room, Walter Everett leaning on his cane and Julie Perkins in a long flowered evening skirt and white blouse, walking, chin forward, with the confident knowledge that the ship and the world were hers, were and always would be.

Harry Flemming was still standing, watching, his eyes shining. "That was Julie Cooke," he said in that certain slow word-swallowing accent that seemed to come and go depending on composure.

"I thought he said Perkins," said Ardys. "Julie Perkins."

"She was. An attractive girl. You've heard of the Cooke Mills, I'm sure."

"No," said Art.

Harry looked away. "Well, anyway, that's Julie Cooke."

"And *that* was Walter Everett," said Ardys.

"Nice feller," said Art. "A real nice feller. Wonder what happened to his leg? D'you guess he's got a false one?"

"No, for godsakes," said Harry. "But he was pretty bunged up. My family and his are *awfully* good friends."

"You said that before," said Ardys.

"Nice feller," said Art again.

Winky said nothing. She had not liked Walter Everett.

There was something, she didn't know what exactly, something forced perhaps; too conscientiously what Art said, "a nice feller." Or maybe it was Julie Perkins she had not liked. For some reason Julie Perkins seemed the correct prop for him, belying the kinder face, the wounded hero, the gentle manner. Winky never missed on first impressions, she prided herself. At any rate, she promptly dismissed Walter Everett.

✺

Winky avoided the students in the main. She realized just how far she had come in the few years since her own college days. Or maybe she had lost something. There they were, the students, straight out of the classroom, parroting theories on war, poverty, death and life. They knew all the dates of latter wars, all the names, all the initials of obscure government offices. Perhaps that was good. She was certain it was. But, as a whole, she found the students dull with their fads and sad intensity.

What did intrigue her was the beauty of the North—the wild yellow iris they saw at Oban, Scotland, and the purples, blues and reds of the North Sea sky. How strange it all was—for her—born and bred in the American South. The chilled Northland with its lonely high beauty. Light, day and night, terrible purple skies, so vast, everlasting sunset. Far, far. A voiceless world.

"Is it like Charleston?"

Winky was leaning against the rail. The voice startled her. It was Walter Everett.

"Oh, hello."

"You've been standing here about one half hour. What do you see out there?"

"It's so beautiful."

"You should go farther north. The Lofoten Islands. Truly beautiful."

"You've been there?"

"Once, years ago. With my parents. But I still remember it."

"I don't think I'll ever forget this."

"You're a strange girl."

Winky glanced at him, startled. "Why?"

"I don't know. I've watched you. Why are you trying to avoid everybody?"

"I'm not."

"I grant you there's not much choice."

"It isn't that."

"Is Charleston really so closed a door as they say it is?"

She laughed then. "Not really. It used to be. It still is in some ways, I guess. It was a kind of protection."

"Protection from what?"

"I don't know exactly."

"From Yankees? Like me?"

"There're some very nice Northerners living there now."

"Are they accepted?"

"Yes, some. But why are you so interested?"

"Just interested. What do you do there?"

"Sail, garden, go to parties. Like any place, I guess."

"The Charleston regatta. I've heard of it."

"Have you?" Winky turned from him. "Oh, look! Isn't it lovely?" Shades of pink were threading through the purple skies, and the white caps shone pale.

"You have a beautiful profile, you know—classic."

Winky glanced at him and then away. She wanted to put her hand to her face, hide it. She gave a short laugh.

"You see, you *are* human. You're not as cold as you seem."

"This seems to be my week," Winky said. "Someone else said the same thing."

"Who?"

"Ardys—Ardys Langenberry. You met her at our table."

"Let's have a drink."

"And miss all this?"

"It'll be here tomorrow—and the next."

It was late, and the bar was still crowded with students. One rather voluble young man was speedily seeing his way to oblivion. His face, gleaming with sweat, was fire-ball red, and the other students seemed to delight in his passing:

"Hey, Polk, what was that you said about Lynda Bird?"

"I shaid I was in love with her, godamn it! Cancha get that straight? I just luuuuve Lynda Bird and Lady Bird and all the birds!"

"But she's gone and left you, Polk. Flat."

"I shaid—"

"You know," said Walter, obviously finding no amusement in the antics at the bar. "I'd like to see some of those youngsters headed in another direction."

"Vietnam?"

Walter nodded. "I guess I would. But there're such damned innocent kids."

"Weren't you? Once? I seem to remember—"

"Remember what?"

"When I was at Wellesley . . ."

"So you went to Wellesley. Where was I? Why didn't I ever see you?"

"You were too busy with other things."

"How do you know?"

"Everybody knew. You were a kind of *guru*—but untouchable to most of us."

Walter laughed then. "That's when I was going to save the world." He touched his glass, circling his finger round the top. "I had a lot of theories. The ideal society. Bread for everybody like the old Corn Laws of Rome. I was almost winning, too."

"No longer."

"What?"

"Socialism."

"No."

"Why?"

"I don't know." He leaned back. "If I told you, you wouldn't believe me."

"Perhaps I would."

Walter sipped his drink again, and Winky noticed she hadn't touched hers.

"It was all so damned crazy—Vietnam, a mess, and we kept hearing the reports from home. You know." He gazed at her. "Hell, you won't believe me."

"Perhaps I will."

"It sounds manic."

"Maybe not."

"All right. Something like this. One night the company was on patrol, a tiger patrol, trying to bring out the V.C. We did that a lot and then the air force would bomb hell out of them. Sometimes." He was gazing down at his drink. "One night I thought we'd had it—ambushed, deadlocked—the captain, me, all of us. And you know what I wanted? When I had time to think? What I wanted most of all?"

Winky said nothing.

He took up the straw from his drink and began twisting

it. "What I wanted most of all— I wanted to be home, any-where, sitting with my big feet up and listening to a damn soap commercial. No, don't laugh. I wanted to see a white dove fly into Mrs. Whosit's kitchen and see some Indiana housewife point out that white dove in her nice clean kitchen and listen to that voice telling all the housewives of America how good that soap was." He gazed at Winky as if he were studying her reaction. "And I said to myself: 'Everett, old boy, here you are, fighting for a goddamn soap commercial.' Does that make any sense? Do you want to laugh?"

The circles beneath his eyes were darker than Winky had first noticed. "Not completely."

"It was just about one hundred and eighty degrees dif-ferent from anything I'd ever thought before. Me and John Wayne—the big overgrown Kiwanian, God-in-Every-Fox-hole Everett.

"I wasn't thinking about Maine, or sailing, or theories or even a girl named Kai. Anything. Just that commercial, and I was wondering if they still had it. It all seemed so safe, even right somehow." He leaned back and tossed the straw into the ashtray. "Manic. Paranoid."

Winky kept looking at him. She was trying to unravel his emotion. Anger? Weariness? Trickery? Amusement?

"You're not saying anything. I can't blame you, I guess. Pretty stupid."

"I was just thinking."

"What? That I'm a poor corny shell-shocked veteran re-turning from the wars?"

"No. Just wondering. *Was* there, as they say, a god in the foxhole? Yours?"

He looked at her a long while, too long. It was as if he were daring her to hear his answer. She looked away first.

"Yes," he said. "For me." And he rose from the table and left her.

Winky sat there, watching him go. She felt weightless, stunned.

At the bar the chant continued: "I shaid Lynda Bird! Lynda Bird! Fly to me, angel. Take me on the trip!"

Roars of laughter.

The university, at Blindern, where the American students stayed, was different from anything Winky had ever known, a mingling of the new and old like the country itself with its modern cities and rural old Norse villages. Night was a continuous twilight, and the campus, rolling green, smelled of ripening apples, a northern smell mingled with birch and the sounds of Grieg from the concert hall and the lilt of the young women's voices: "*Tak, tak. . . .*"

"I'm happy," Winky said to herself one afternoon as she rode her bicycle back to the dormitory. "I'm actually happy." She had never said such a thing to herself before, and she was to think of the moment many times later in her life, the one moment when the wind blew in her face, a pianist played Grieg, and she was young in a northern land.

The note from Walter Everett came two weeks after they had been at Blindern:

> How about adding a bit of Charleston to our own private regatta Saturday. If you don't call, I'll be by for you about ten in the morning. Okay? Are you homesick for the big PX (the G.I.'s quaint term for our fatherland)?
>
> Walter (Everett)—in case you have forgotten

The note was typewritten save for the signature, an ordinary, tight, slanted hand, a school boy's hand really, firmed through the years but still the boy that was. It was a handwriting similar to others Winky had seen and, as before, it always surprised her, told much, seemed so vulnerable.

But there it was, his name, part of him, the untouchable Walter Everett, and he was writing to *her*, wanting to see *her*. It occurred to Winky she had always been in on the end of things. People, events never reached her at their peak, but only as the glory began to fade. No matter. She ran back to her room. Ardys was not there, and the excitement was so high in her she walked up and down the small room, then looked at herself in the mirror above the bureau as if the face there might tell her something, answer something. Her face was flushed, and she put both hands to it, seeing only her eyes looking back at her, coy, even mischievous. "He likes me."

She lay across the bed, holding the letter high, tracing the signature with her hand. "I *knew* he would—" She wanted to cry and laugh at once. And then a fear came to her. She knew, looking at the signature, the awkward L's and T's, that hereafter her own days, even life, would never be the same again. How odd, how strange. And yet she knew and was afraid.

Ardys entered the room, and Winky calmly showed her the note. Calmly.

"Oh, Win-ky!" Ardys looked at her.

And just as calmly she said: "I'm going to marry Walter Everett, Ardys. No, I'm not insane. I just am, that's all."

He arrived on Saturday one hour late. He was driving one of the small Norwegian cars Winky had seen curving in and out of the neat little roads. He looked better than he had on the ship, his face darkly tanned against the white T-shirt.

He was standing outside the car and standing so tall the car looked as if it might have been a toy car one sees at an amusement park.

"Hello," she said, her breath coming quick, trying to hold back the burst of a smile she felt inside. She wanted to look away. She put her hand gently to her hair. "Your cane," she said. "You don't have it."

"I threw it away." He made a gesture with his hands. "This place has cured me." He opened the car door. "Enter."

Before he started the car he looked at her. "Say something."

"Oh, Walter."

"O-ah, Wal-tah," he mocked and shook his head. "I'll *never* understand it."

"Will you put me in a play some day?"

"If I did, nobody could understand it. How did you know I was a writer? Or, better put, want to be?"

"People told me."

"The roommate again?"

"No, just people."

"People, people, people." He started the car. "We'll go by the house first. Okay?"

"What house?"

"Where I'm staying. The people I'm visiting."

"Oh?" And there was the old apprehension again, the timidity that came with meeting strangers. Winky had been what Aunt Pett called "a timid child." Through the years she had conquered most of it, but the effort was still wearying, the effort to please. Especially did she not wish to appear wrong now. And as if he sensed her feeling he put his hand over hers. "You'll like them. They're all very easy people to know."

Winky withdrew her hand and lighted a cigarette, but the touch was still there between them.

Walter's hosts were in shipping, he explained, as they approached the entrance to the drive up to the house. "The company goes back as far as Leif Ericson or something."

The drive to the house was lined with mountain ash and birch, and somewhere amongst the lawns and fields there was the smell of ripe berries. The house overlooked Oslo Fjord, not from a mountain top but from a hillock from which green lawns slanted downward toward the water. The house itself was a two-story gray rectangular structure, simple in design with a high arched doorway. Inside the hallway startled in its whiteness, white walls, marble floors. One looked straight through to the rolling green lawns and beyond to the water where the tip of a blue sail shone against the sky. The sail and the sky were like the blues in the large gilt-framed Carpaccio painting which hung on the right wall, matched on the left wall with one of Munch's painfully wrought pictures of a man, the anguish written on his face through the colors and strokes of the brush. Winky caught a fleeting glance through the other rooms, the Gobelin tapestry in the dining room, other pictures, some Italian, Norse ancestors, lace collars and cuffs, glass, woven rugs, old woods stripped of finish, high polished cabinets and tables, their legs meeting bare floors, and in the drawing room there was one large glass vase filled with green leaves and red berries. But the whiteness, the very purity of it, made one fearful that one error of voice or touch might soil this grace, this pure perfection.

"Everett," called a voice from the terrace, a New Yorker's voice, rather young, male.

Walter guided Winky to the terrace beyond. The first person Winky saw as they came onto the terrace was Julie Perkins from the ship. She was dressed in a tennis dress, sitting with her bronzed legs resting on another chair. She recognized

Winky's and Walter's presence with a slight lift of her racket. By her side was another young woman, but whereas Julie Perkins had what might be called "a kind of style," the other had true beauty. She wore no make-up, her hair was dark, and her face was like a sunburst in its radiance.

She immediately rose to her feet. "I am Kristin, the daughter of the house."

Winky shook her hand lightly. Norwegians were always shaking hands. She had formerly been Kristin Walle-Vidkusson, but was now married to a New Yorker and living on Long Island.

"How lovely you could come," she said in a voice almost lilting. "You should meet to know my mother, Mrs. Walle-Vidkusson."

Winky looked toward the chaise-longue. A woman, perhaps in her late forties, it was difficult to tell, lounged with a small puppy in her lap. She was tall, slender, wearing white pants, a black and white striped shirt, and her hair, brownish, was tied back with a bright blue scarf which emphasized the color of her eyes. There was the daughter in the mother's face, the high cheekbones, sunken cheeks, blue-green eyes, strong nose, thin lips, yet the combination did not give one the feeling of radiance as in the daughter, rather a sense of aloofness.

"Miss Carr?" she said with scarcely a trace of accent. Her voice was low.

Winky took hold of her hand.

"I have been to your city. Charleston, South Carolina."

"Oh?"

Walter laughed then.

"Yes," said Mrs. Walle-Vidkusson.

"How did you happen to be in Charleston?" Winky asked.

"I had heard of it from friends, in New York, and we took a trip there. I remember the gardens and the houses. You come to us from a beautiful place."

"Thank you," Winky said. "Visitors sometimes can be disappointed in Charleston. I think it takes time to appreciate its mood and difference."

"Not at all. Mr. Walle-Vidkusson and myself thought it rather choice."

"After this?" Winky asked. "This is so lovely." She looked beyond to the water in the distance.

"Thank you veddy much," said Mrs. Walle-Vidkusson abruptly as if she might be shy of compliment.

"And what about me, Everett?"

Winky turned still smiling.

"Winky," said Walter, "this is George. George Perkins. He's good, upstanding, and teddibly stuffy except for his dear wife Julie."

George Perkins, horn-rimmed, dark-haired and also in tennis attire slowly got up from his chair. "I'm stuffy because I don't like to see males sitting on rocks without any clothes on."

They all laughed.

"I'm afraid the customs of some of our people have shocked Mr. Perkins," said Mrs. Walle-Vidkusson. "We were sailing yesterday and many were swimming, you understand."

"They weren't swimming," said George Perkins. "They were sitting on rocks, like mermen."

"Please, Miss Carr. Do have some coffee. We are very lazy today."

Winky looked at the blue porcelain coffee service.

"No, no coffee," said Walter. "Charleston and I are going sailing." He looked at his watch. "Just a-bout one second from now."

"Poor dear," said Julie Perkins from her reclining position. "He nearly drowned us yesterday."

Mrs. Walle-Vidkusson picked up the small puppy again. "You do like to sail, Walter, don't you? Actually, you're very good."

"Hah!" said Julie Perkins.

"Control yourself," said Walter to Julie. "You get so hysterical about little things."

"Oh, and yes, Walter," said Mrs. Walle-Vidkusson, "I think Ingrid has prepared a little lunch for you and Miss Carr, if you care to take it with you."

"Very nice. Thank you," said Walter.

The sloop was rigged and moored to a small pier.

"Oh, *blue* sails!" Winky said.

Walter grinned down at her. "I still can't get over it."

"What?"

"Charleston, South Carolina, invading Norway of all places."

Winky laughed, almost a giggle. "I adore this place. You know, I don't think I've ever been so happy."

"It's all because of me. I'm sure of it."

"Of course!" She smiled, looking away. "Your friends are delightful, truly charming, but I don't understand . . ."

"Julie."

"I guess so."

"She's all right—a spoiled peasant, that's all."

"I thought she was a friend of yours."

"She is, but she's still spoiled." Walter knelt and began unwinding the line which held the sloop to the pier. "They're beautiful people, Kristin and her family. You'd like her husband, too. Paul's great. I noticed you with Mrs. Walle-Vidkusson."

"She frightened me a little, I think."

"Why?"

"I don't know. The Garbo look or something."

"You stood well," he said.

"What do you mean?"

"Julie comes off badly next to her. But she didn't diminish you."

"Diminish me?"

He looked back at her. "Probably all that Charleston breeding oozing out."

"Probably," Winky said.

He grinned. "Okay. Let's get going."

Walter took her hand and, steadying the boat with his foot, helped her in.

"Can you take the tiller for a minute?"

"Gladly."

They cast off and for the first time since Winky had been in this country she felt instantly at home. She was thinking she had only to close her eyes. All the familiar sounds were there, the water, the sound of the headsail struggling against the wind. Everywhere there were small boats filled with families, small children.

"Let's make this thing go," Walter said, taking over the tiller. "Can you coil the sheet?"

Winky adjusted the sheet and all at once the blue sail blossomed like the sky.

"Okay, skipper," Walter said. "Well done."

The spray pricked Winky's face. She leaned back. How wonderful it all was, the trees and hills on either side, the sound of water beneath and the wind against the sail.

"You're all right, Charleston. I didn't think people down there had the energy."

"Energy for what?"

"Sailing."

"What did you think we did?"

"I don't know. I thought they probably did what Faulkner said they did—spat at the snakes or something."

"Not today," Winky said.

"What?"

"Faulkner."

"You know, you even look Scandinavian. How did that happen?"

"I don't know. I— Walter! Our lunch!"

The basket packed by the Walle-Vidkussons' young servant was drenched with spray. Winky opened the lid. The linen napkin so carefully placed over the top was soaked.

"Wet herring," Walter said.

"I wasn't famished anyway. Were you?"

"Yes, of course, I was."

"Sorry."

Walter was smiling, easily, it seemed to Winky. Again she thought how really much better looking he was than she remembered from the ship. It was his nose, more prominent than other features, large, straight, yet thin about the nostrils, that marred what others might call a truly handsome face. He also stood and sat slightly stooped and Winky wondered if it had been a stance of childhood, a young man to whom height had come too early. Yet he had wonderful eyes, darker than his brows, and a firm, strong mouth, perhaps his most appealing feature.

"Why don't we have an early dinner somewhere then?" he said.

"Like *this?*" Winky was wearing khaki bermudas and a sweater.

"This is Norway, remember. Half the people don't wear anything."

"Don't be ridiculous."

"Where's your good beatnik sporting blood?"

"In the fjord."

Winky tossed her head back and let the spray and wind strike her full-face. "All right." She opened her eyes to see Walter looking at her, his eyes intent, perhaps even curious. Or were they sad? How quickly his moods changed. She smiled back at him, an asking smile.

They sailed most of the afternoon, and by the time they were seated at a restaurant it was six o'clock. Between them there was the shared fatigue which comes after much physical exercise. Walter had chosen the Dronning, a restaurant on the water, where one could see the lights of Oslo and the anchored ships twinkling in the twilight.

"Look," Winky said. "You can almost touch the water." Their table was near a window, and Winky felt if she leaned far enough she actually could tip the water with her fingers.

"Try it," Walter said.

"I couldn't if I wanted to, not after a whole day with you."

"Wait until tomorrow."

"Tomorrow?"

"I'm going to show you my Norway."

"I've already seen it."

"Not with me you haven't. But right now let's order. I'm starved."

He ordered for the two of them without once glancing at Winky. It didn't matter. Nothing mattered.

Aquavit, crayfish, beef fillet. . . . "And champagne, yes champagne for South Carolina's star skipper!"

"Crayfish?" Winky asked.

"They're good."

"How did you *know* I wanted them?"

"Because I like them."

"I see."

The aquavit was ice cold, served in small jigger glasses. It burned as it went down Winky's throat. She coughed. "This tastes like paregoric."

"You're not supposed to sip it. No Viking would do that. Just toss it down, like this." Walter drained the small glass in one gulp. "That's the way you're supposed to drink it."

"No thank you." Winky continued to sip it, meanwhile trying to hold back the smile that wanted to play about her lips and the instinctive urge to lean forward.

"How old are you, Charleston?"

"Twenty-five, soon twenty-six."

"And not married? Well, well."

"It's a disappointment to my mother, of course."

"What?"

"That I'm not blissfully wed to some fine, young Charleston youth."

"Why aren't you?"

"Why aren't *you?*" She leaned back in her chair.

"I don't know. Once, *once* it was pretty close. But she couldn't speak English, and I couldn't see myself sitting up all my life saying: 'DO-You-Do-THAT-In-Hong-Kong? We-Don't-in-A-MER-I-CA.' I don't know."

"Hong Kong?"

"She was Eurasian. A long time ago."

Did he still care for the girl?

"What is your mother like?"

"Mother?" The question startled her. These sudden changes in direction had puzzled her all afternoon. "Mother? Mother's lovely, a truly lovely woman."

"Like her daughter, of course."

Winky lifted her glass slightly. "*Tak.*"

"And your father?"

"Why all these questions?"

"Just interested."

"The writer in you?"

"The would-be."

Winky leaned back in the chair. "My father's marvellous! He should have been a teacher, professor somewhere. He writes, too."

"Oh?"

"Not plays or novels, mostly things about Charleston. He was a Rhodes Scholar."

"What does he do now?"

"Insurance, real estate."

"Oh, my god."

Winky laughed. "*Every*body in Charleston is in insurance."

"Everybody?"

"No. It just seems that way."

"You're very fond of your father, aren't you?"

"Yes." Winky was looking at the lights of the Sagafjord in the distance—tiny lights everywhere, but she was seeing the tall, lean figure of her father, his face so very thin. She looked back at Walter. "Why do you ask?"

"Just interested."

"Was it Proust who said one loves only one's own image, not an individual?"

"Something like that. I don't know whether he was completely correct."

"But what about you?"

"What about?"

"Why did you volunteer for Vietnam?"

"—I thought we were talking about love, a much more absorbing subject."

"Why did you?"

"I'm asking myself that now. I was politely asked out of Williams, you know."

"I heard."

"You've heard everything, haven't you?"

"No, not all. But why?"

"Why what?"

"You were in the English department, weren't you?"

"Yes, teaching sophomores—"

"And what happened?"

"I guess I wasn't *asked* to leave, not technically. They just said I went a little beyond 'academic freedom,' whatever that means." He lighted a cigarette. "Actually, I didn't like teaching anyway, so I left."

"Just like that."

"My brother was killed in Korea. I don't know. After my play was such a flop I just volunteered. That's about it. No heroics. No beliefs. Maybe I just needed a war."

"Your brother was the oldest?"

Walter nodded. "The hope of the family. Nothing seemed right after that."

"You mean with your family?"

"I guess so. All they had was my sister and myself. My sister is married to a fine, upstanding lawyer, who is about as dull as soil erosion and so—there was just Walter, the heir and hope of Everett Steel. I said no thanks."

"Why?"

"It just wasn't for me—"

Winky said nothing. Somehow the puzzle seemed to fit.

"My father keeps saying 'any young man in this country would be *grateful* for just half the opportunity you have.' "

"I suppose he's right."

"I suppose so."

"What about your play? What was it about?"

Walter shook his head. "Damned if I know."

"You must have some idea."

"I guess I did in the beginning—there was the East-West business, conflict, and a lot of symbols. I'm a symbol guy, they say. Some of the critics liked it, scared not to, didn't want to be caught not getting the point. One of them said I was looking for God." He leaned back. "Big surprise, that one. But, unfortunately, the other critics got the point and crucified me."

"But at least you've had a play *produced*."

"Two nights. Never again."

"Why not?"

"For one reason I can't stand another hangover like I had the next day."

"What will you do now then? Write fiction, novels?"

"Novels, short stories, starve to death."

"For some reason I can't see you in the role of the starving poet."

"Nobody can."

"And for some reason I don't think you will."

"I still can't get over how Norwegian you look!"

Winky put her hand to her face. "Why not Swedish? They're supposed to be more aristocratic." She laughed. "Your dear friend, Harry Tosdale Flemming III, our seating companion on the ship—"

"No *dear* friend."

"Any-way, he said Norway was the slum of Sweden."

"Rot. The only difference in the two places is Sweden never fought a war, at least not Hitler's brand. This little country fought like hell. It's tremendous."

"It *is* wonderful." Outside, it was growing faintly darker.

"A Carolina Viking. Who would have dreamed it?"

Winky lifted her champagne glass.

They both laughed, and there was the distance of the table between them as they leaned forward.

It was midnight, still light, when they reached the dormitory at Blindern.

"Tomorrow. At eight o'clock," Walter said. "You'll see *my* Norway."

"*Eight* o'clock?"

"Eight o'clock."

Walter reached across Winky and opened the car door on her side. The gesture caught her unawares. She looked at him wide-eyed.

"Goodnight, Charleston."

"Goodnight," Winky said, and as she watched him drive away she wanted to cry.

Chapter 8 ❧

"Just *where* are we going?" Winky finally asked Walter. They had driven past the outskirts of Oslo, and the open road lay before them. Walter had a thick gray sweater thrown around his shoulders with the arms tied loosely together in front. Yesterday's picnic basket, open and empty, was resting on the back seat.

"Mrs. Walle-Vidkusson and Kristin thought you were charming yesterday. That's a quote."

"I said, where are we going?"

"I hate to tell you, but dear Julie didn't say anything. You know, I don't think Julie takes to Southerners very well. Peculiar girl, isn't she?"

"Yes, I would think so."

"Peculiar girl."

"You know, I have an odd feeling I'm being abducted."

"I started to bring a bicycle, but I was afraid it would be too much for you."

"What would be too much?"

"You tire so easily."

Winky crossed her arms and said nothing.

Walter glanced at her. "Are you becoming petulant? I despise petulant women."

"Pity."

"It's a foreboding of things to come. What is it about women? Once they're married, anchored, they suddenly become tyrants, paranoid. I've made a pact with myself. I've decided before I marry I'm going to take my betrothed on a

125 ❧

trip around the world and then if I can still stand her I'll marry her."

"How humble of you. Are we starting out now?"

"Why, Charleston, you're asking me to marry you! What would your mother say? *You* married to a poor crude Pittsburgh boy?"

Winky laughed then for the first time. She really didn't care where they were going. She didn't care about anything. She leaned back in the seat. They were in open farm country, neat rows of green with hay piled in bundled stacks, row after row, like crude children's drawings.

"We're going to church if you must kn∮w," Walter said. "It's Sunday, and we're going to church."

"To *church?*"

"Uh huh."

"Couldn't you find one a little closer?"

"Not like the one we're going to."

A marker on the roadside read "Lillehammer," pointing straight ahead.

"You'll like Lillehammer," Walter said.

"I'm glad. How far is it?"

"How far? Why?"

"I just want to make sure we'll make church on time."

"We will. It's always there."

The land was becoming more rolling—green, green meadows, small houses, red barns and colorful flowers, yellows, reds, whites.

"Sigrid Undset died in Lillehammer."

"The writer?"

Walter nodded. "I went to see her once, she was living in a nunnery. She finally consented to see me, and it was the worst hour I ever spent in my life."

"Why?"

"She just sat there with her arms folded and those great eyes looking straight through me. She didn't say one word."

"Not one?"

"I was only fourteen. She had a basso voice, and the only thing she said was 'I de-spise New York.' "

Winky laughed. She was thinking of him as a boy of fourteen—tall, gangling.

"I liked her, though, I don't know why. My parents never believed I actually went to see her. I was a notorious liar when I was fourteen."

"But you improved?"

"Immeasurably."

"Walter, are we really going to church?"

"Yes, of course."

And then he fell silent. It was difficult to reason his silences. Yesterday, sailing, there had been an hour or more when they had said nothing. She leaned her head against the seat and watched the clouds in the sky. It was a perfect day, cool with the sun high and the sky blue, bluer, it seemed, than any other place she had ever seen.

They drove the rest of the distance in silence, Walter only once asking her for a cigarette. She handed it to him, saying nothing, wondering how many girls, women, had sat just so beside him in a car asking themselves what thoughts turned through his mind and why, when not talking, his face was older, the look in his eyes so far. He's been hurt, she thought. *By whom? When? Why?* . . .

Lillehammer was more rolling than Oslo, and the town with its Sunday feel was spare of people, almost deserted with its small shops, some wooden and brightly painted, standing in rows, inviting, modest, even proud.

"We have to go to *two* services," Walter said finally.

"Two?"

"One we'll just glimpse, and the other we'll remain. Incidentally, what are you?"

"What *am* I?"

"What church do you belong to?"

"The Episcopal church. You?"

"Presbyterian, I guess."

"Why do you guess?"

"I don't know. There's the Victoria Hotel. On the right. I stayed there once."

"They have a plaque on the wall, I'm sure."

"You just don't trust me, do you? You don't trust me at all."

"I wouldn't say that exactly. But you *do* know where we're going, don't you?"

"I stayed here for a whole month once."

"Why here?"

"Because I liked it."

"Oh?"

"You know something, Charleston? You've been imprisoned too long."

The remark startled Winky, and she half laughed.

"No, I've been watching you. Quit fighting. You've never learned the art of living. Why not?"

"Now, that *is* a statement."

"Just an observation."

"A rather hasty one, too, wouldn't you say?"

"No."

They were entering a park, a drive dark with trees.

"We'll walk," he said as he parked the car. "Okay?"

"If you say so."

He turned to her. "I'll say it again—I could listen to you talk forever, but you're not much of a talker. Thank God for that." He leaned over and opened her door just as he had the night before. "Exit."

"Your favorite word?"

"What?"

"Exit."

"Petulance again. I detect a slight . . ."

Winky got out of the car and slammed the door.

"And she has temper, too," Walter said as he caught up with her.

"No, I've been imprisoned too long."

"Now, Charleston, you're not entering church with the right attitude." He grinned at her.

"Oh, Walter." She gave up, met his smile.

"Now, that's better. Much better."

The trees met overhead closing out the sky like a cloister. It was dark, damp, and the smell of earth and leaf was pungent. In the distance Winky saw a stone wall and, beyond, a lake.

"Now, from here," Walter said. "See my church."

"Church?"

"No, look, through the trees." He placed both hands on her shoulders. "See."

"Yes. Is it a church? Really?"

"One of the oldest in the world. Come."

Winky followed his long striding steps, and she noticed he still favored the right leg.

"There she is," he said, standing still. "A Garme Stave Church, built in the year 1050."

Before them rose a small wooden structure, the wood shingles darkened by centuries of weathers, roof upon roof, dragon design, with a small steeple rising in a clearing of trees.

"It *is* a church," Winky said.

"One of the few stave churches left, but I have a special feel for this one."

"It's lovely."

"I used to come here often. On week days there were very few people. Can't you imagine the Vikings? 'Deliver us from the wrath of the Vikings.' You Church of England people used to pray that. But this particular church was new before the Battle of Hastings, older than Charleston even. Imagine."

"It's fascinating. Really."

"There's nothing like it anywhere in the world except, of course, at Bygdo. Now we can go to our other church." He started back toward the car.

"But we haven't even seen—"

"Not much time," he called back.

Winky stood for a moment, looking from the entrance of the church, across the water to the hills.

"Hurry, we're late."

She looked up once again at the steeple.

"Now," Walter said when she caught up with him, "I want you to meet my best friend in all Lillehammer."

"I thought we were going to another church."

"We *are*, but we have to meet my friend first."

Winky stopped walking. "Walter, you *are* mad. Absolutely mad."

"Come on. Not much time."

They drove through the village again and out into farmland. Shortly they entered an unpaved drive and stopped in front of a small house painted pale yellow with black trim.

Through the open windows Winky could see freshly laundered lace curtains.

As they stopped the car an elderly woman dressed in a black dress with lace cuffs came through an apple grove from the side of the house. She held a huge dog by a chain, and when the engine of the car stopped, she, too, stood still. Her white hair was rigidly pulled back from her face, and her thin lips and piercing blue eyes seemed to show anger.

Walter got out of the car, and the woman stood still, her expression never softening. The dog began to bark fiercely, trying to leap itself free from the chain. Yet, there was still no response from the woman, not the slightest sign of recognition. Winky glanced toward the house. There was no one else about. But when she looked back again the woman was shaking hands with Walter, the thin lips smiling but the eyes still piercing. And then, at once, it came to Winky: the woman was blind.

As the two came toward the car Winky could hear the woman speaking—half Norwegian, half English. She caught the words, "Your wife?"

"No, no, no," protested Walter.

"Still the sea gull, Mr. Everett?"

"You remember too much," Walter said, and then he began to speak in Norwegian. He had the words but not the voice, not the lilt nor the rhythm, but the woman seemed to understand and never marked in her expression the faults surely her ears must have taken strangely.

Winky got out of the car.

"Mrs. Baarli, this is my friend, Miss Carr. She is from the southern part of the United States."

The woman nodded and extended her hand. Winky took

her hand, veined and slight. The handshake was surprisingly firm, positive.

"I am not able to see you," said Mrs. Baarli matter-of-factly.

Winky wanted to avoid the eyes, so blue, the look from them so penetrating.

"But your dog sees for you," Winky said, trying to pet the dog who had quieted now. "A beautiful dog."

"Yes?" And then she continued in Norwegian to Walter.

Walter answered, seemingly not struggling for words. And then in English he said: "I have something for you. From New York." He reached inside the back of the car, and the woman stood straight, her chin lifted, waiting.

"Never let it be said I haven't been thinking of you." Walter handed her a small package tied with a silver ribbon. "You must open it," he said.

"I will," she said with a dignified nod of her head. She handed Walter the dog's leash and without the slightest show of emotion began to unwrap the package. Inside was a small pearl bracelet with a diamond clasp. She felt it carefully and then the glimmer of a smile shone on her lips, followed presently by a true smile, wide, almost child-like. She looked up at Walter. "Pearls?" she asked softly as a younger woman looking into the eyes of a small boy weeping might say the single word "tears?"

Walter said nothing. He took the bracelet and fastened it round her wrist. It hung there on the frail wrist like an unnecessary thing.

The smile lingered on the woman's lips.

"Now," said Walter. "You can do something for *us*."

"Yes," said the woman gravely.

"Are you still the best cook in all Lillehammer?"

"*Ja*," the woman said, accepting the truth.

"And you still sell to the shops? *Lefse?*"

"*Lefse? Ja.* It is Sunday."

"I know," said Walter. "But we cannot buy because it is Sunday."

Mrs. Baarli then understood. "Oh, you must come." She took Walter's hand gently. "Come."

They entered the front door of the house. The living area was larger than Winky had first supposed, or rather there was the feeling of space—a room sparsely furnished, a table set with a porsgründ coffee set, a woven rug and paintings on the walls, paintings everywhere, it seemed, one above and below another. And in the corner of the room was a fireplace, rounded, oval. Winky had never seen a fireplace built just so and she remarked on it.

"Typically Norse, rather old Norse," Walter said.

It was a charming room with the spotless lace curtains, the woods gleaming. The curtains gave an old-fashioned tone to the room as if they had walked back into time. Yet some of the paintings were modern bright, raw colors.

"Will you have coffee?" said Mrs. Baarli.

"No," Walter said. "Thank you. We haven't much time today. Miss Carr studies at the university, and we must return to Oslo."

"I understand," said Mrs. Baarli solemnly. "You have your duties."

"I will be back, though," Walter said. "I want to have a long talk with you."

"Yes, we will visit. I have your letters. The war. You are well now, Mr. Everett?"

"Oh, yes."

"I shall go now, prepare for you."

"May we help you?" Winky asked.

Mrs. Baarli obviously didn't understand or hear. She disappeared into the back of the house.

"She doesn't want anyone to help her," Walter said. "Actually she does very well. See these paintings. Most of them were done by her son Leif."

"Oh, does he live with her?"

"No, he was killed in the war. The Germans shot him as he was fleeing on skis."

"Then she's all alone?"

"Completely. She has this farm, and she sells her baking to some of the shops in the town. She's perfection."

"And lonely?"

"Perhaps."

"It's sad."

"Not at all. It's magnificent."

Winky was looking at one particular painting, and she couldn't take her eyes from it. A blond young girl, her face flushed with excitement, was holding out a large bouquet of lilies of the valley as if she were presenting a gift. It was a work done by a man with an obvious reverence for living things—caught like a moment on the canvas, the one glorious time before the flowers withered, before the girl grew older. There, in color and line, was all the vitality and miracle of a fresh new life meeting the joy of a young day.

"They sell the flowers in the spring, in May," Walter said.

"How beautiful."

"Lilies of the valley. You see the young girls with them everywhere. I believe the flowers grow wild."

"I wonder what ever became of her, the girl?"

"Who knows. But at least she had that one day, didn't she?"

Winky looked at him. His eyes were bright as he studied the picture, an excited look.

"Have you ever had a day like that?" Winky asked. "A perfect day?"

He kept looking at the picture. "I think so. Here, once, a long time ago."

"You're very fond of Mrs. Baarli."

"Yes."

"It was lovely of you to give the bracelet."

"Not at all. I owe her a lot. I'll tell you about it some day."

Mrs. Baarli had returned. She was holding Mrs. Walle-Vidkusson's basket. Walter immediately took it from her.

"For your journey," said Mrs. Baarli. "And . . ." She went over to a side cupboard, and, bending low, fetched a bottle of wine. Her face brightened as she presented the gift.

"Your last?" Walter asked.

"You must take." She then extended her hand to Winky. "Thank you veddy much to come," she said.

"Oh, thank *you*."

Walter took her hand. "I will be back. Perhaps next week." He then said something in Norwegian, and Mrs. Baarli laughed—for the first time.

As they drove from the house Winky looked back. Mrs. Baarli stood, a lonely figure, seeming to look after them until the car disappeared.

"Some day I'm going to live here," Walter said. "Right here in Lillehammer."

"And you'll write novels and short stories. Won't you be lonely?" She lighted a cigarette.

"Never."

"What will you write about?"

"War and peace. Love and death, growing old."

"And you'll become famous. Just think, some day I'll read about you with a dateline 'Lillehammer, Norway,' and I'll say 'I knew him. I knew him quite well.' Maybe I'll even exaggerate and say, 'I know him very well. He likes to sail and he eats crayfish and drinks aquavit and he's a little mad.' How impressed my friends will be."

"That will never be."

"Why?"

"Because nobody'll give a damn."

"I will."

He glanced at her. "Thank you, Charleston." His voice had an odd ring to it. She had started to continue her chiding, but she saw how serious he was.

"Where are we going?"

"To church, I said." And surprisingly he began to sing in Norwegian. He had a good voice.

Winky listened to him. He was happy, very happy. And she was to think of him like that many times later, a young man driving along a northern road singing. How simple things had seemed.

Walter's "church" was a hillock above a meadow where, below, wild daisies grew. They had parked the car far below and walked perhaps a mile or more through the meadow, over small stiles, through groves of pine and birch until at last the rolling green and the daisies lay before them, and Walter said: "It's every bit just as I remember. Breathe the air, see the sky."

It was so quiet, only the daisies bending in an unheard wind. A bird flew high in the sky. But the quiet and the heavy rolling land—

"Doesn't it frighten you a little?" Winky asked.

He looked at her. "What?"

"I don't know. Something—something almost biblical—The land, the sky, will always be here, and we won't. We'll be—"

He kept looking at her. Finally he said: "I didn't bring you here to talk about death. You're obsessed with the subject."

"Not really. I never think of it actually."

"That means you never think then, doesn't it?"

"Why?"

"Tolstoy said the only time a man thinks is when he thinks of his own death."

In the distance Winky could see a small house. The roof of the house was thatched; and were those children moving about the little garden?

"See the farms, like small squares. The land is very precious, they make use of every inch of it. See."

"Uh huh."

"You're not looking."

"I *am*."

Walter sat down.

Winky cocked her head at him.

" 'Come, let us sit on the ground and tell sad stories of the death of kings.' "

"Sad stories?" She sat beside him.

"And to begin with you can open the basket and see what's inside. The wine first, please."

Winky opened the basket. There were two cups. She held one out as Walter poured the wine.

"Ignore what floats," he said.

"We'll have to return these things."

"I will. Next week."

The wine was good, warming.

Walter leaned back. His eyes were scanning the hills. "I never thought I'd be here again. Never in a million years, and here I am with a beautiful blonde who can't speak English and a bottle of wine with cork in it." He turned to her. "Not bad, huh?"

"Not bad, but inaccurate."

"You don't consider yourself beautiful?"

"Of course. And my English is perfect."

"You're vain. That has never come out in your personality before."

"There're many things you don't know."

"But you are beautiful and you don't know it, and I like you for it."

Winky felt the color rise to her neck. She touched her face lightly with her finger tips.

"You're afraid of compliments, aren't you?"

Winky nodded.

"Why?"

She shook her head, looked at him sideways. "I don't know why." She had been an ugly child, and the bruise was still with her. She could still hear Aunt Etoile trying to help: *"But she has such charm. She'll be all right one day, Ann. Just wait . . ."*

"Is it difficult?" Winky asked then, trying to change the subject.

"What?"

"Your being here and thinking about—Vietnam, everything there, people—" Her voice faded.

"Do you mean do I feel guilty?"

"No, not that exactly."

"In a way I do, I guess. I felt more that way on the ship and now in Oslo with Julie and George."

Winky kept looking at him.

"How about more wine?" He picked up the bottle. "What is that from Aladdin and the Jinn? How does it go?

> 'Bring me old wines,' said Aladdin.
> . . . That will comfort the stale and the sad,
> For I would be mending my spirit,
> Forgetting these days that are bad,
> Forgetting companions too shallow,
> Their quarrels and arguments thin,
> Forgetting the shouting Muezzin:
> 'I am your slave,' said the Jinn . . .

"Something like that," he hesitated. "I've even forgotten poetry."

"Vachel Lindsay," Winky said.

"More wine?"

Winky handed him her cup.

"And don't look at me that way."

"What way?"

"I wouldn't want to have an affair with you right here in church."

Winky quickly looked away.

"And she blushes, too, our fair Southern maid."

She was blushing; she felt her face hot.

"I said not in church." He opened the top of the basket. "Let's see what else Mrs. Baarli has for us. Yes— I shall now show you how to eat *lefse*." He handed her a napkin and took one for himself. "Just watch me."

Winky watched as he unwrapped what looked like a wide, paper-thin pancake. "What's it made of?"

"Potatoes. Now, you see, you must butter it—all over,

and then—sprinkle a little—sugar—just so, then you roll it up—very carefully. Great." He handed it to her. "All yours."

"Are you sure?"

"Go ahead. Try it."

Winky bit into the rolled top. Walter was watching her. It was delicious. She said so. "How do they make it?"

"No idea. But the women bake it here in Lillehammer, and I have a friend in Duluth, Minnesota, who used to send it to me. I met her here, in Lillehammer, as a matter of fact."

He sat up then, made his own *lefse*, poured himself another cup of wine. When the cup was empty he lay on the ground, his hands beneath his head.

Winky felt easier with his silences now. She leaned back, resting on her elbows. Above, the branches of the birch tree were white against the sky. The wine had been good, and a kind of euphoria was with her. "How good this day," she thought idly. After a time she glanced over her shoulder at Walter.

"Have you ever been in love?" he asked.

"Many times."

"I mean really."

"Once. I thought of marrying someone once."

"Why didn't you?"

"It just went . . ." she raised her hand, ". . . spftt. All at once."

"Just like that?"

"Just like that."

He sat up. "You know, your eyes aren't blue at all. They're green, and they have orange specks in them." He put one hand over his right eye and narrowed the left. "Yes, they're orange."

Winky laughed.

"You don't like me very much, do you? You still don't trust me?"

"Yes, I like you."

He kept looking at her. "Uh huh, orange eyes." He suddenly stood up. "Let's go, Charleston."

Winky looked up at him. "Go?"

"Church is over."

And below the hill by a clipped lilac tree he kissed her.

". . . Why, Winky, you're crying."

"I know. I don't know why." She was trying to laugh, too. "That's the first time you've called me Winky."

He kissed her again. Her cheeks were wet with tears.

"You—" He held her from him. "My god, Everett. Oh, my god."

"I—"

. . . And that was the day Winky considered the happiest day of her life.

Chapter 9 ∿

She awoke early the next day, and yesterday came to her like the morning sun streaming through the window. No, it had been no dream.

"*Good* morning, Ardys!"

Silence from the other bed. The downed comforter that Ardys had never quite adjusted to was half lying on the floor, and Ardys lay curled like a fetus with a wool bathrobe over her.

Winky got out of bed and, giggling, plopped the comforter over Ardys. "Up. Arise! It's a beautiful day."

"For godsakes, you're acting manic," said Ardys, turning over. "It's not even seven yet."

"Do you know what?"

"No!"

"I'm going to have herring, eggs, and even some of that goat cheese for breakfast."

"Good luck."

"Ardys! I've got a thousand things to tell you."

Silence.

Winky went over and pushed open the windows. She stood there for a moment looking at the golden green of Blindern, and looking she tried to form a mental picture of Walter's face—eyes, nose, mouth. The image was confused. She had heard it was this way sometimes, that people in love could never sharply define the other's face. His expressions were so changeable. But there, now, she saw his mouth— thin, sensitive and— Something turned over in her, and she put both hands to her face, her body rigid with the excitement that filled her. "Oh, Ardys." She half whispered.

Ardys sat up, her eye mask snatched from her eyes. "Winky, honestly. If it isn't bad enough having sunshine at midnight without your flitting around like some paranoid butterfly—"

Winky went over to her. "Ardys, he likes me! He really does."

"Cheezus, Winky. It's too damn early."

"But he *does*. Honestly."

"Well, good." Ardys straightened the comforter and turned over. "Pull the curtains!"

Winky dressed hurriedly and outside found her bicycle. She was hungry for breakfast. She had never been before. And then she remembered the *lefse* of yesterday. "We never really ate anything," she said to herself, "all day yesterday." She smiled and wondered if Walter were up now, probably having breakfast at the Walle-Vidkussons'. Would he be having herring and eggs and—

The morning was cool and smelled of odd spices. She tossed her hair back as she coasted down the way to the dining hall. She passed two young men, one from Rhode Island, the other a Norwegian. She had had coffee with the two of them one afternoon and rather liked them. "Hi," she called out as she passed.

"Hey, you all," called the young man from Rhode Island. "You all all right this mornin'?" The mimicry reminded her of Walter.

She laughed. "Fine!"

Yes, she was indeed fine.

Just when the day began to pale she didn't know exactly. She and Byrnes Walker, a student from Georgia, played tennis that afternoon, doubles. They played with the one married couple attending the summer session—the wife, a tall blonde with her hair braided at the back of her head and her husband, a lanky Californian with slender, almost fragile looks. Winky and Byrnes won the match. It had been a good afternoon. Then going back to the dormitory she decided to stop for the mail. There was a note from Aunt Pett saying she had just returned from Hilton Head and that she really hadn't missed Canada this summer at all; she had seen many friends she hadn't seen in years and the weather, though warm, was fine. There were many young people there from Charleston. But it all seemed so far away and dull that Winky wondered how she could ever have enjoyed Hilton Head or any of the people who had taken to gathering there, family groups like symmetrically arranged units. How insular it all seemed. That was her mail. There had been no notes, no messages that anyone had called, tried to reach her. Then, there, like a pin-prick of pain she realized Walter had said nothing about seeing her today or tonight or, for that matter, any time. Somehow she had taken it for granted there would be every day, every night, the two of them in the remaining weeks.

And as the night fell anguish fell with it. Yesterday meant nothing to him, she reasoned at last, only an idle afternoon. Had it been otherwise, had his feelings matched hers, surely he would have called; he would be here, now. She went over and over the day, everything he had said, the final kiss before she left him, the odd gentleness. She shut her eyes. Maybe he was with Julie and George, maybe they had planned something. That was it! Yes. After all, it was only one day. And she slept hugging her pillow like some yielding body she refused to loose from her.

But there was no word the next day nor the next. At

last a week passed. Each morning she got up, her body heavy, her eyes burning, fatigued from the sleepless nights and the deadly expectancy of the days. She ate little and routinely went to classes, not listening to the sing-song voices of the professors, just writing over and over the initials W.S.E. The S stood for Sayers, his mother's maiden name. He had told her that driving back from Lillehammer. His mother was from New Hampshire, a rather cold, orderly woman. He had never seen his mother cry. They had said very little driving home, Winky leaning her head on his shoulder, hating to leave him, hating to leave the clasp of his hand. And when she did leave she felt confused, single, so peculiarly alone. How silly she had been! But it *was* different. It *was*.

Then in a senseless act of madness she called the Walle-Vidkussons one night. A voice she didn't recognize, a man's, answered. She asked for Walter.

"Pardon," said the voice in the hesitant way many of the Norwegians used when speaking English.

"Mr. Everett. Mr. Walter Everett. He is a guest there?" Her heart beat hard. What would she say to him when he came to the phone?

"Oh, yes. Mr. Everett. He and the other guests are salmon fishing—at Bolstad." He didn't know when the guests were to return. He could ask Mrs. Walle-Vidkusson when she returned from a dinner engagement.

"No, that is all right. Thank you."

Did the lady wish to leave a name?

No, the lady did not wish to leave a name, but thank you.

She replaced the receiver with relief. She had been stupid to call.

The next day she asked everyone about Bolstad. She even

asked Harry Tosdale Flemming III. "Incredible fjord country," said Harry. "On the Vossa River. Great salmon fishing. The ambassador goes there frequently. Why?" he asked her. "Are you going there?"

"No, no. Just curious."

"Extraordinary place, really."

But she was angry, angry because she was made to feel foolish, remembering passing kisses like a country maid. That night she joined a group celebrating Ardys's birthday. She drank too much, and the next day she was ill and vomited. The weather turned unseasonably cold, and she longed for the beaches of home and the friendly womb of it, her drawling, lazy Carolina. She hated Walter Everett. Their lives were too different, their weathers were strangers. How near she had come to losing every vestige of pride. The thought made her shudder. She *hated* him!

Then hatred gradually fell into sanity again. Hard work, resignation and routine were good enough things to base one's life on. She listened to all the lecturers invited to the school to speak to the American students. She even took notes, thinking she might write some articles. She attended concerts, wrote letters: "It is all so beautiful here. It is all so . . ." But inside her all the while was the faint voice weeping: "What is to become of me? What is to become of me?" One of her professors, a young man from Bergen, who taught Norwegian literature remarked in class one day that the "excitement of life" was the unknown, a state to bless rather than fear: "Each day, hour, holds discovery." It was a youthful remark, a youthful spirit, even pathetic in its touching naiveté. For she knew her days. She saw them there in the future: pat, gray years, each as predictable as the rise and setting of the sun.

You've never learned the art of living. Art of living. What had Walter meant by that really? She looked inward, trying to see the depths of herself and why. As a small child she had been shy, afraid, afraid even of the smallest things. But of what? Darkness, sounds, seas, rivers, people. Gradually the child's fears had given way to others more unidentified. She had never embraced life with any sense of forgetfulness or freedom, but had held back, never the participator. She followed rules, would never have led a revolt, had her likes, dislikes, some hearty, some mild. In school she had been liked in spite of an aloofness on occasion. She had never been a leader. In her late teens she had discovered a God, dramatically and emotionally, and just as undramatically gradually lost Him, not completely, only intellectually. She knew, however, that the true despair is a life with no faith. Yet she felt— Ah yes, she felt. She felt pride and grief and laughter and love and the aching loneliness that all humans come to know and suffer. And she embraced *their* pride, *their* warmth, *their* wants.

Still, what chains held her so? At times she envied the Negro, the rural Southern Negro. He, alone, it seemed, had a freedom, shouting out his love for his God, crying out his grief, moaning his hatred, clapping his hands in gaiety, body and soul. How good to lay waste these griefs, joys, in simple abandon.

Yet she could not.

Why?

The art of living . . . .

Hard work, resignation and routine.

She began making plans for a future outside Charleston. She would quit her job on the newspaper, take work in New

York or Washington. The promise of it rather excited her, and Ardys said she would help her find something to do. They would share an apartment.

"I don't know why you haven't thought of it before," Ardys said. "Except, of course, there was Ted."

Yes, there was Ted. She probably should have married Ted. She might even have discovered some facsimile of love. The thought rather sickened her, pretending for the rest of life. Still, it would have been better than the stern staleness that held her now.

" 'For I would be mending my spirit,' " she said aloud.

"What did you say?"

"Nothing, just quoting."

She was eager for the school to close. She said so. Its newness had worn. She wanted to see more of Europe before she returned. Ardys would not go with her as they had planned. The associate editor was writing daily.

"You'll probably marry him," Winky said, "and then where will I be? I can't move in with both of you."

"You can have my apartment in that case. I said *in that case*."

Then one afternoon as she came out of the *Studenterhjem* there was Walter, sitting casually on the steps outside the entrance as if it had all been planned. He was darkly tanned, and his cheekbones were faintly reddened as if just a moment ago he had left the sun.

"Hi." He lifted his hand, almost saluting. He was wearing a dark blue sweater and the whiteness of the loosened collar at his neck made his face look even darker.

"Hi," she said, but anger and excitement both struggled within her.

"Are you ready?"

"Ready for what?" She tried to fight the anger, to show only she was meeting a casual friend. "What *are* you talking about?"

"To go."

"Go where?"

"Blom's. We had a date to talk. Remember?"

"No, I don't remember."

"Poor, poor memory." He shook his head. "You're failing, Charleston."

"How have you been?"

"A fat fifty-four pounder."

"What?"

"I caught a salmon—fifty-four pounds. They took my picture. I was a hero. Didn't you see it?"

"No, I didn't."

"Uh huh." He tossed a stone in the air and reached to catch it. "Incidentally, this place doesn't seem very scholarly to me."

"Oh?"

"Looks more like a lonely hearts club. Lovers strolling here and there."

It was true, in a way. Most of the younger students had paired off, found their summer romance or whatever.

"Maybe so. But we do have exams coming up."

He glanced up at her. "Ready to go?"

"Walter," she forced a smile. "I have to study."

"Oh? Sorry. I'm leaving tomorrow."

"You're leaving?" she managed. "Where will you be going?"

"Around."

"And then?"

"Home. New York."

"And the great American *Erfolg?*" She tried to smile. "Joke."

He looked at her. "Cut it out, Charleston. Let's go." He stood up. "I've just gotten back from Bolstad—*and* Lille-hammer."

"How was Mrs. Baarli?" *He's leaving.*

"Mrs. Baarli is fine. I didn't want to go to Bolstad."

"I wondered where you were," she said softly, her face burning.

"We'll go to Blom's, have a few drinks." The lines on his face showed through the tan.

A few drinks and you'll be gone. She looked down at her hands. They were trembling.

"Okay?" he said softly. He was looking at her, narrowing his eyes as if he meant to say more.

"All right," she heard herself say. She was nodding. Her legs felt weak. "I'll be with you—in a minute." She walked away.

"And hurry," he called.

She didn't look back.

Blom's was an "artists' " café. Ibsen, Gustav Vigeland, most of Norway's writers and artists had at one time or another spent time there, or so said the billing. Their pictures lined the walls and with its darkness, unobtrusive piano player and meticulous service the place was sought after more by tourists now than by artists.

The room had a winter feel about it, *gemütlich*, and Winky preferred to think the two jolly Norwegian women across the way had some vague connection with the arts rather than being what they undoubtedly were, two housewives on a late afternoon spree.

Walter ordered two beers, and the two sat in silence.

The pianist, an unhappy looking Norwegian whose blond hair was in need of a haircut, was playing something from Sibelius, vaguely familiar. Winky only half listened, but the music, melancholy, lonely, touched the same chords within her body.

Walter sat holding a burning cigarette near his mouth, not smoking it. His hand partially covered his mouth, and the smoke curled upward toward his eyes. Why had he come back? How much simpler to have merely left. She would never have seen him again, or thought of him, not really— only a face vanished in time.

Was it possible that one person could feel so deeply and the other nothing? Was it only women who felt these things? For no matter how she explained it away she knew, sitting there, listening to the pianist, waiting for the hour to go, she knew she could not bear his going, vanishing forever from her life. Love *was* a kind of madness—for women, at least. She had never known what the word "love" meant. It was only a word, unidentified, untranslatable. But— "Oh," she said aloud and turned her gaze from the pianist.

"Something wrong?" Walter asked.

"No. The music maybe. He's good." Her voice had an odd hoarseness to it.

Walter mashed out the cigarette into the ashtray. "All right. Let's quit the chess game."

Winky only looked at him.

"I've missed the hell out of you, Charleston. I wish we'd had more time."

Winky met his look and flushed deeply. She put a matchstick over the still burning cigarette.

"God knows I didn't want to miss you. I don't need any more complications just now."

"I know. I . . ."

"And quit the tears. Don't do that again." He handed her a handkerchief.

Winky put the handkerchief to her nose. "My mother says a lady always has a handkerchief. And I don't have one." She put her fingertips to her eyes. "When will you be leaving?"

"Tomorrow morning."

"Why?"

"I've got to get back."

"You're going straight home? Fly?"

"No, I'm stopping off in Copenhagen and I want to see some people in Paris."

"But—" Winky folded the handkerchief. "I don't know." She put her hands to the back of her neck and leaned her head back.

"I know."

She looked at him and smiled. "I had a lovely day that Sunday. I'll remember it as a lovely day."

Walter turned from her, not saying anything.

"I'll never see you again." Her voice came weakly, childlike.

He looked back at her. "Yes, I'll see you."

"No, I don't think so. That's the way things go."

"It's the age of the jet, you know."

"And things move so quickly."

He took hold of her hand.

She looked at him questioningly.

The hold on her hand tightened. "Come with me."

Winky tried to withdraw her hand.

"It will be all right."

She could not say a word.

"I'm not suggesting anything. Believe me."

"Suggest?"

"Winky."

"Yes?"

"I couldn't hurt you."

"I know."

"Will you?"

Winky closed her eyes. The grasp of his hand asked once more. She felt dizzy, and his eyes burned in his face. "All right."

He looked at her for a long while, saying nothing. Then he said "Let's go" and they left the café, still saying nothing. They drove in silence back to Blindern.

"Eight-thirty at the airport," he said.

Winky nodded and left him.

But far into the night she lay sleepless, her eyes watching as darkness finally came with a hush full of awe and fear. Life was speeding to her, and the wonder of it overpowered her into sleep at last.

Chapter 10 ᷒᷒

When it was all over Winky wondered if she exaggerated those days with Walter, made them seem gayer, easier than they really were—like the bereaved remembering the dead, she sometimes thought, the mind clinging so everlastingly to the virtues, the good, forgetting the flaws, even one's own. Yet taken all in one she seemed to remember the time as one long Tivoli—lights, fountains, colors, laughter and the faint, ever so faint, feel of autumn there at the end in Paris. If there were flaws she couldn't remember.

Whatever, she knew there would never be a time quite like that again. Even with Walter. But she held no regrets, no real ones; only that it could never be repeated, matched or even captured. So it was true, she came to believe, that remembered happiness can pain equally as much as grief, if not more so. The winds of fortune did spoil, a few days scattered into wastelands like leaves from an old calendar. She wondered why it was that the secure always rationalized to the lonely: ". . . at least you had *that* time; some don't even have that." It was a careless statement, useless. Better never to have had the time at all, better to have etherized the brain. How thieving the pitiable brain.

She had packed that morning with grim determination all the while hearing Ardys's admonitions:

"I gave you credit for having *some* sense." (Ardys was always giving somebody credit for something.) "Winky, you're a fool." (No credit.)

"Maybe so," Winky said and, tight-lipped, methodically folded a sweater and put it in the open suitcase.

"What do you want to be—like the rest of them? You *know* about the rest of them." (Why the prim smile on her lips?)

"No, I don't," Winky said.

"Well, you should. And you know now."

"Uh huh."

"Winky, get some sense!"

Winky glanced at her.

"It's just no good."

Winky slammed the suitcase shut.

"You're really going." Ardys was looking at her in utter disbelief. "You're really going."

Winky picked up the suitcase. "Don't worry. I know what I'm doing. Really."

"If it's what you want—"

"It is."

Ardys just looked at her, her mouth hung open. How unattractive she looked.

"I'm not going to die," Winky said. "Just the opposite."

But the doubts came. Riding to the airport in a taxi Ardys's words came back to her: *You know about the rest of them*. The statement teased in her mind. Had there been others? Someone who had sat across from him in a dark café and, abandoning all sense, said "yes"? How many? Last night and the rightness of her decision seemed so hazed now, a decision made in a dark dream. The morning was so bright it almost hurt her eyes to look at it. For a moment she started to tell the driver to turn back. What would they say of her at home—her mother, father, all of them? She thought of them there, so innocent in their stern Protestantism, and picturing them she felt a longing to see them, to be there with them the girl she was, protected, loved, the daughter of the house. But had it been like that really?

It was in this mood she arrived at the airport. But when she saw Walter all doubts left her. He was in a festive mood, wearing a raincoat and khaki fishing cap. He waved the cap at her as soon as she entered the airport.

"I thought you'd never get here." He looked so very young. It was the cap, set so jauntily on his head.

"But I am," she said almost shyly.

He took her bags. "Hurry, they have a ticket for you. Check in, and then *I* have a surprise."

Her hands trembled as she took the ticket from the young woman behind the counter. Walter quickly led her outside to the waiting planes. And then she saw the two champagne glasses, resting elegantly atop an old typewriter case.

"Walter?"

He popped open a bottle of champagne, and a middle-aged couple nearby, tourists, Americans, laden with cameras and straps, smiled.

"For our voyage!" said Walter, handing her a glass with an exaggerated bow.

Winky tossed back her head. "Oh, Walter, how wonderful! How *simply* wonderful!"

And so it was—the short flight over, the blue sky, silver wings: "On a blue day I flew to Paradise on silver wings." And below, finally, the city. Copenhagen. Bicycles. Copenhagen—like the glass of champagne, bubbling, gay, festive, as deceptively innocent as the poor boy from Odense, who saw the city as a children's city and wrote his haunting tales. Bicycles. Gay, gay, sad city.

There was not one hotel room to be got in the entire

city. Walter had planned to stay at the D'Angleterre. "The only place," he said rather grandly on the flight over.

"But it's the height of the tourist season," Winky had told him.

"So?"

"Tourists."

"Forget them," he said. He knew somebody at the D'Angleterre, Per Lundquist. Per would give them rooms "no matter what."

But Per was "not with the D'Angleterre any more. He left for Rome over a year now." And the tall clerk behind the desk merely shook his head—graciously, but firmly "no."

"But where will we go?" Winky pleaded with the clerk.

"It is a busy season here, Madam. All rooms in Copenhagen are reserved in advance. But perhaps—" He looked at Walter. "You wish two rooms, sir?"

"Yes."

He glanced at Winky.

"Two rooms," Walter repeated.

"You are not—pardon—married?"

Winky looked straight at the man. "No, we are not." She didn't care. She didn't care about anything.

"Then perhaps. Pardon for a moment, please."

When the clerk disappeared Winky looked at Walter and giggled.

" 'You are not—pardon—married,' " Walter mocked the clerk, the pursed lips, the dull eyes looking into space.

"There're always park benches," Winky said. "Or do they do that in Denmark, you suppose?"

The clerk returned holding a small piece of paper. "There is a lady who rents rooms on occasion. She does not serve fare." He held out the paper.

The name written on the paper given by the clerk was Mrs. Ragnar Lundberg, and it soon became obvious that Mrs. Lundberg was not overly pleased having two Americans in her house.

She met Winky and Walter at the door of a two-story brick town house. A pale, severe-looking woman in her early sixties, she only cracked open the door. "*Ja?*" she asked, looking from Winky to Walter and back at Walter again, an instant signal of danger in her eyes.

"We were sent here by Mr. Keilhau—at the D'Angleterre," said Walter.

The door did not open, and the woman continued to frown at them. "Americans?" she asked with a whisper in her voice. At least she spoke English.

"Yes," Walter said. "I understand you have rooms?"

"*Ja!*" Silence.

"Well, we're here," Walter said, jamming his hands into his raincoat pockets.

The woman looked back at Winky.

Winky smiled at her, a female language that sometimes worked.

"We have no luxuries here," said the woman.

"We only want two rooms," Walter said. "Do you have them?"

"Americans?" she asked again.

"Yes. The United States of A-mer-i-ca," Walter said testily.

"How long must you stay?"

"Only one night. We fly to Paris late tomorrow afternoon."

Winky continued to smile at her.

"You may come." She opened the door hesitantly.

The hallway was dark. A high stairway met them almost immediately. "I have only a flat, you must understand," said Mrs. Lundberg. "The lower floor is that of another."

Winky and Walter said nothing. They followed in silence as Mrs. Lundberg in arch dignity led her pilgrimage up the stairway. There were signs the house had seen happier, more glamorous days. The Reeding molding along the ceiling was a reminder, but the stairway itself, neat, practical and blond, was new five years or more.

Once upstairs Mrs. Lundberg turned to them again. "We have no luxuries." There was pride in her voice, and Winky wondered exactly what she meant. She glanced at Walter, who was frowning, pointedly disgusted with the entire affair. The urge to laugh came again.

"The gentleman must stay here," said Mrs. Lundberg, opening a door to the left. Winky and Walter both followed into the room. The room was spotlessly clean with high ceilings, containing one brass-posted cot with the same comforters they had in Oslo. There was a table on which sat an enamelled bowl and pitcher and near it one chair. But on the right side of the room there was no wall, only one long curtain, dark with faded rose-colored flowers.

Both Walter and Winky stared at the curtain. It had a vaudeville look about it. There was no explanation from Mrs. Lundberg, and she found it not amusing when Walter pushed it slightly aside.

"Another room?" Walter asked.

Mrs. Lundberg touched her hands together in front of her and lifted her head. "The curtain divides the rooms."

"I see," Walter said, lifting one eyebrow.

"The other room belongs to my brother-in-law. He does not like to be disturbed. He has late hours, until midnight."

"I see," said Walter.

Winky covered her mouth with her hand and turned from the woman.

"Now, Madam, I will show you to your chamber."

Winky's room, down the hall from Walter's, was solid, no curtains anywhere.

"This is very nice. Thank you, Mrs. Lundberg." Winky stood straighter, meeting the woman's dignity with her own. "A bath? Do you have a bath here?"

"You wish to bathe?" asked Mrs. Lundberg incredulously.

"No, I just wondered—a room somewhere, maybe? Nearby?"

"Come." She frowned at Walter. The two followed, through a small hallway, through a parlor, dining room. "In, please." She pointed to a closed door.

Winky looked inside. It was complete. "Well, thank you, Mrs. Lundberg. We do appreciate your having us."

Mrs. Lundberg nodded her head, and then looked sideways at Walter. "You do not keep late hours?"

"No, no we won't keep late hours," Walter said.

"Then," Mrs. Lundberg looked back at Winky. "I shall give you a key to enter for the evening."

She handed the key to Winky.

"For the *front* door?"

Mrs. Lundberg nodded. "You may leave the key in your chamber when you depart."

Walter cocked his head. "You've been so gracious, Mrs. Lundberg. Thank you. Thank you. I—"

"Good evening." She vanished.

Winky hurried back to her room and fell into a fit of

laughter. When she glanced up Walter was standing at her door. "Dear god," he said.

"That curtain. You shouldn't have peeked. She thinks you're a gangster."

"Hell, I didn't know *what* she had back there."

"But you and brother-in-law will make such a cozy couple—all divided by a curtain and everything."

Walter laughed then and went over to her. He cupped her face in his hands. "You're a lot of fun, Charleston, a good sport. And you're—" He started to kiss her.

"Not here. Mrs. Lundberg wouldn't approve."

Walter dropped his hands to his side. "What a mess. Let's get out of here. This beautiful city, and here we are."

Tivoli was a fairyland, stars in the trees, dazzling fountains, flowers, music, lights, colors, children.

"All the men look like Hans Christian Andersen," Winky said. She seemed to see him everywhere, the tall lean body, straight carriage, prominent nose, thin lips, blue, blue eyes.

And the children, blond, bronzed—wide, wonder eyes, shy of the glory about them.

"It's like a music box I had when I was a child," Winky said. "I always thought the world would be like that music box when I grew up."

"And now it is," Walter said.

They had a drink at one of the garden restaurants, and then walked hand in hand through the grounds, as children do, lost in the gaiety of the night, pausing once to hear the symphony, then on to watch the young couples dancing and all the while the fountains upward, upward, multi-colored. They stopped once to look at the ducks in the pond.

"Where is the ugly one?" Winky asked.

"There isn't one. It was only a story. Didn't you know?" Walter tightened his arm about her, and Winky lifted her face. He kissed her. There were people about; Winky didn't care.

"It's a dream, isn't it?" she said. "I'm so happy." She closed her eyes. "Are you?"

"Let's stay here. Let's don't go to Paris."

"All right."

"But I want to show you Paris."

"All right."

"Very agreeable, you are."

"You're wonderful."

"*Hjertelig tak.*"

"Because you speak such be-utiful Danish."

Walter held her at the waist, looking at her. "You know, I think I'm a man who is about to—"

"What?"

"I'll tell you at dinner."

"Dinner? What's that?"

"I'll show you."

"Here?"

"No, another place . . ."

Walter found a restaurant on Gammel Strand. It was a small place, though rather formal, even elegant, an elegance Winky had come to learn as markedly Scandinavian, pristine, pure, graceful, correct and yet doll-like; yes, as the chandelier above—light, gay, one a child would admire, want to touch.

"Do you suppose *anyone* is unhappy here?" Winky asked when they were seated.

"Think of the suicides."

"Isn't that somewhat exaggerated?"

"Perhaps."

Winky suddenly sat straighter. "Walter! Please, I want a cigar."

"A what?"

"Look at the lady there."

A young woman, her blond hair piled atop her head and wearing long jade earrings, was smoking a cigar. Winky had seen others at Tivoli, and it seemed so incongruous—the woman with her slender femininity and graceful movement of head and hands holding a cigar so delicately.

"Awful. Terrible," Walter said.

"I think it's fascinating. Why do they do it?"

"Cheaper."

"What?"

"Cigars are cheaper than cigarettes. I'll divorce you if I ever see you smoking one of those."

"You know," Winky said, smiling at him, "you have an accent, too."

"An *accent*?"

"You say, ci-*gahs*. You sound so teddibly propah and bored. When I first met you I thought you were a terrible stuffed shirt. It was the way you spoke. I couldn't imagine how the world had ever taken you in. You were so painfully understated."

"And I thought you were the coldest damned woman I'd ever met."

"Am I?"

"Not so far."

Winky looked back at the woman with the cigar.

Walter took her hand. "Slender fingers, long. Artistic."

"I'm sad," Winky said.

"I thought you said you were so happy."

"I am—sad and happy and—"

A waiter in a red coat and brass buttons appeared. Walter glanced up.

The waiter smiled at them.

"We *are* here for a purpose, aren't we?" Walter said. He took the menu. "Aquavit, first, please. The plaice, your mousse with truffles—and . . ." He looked at Winky. ". . . champagne?"

Winky nodded.

The waiter disappeared.

"You're so absolutely worldly, aren't you?" Winky said and grinned.

"And you have such an immense sense of humor."

Winky leaned forward, her elbow on the table and her hand curved beneath her chin. "You'll be the greatest writer in the world. I know."

"Not if you're around."

"What a really nasty thing to say. I could help you. You could read me what you've written. I'm a very discerning critic."

"You probably are."

"Don't look so serious. I was only joking, but I do think I have *some* taste."

The waiter brought the aquavit and Walter sipped it.

"I thought all Vikings gulped it in one great gulp," Winky said.

"Oh?"

His mood was changing. Winky could hear it in his voice, the "oh?" almost arrogant. She began toying with the glass before her.

"But I am going to write," he said.

Yes, the mood had changed. She didn't want it. "I didn't know there was any doubt about *that*."

"Very much so."

"What?"

"I wanted to go into the ministry."

The surprise must have shown on her face.

"I shock you."

"The *mini*stry!"

"I have shocked you."

"A little." She searched his face for something new, or perhaps old. How quickly one's view of a person could change, just in a moment, a few words. Someone had told her once it was the first impression of a person that really mattered; no matter to what depths one finally learned another, eventually the first impression always returned, was the truer. She didn't know.

"I guess it was there all the time," Walter was saying, "even when I was teaching. I considered myself a nihilist, even bragged about it . . ." he gave a short laugh, ". . . but I guess I was as the bard says—protesting too much."

Winky took up her glass. A puzzling reaction was settling within her. She felt closed out, cheated, and because of it there was resentment, too. It was as if he had mocked her these weeks, let her prattle foolishly. It was a fault of the spiritual. She had seen it before like the rich posing as the poor. Why hadn't he shown her this side of himself before? He had hinted at it once, that time aboard ship when she first met him, but she had confused what he said with his rudeness when he so abruptly left her, the latter taking most of her thought.

"I don't know you," she said aloud.

"I'm trying to tell you."

"It just doesn't make any sense." She regretted the irritation in her voice.

"What doesn't make any sense?"

"I don't know. Everything about you. At times you seem so urbane—so—" He seemed to be looking at her mockingly, amused. "Even the way you look, dress. If I looked at you—I mean as a stranger, I would say, 'Now there's somebody who's had everything, never really been touched by any of the harshness of life, or even cared.' The accent is so right, the tone of voice, the walk, the complete assurance. You look like somebody who's saying, 'Look, people, Mother and Daddy sent me to all the correct schools and see—I've learned *this* and I've learned *that!*' And I would say, 'You, young man, should go to your God and pray for the sin of arrogance.'" She dropped her head. "I'm sorry."

"Come now." He lifted his glass. "Not tonight. Hey, my glass is empty."

Winky smiled at him, yet an unevenness had come between them. They had lost the lights of Tivoli.

"Please smile again."

"I am."

"Not really."

"Yes, I am. See."

"I think I love you."

Winky looked at him wide-eyed. "What?"

"There. See. There's the look again. Alive. My real Charleston."

"But . . ." She brushed her hair back from her face.

"I do, you know. I really do think I love you."

"Walter, Walter, Walter." She put her hands over her face. "I don't understand you. I just don't."

"If you cry again I'm going to walk right out of here, fly to Paris, leave you with Mrs. Whatever-her-name-is and her snoring brother-in-law."

Winky relaxed her hands. "I'm not crying." She moved her head slowly. "I'm just—"

"Finish your drink. We've got more places to go before this night is done."

It was four-thirty in the morning when they returned to the "House of Lundberg" as Walter called Mrs. Lundberg's establishment. Darkness had come, but the night had been light, filled with music, dancing and Danish laughter. They had gone to Sollerod Kro, then to the north where the chalk cliffs overlook the Baltic Sea and where behind them were the windmills and woods as mysterious as the sea itself. They finished the night with a final salute to the last and lonely mermaid forever bathing in her wonder world. Walter was gay, gay.

"Shuhh," Winky said. "We'll wake up Mrs. Lundberg."

"Charleston!"

"What?"

"I've lost the key."

"I gave it to you."

"I know, but I've lost it."

"Oh, no. Look in your pockets."

"I have."

"What'll we do?"

"We'll have to ring the bell."

"We *can't*. We'll wake her up. Look again."

Walter walked out by the street lamp, removed his coat and began searching the pockets.

Finally, success.

He fumbled with the key in the lock.

"I feel like I'm back in school again, naughty children sneaking home after hours."

Once inside the dark hallway, Walter carefully closed the door. Winky began to giggle. "I can't *see*," she said, feeling blindly for the stairway railing.

"Hey," Walter whispered.

"What?"

He took her by the hand. "Wait a min-ute." And then she was in his arms, lifting her face to meet his kiss, his body so close she was senseless. He kissed her again and when he placed his hand over her breast she felt he would take her very heart so rapid was its beat inside her.

"Winky?"

"Yes." She could barely speak.

"I meant it."

"What?"

"I think I love you."

She covered his face with kisses. "I'll take care of you. I will."

He held her from him then, gently, saying nothing, with his arms around her waist. It was a conscious gesture as if some thought had suddenly come to him. Winky could scarcely make out his features, the forehead, nose, the thin lips, the boy-like head. It was the boyishness of the head that touched her, and she wanted to take his face in her hands, soothe it, so that the lines made there would fade forever.

"I could never hurt you," he said.

She put her hand gently over his mouth. He took her hand, kissed the palm.

"I'm you," she said. "I am. I'm *you*."

How long they stayed thus Winky could never remember.

Chapter 11

"The French are ruder than ever," Winky wrote home on a postcard to her parents, explaining she was traveling with a friend and would fly home in a few days. "The people are the only thing wrong with Paris." She was parroting Walter's sentiments, of course, and some of her own.

Their entrance into Paris had been an indelicate, to say the least, encounter with an hysterical taxi driver, who felt his "pourboire" insufficient and had dumped them, oaths, shouts, baggage and all on the Avenue Montaigne, two blocks from the place they were staying.

Tired after the flight over and irritated with the driver's (purposeful, it seemed) inability to understand the correct address, Walter made a passing, not too complimentary reference to General de Gaulle's Fifth Republic. That, in turn, stoked the already fuming flames so at the end the wild shouts of the man reached almost soprano heights causing not a few passersby to stop and witness the meeting between the two Americans and the loyal Frenchman.

Paris was not Copenhagen. And Winky found herself already missing the "civilizing force," as someone not very originally put it, of Scandinavia. She even missed Mrs. Lundberg. They had left her, too, under rather uneasy circumstances: Drugged by sleep after their night in Copenhagen, Winky rose late the next day, and, slightly headachy, slipped on her bathrobe, took up her toothbrush and carefully made her way down the hall, through the living room and into the dining room, only to find Walter similarly clad and equipped and Mrs. Lundberg stonily entertaining guests for luncheon.

Winky had caught only the words "Americans" and Walter's ceremonious "Good morning, ladies and gentlemen" as she "queenly marched," as Walter later described it, through the room, out into the hall and into the bathroom, abandoning Walter to his own fate of four black-suited, stiff-backed gentlemen and three pairs of icy-blue female eyes.

Their departure from the "House of Lundberg" had been less than gracious, though with a different texture than that of the taxi driver.

The urbanity of Paris with its decided Latin malaise seemed unkempt and despairing after Scandinavia. The city was readying itself for autumn. The theatres were trying to refresh themselves with nonsensical avant-garde mouthings; social life was beginning to move. Tourists, both German and American, had had their fill and for the most part fled. The nights were cool but the days warm. Yet the faces of the people bore no seasonal change: routine, ennui, even disgust, a city sickened, its spirit in coma. Or so it seemed.

"I used to love this city," Walter said as they walked along the street that first night. A neon Esso sign winked at them across the way.

"Don't you want me to carry the typewriter or something?" Winky asked.

"I'm all right."

After the driver had deposited them, Walter picked up the three suitcases and typewriter and they walked the two blocks which seemed to stretch for miles. Finally, a doorman who looked every inch, uniform and nose, like General de Gaulle, relieved Walter of his burden. Inside, Walter picked up a key from a small inner office and escorted Winky into an elevator.

"Just where *are* we?" Winky asked.

"You'll see."

He led her down a hallway decorated with red damask paper. Or was it cloth? She touched it to see. Cloth.

The door near the end of the hall opened into an apartment. Winky stood at the door. The rooms were pleasant, dimly lighted, not too large, with long windows opposite the door. There was a mustiness about the rooms, a closed-in effect and the distinct feeling of the presence of a third person like a legacy from the dead. There was a small desk at the right and, surprisingly, a bud vase holding one pink rose. A sofa and chairs faced the desk, and on the opposite side of the room was a bookcase filled with books and a few papers, yellowed and folded, between the books.

"Whose place is this?" Winky asked.

"My father's. Come, look."

Winky followed him through the rooms—bedrooms with the same long windows, kitchen completely equipped, and a small office with a table and typewriter.

"My father stays here when he's in Paris."

"It's lovely," Winky said quietly.

"They keep it for executives, visitors."

"How nice."

"You don't sound like it."

Winky walked back into the living room and opened one of the windows slightly.

"Stuffy," Walter said. "And I told them we were coming, too."

"We?"

"Uh huh. Drink?"

Winky didn't answer.

"My sister was just here with some friends."

"Oh?" Winky imagined the sister older, perhaps looking something like Walter. She wondered how his looks would carry over in a female face, the smaller nose, the wider mouth, dark hair, dark eyes. Strange, she had never given much thought to Walter's family even though he had spoken of them. Yet their presence was very much in the rooms, disturbing, the saner world again. Would they like her, Walter's family? The room was decorated by someone with passable taste.

Walter opened a black lacquer bar. "And typically she probably didn't leave anything to— Ah, yes. All here. We have scotch, gin—"

"Walter, where am I going to stay?"

"Here, of course."

"Have you lost your mind?"

"No." He placed a record on the record player. *La Mer.* "Drink? Scotch?"

"I can't stay here."

"Why not?"

"I'll give you exactly one reason."

"And what, pray, could that be?" Then he laughed. "All right." He led her out the door and down the hall again. "Now, here," he said, taking another key from his pocket. He opened the door into a small bedroom. "This is where all proper Charleston girls stay when they come to visit."

The windows in the room were open, and the curtains blew slightly. The anonymity of the room and the breeze from the window made her feel better. She said so.

"But you'll have to have breakfast with me. No fare in

this establishment either, a bit like Mrs. Lundberg's, though we do have a twitty little maid who comes in and does breakfast. Nine o'clock sharp, no matter what."

She smiled up at him.

"You don't like my cozy little den?"

"There're too many people in there."

"Too many people?"

"Like your house or something, your parents' house. It makes me feel uninvited."

"Quaint girl."

"Uh huh."

"But you will have breakfast with me?"

"I'd love to have breakfast with you."

"Every day?" For the first time his voice sounded almost shy. "For the rest of your life?"

Winky started to say something, but his lips were on hers as if he were trying to void his shyness. As she returned the kiss a strengthlessness eased her body.

"Oh, Walter." She lifted her face slowly, drowsily searching for his mouth again.

"God, Winky. Where are we going?"

She withdrew from him then and turned slowly, drawing her fingers through the back of her hair. Her breath came so heavily.

Walter took her hand. "Let's do go and have that drink. I think we had . . . better."

She smiled at him, a faint smile, and easily went with him.

The record he had placed earlier had spun itself of its haunting melody of the sea, and now the needle grated along the groove. Walter went over to it and stood before it, both hands clutching the table, his shoulders slumped, making no move to change the record. Winky watched him as she sat on the sofa, a melancholy filling her senses. Through the windows she could barely make out the rooftops and chimneys of Paris, small and perky, half-hidden by the lamplit darkness and Walter's shoulders. She felt easier in the room now. It was the first time she was seeing Walter in his own surroundings, a host entertaining on familiar ground, a Walter she didn't know at all. She thought of him coming here in the past, a member of a family, a younger man, gay, indifferent, the rich man's son in a playful city. Or was he ever that way? Really so?

He lifted the needle from the player and quietly and methodically fixed two drinks. Without saying anything he came to sit beside her, handed her her drink. And they sat seeing the rooftops and chimneys, the skyline of the gay, gaudy city. The scotch was warming, soothing, and Winky leaned her head against the back of the sofa, her body relaxing further with the warmth of the drink. She turned her head slightly and was surprised to see Walter looking at her.

"Winky, look," he said quickly. He sat up straighter and put his drink on the table before them. "I—"

Winky's heart began to accelerate, something about the look of him, the positive way in which he set his glass and the tone of his voice—direct, firm, impersonal, a professorial voice giving some rule of logic to a nameless face.

He didn't look at her. "This whole thing has been so damned crazy, hasn't it?"

"What?"

"You, me."

"Maybe."

"It's been so quick, you know."

"What are you trying to say?"

He looked at her then. A shadow fell across the left side

of his face. "I don't know, really. I can look at you and every-thing rational disappears." He lifted his hands. "I guess what I'm trying to say, ask, is—" (The word *ask*—"awsk." Such a small word to point their differences.)

Winky put her drink on the table.

"I don't want us to get caught up in anything we'll later regret."

He looked away again, and Winky studied his profile. He was deadly serious, as if he were talking to himself, choosing, searching. This is the way it goes, she thought, the easing away, the first step, delicate. "Neither do I," she said thinly.

"*That* would be—ve-ry *bad*."

Winky felt her face flush. "Just what *are* you trying to say?"

He didn't answer.

"That—you regret some of the things you've said?"

"No."

"That it's all been a summer thing, a fillip for sagging egos? I've thought of that, too, you know." She was looking at the lamplights outside. The leaves on the plane trees looked silver. Had it begun to drizzle or was it a trick of the eye? "Is that it?"

"It doesn't matter how or why or what season people meet. It's just that—look. I've been an awfully confused person these last years. Nothing has been, to say the least, exactly normal. Vietnam, those months in the hospital, and suddenly the incredible beauty of Norway and—you."

"It *was* rather perfect, wasn't it?" She put the tips of her fingers to her lips.

"Maybe too perfect. Maybe we were—I, at least—just too receptive. Don't you see?"

She looked at him in half amazement, and then a mixture of anger and pride, mostly pride if there was a difference, went through her. "I think I do," she said.

"Do you?"

She lighted a cigarette, immediately put it out, and rose from the sofa. "Walter, I'm leaving. If you want to see me I'll most likely be in Charleston." She opened her pocketbook, placed the open pack of cigarettes and then snapped the pocketbook closed. "Send me a postcard sometime. I'd love to know the end of your journey."

Walter groaned and was quickly by her side. "Winky, for *god*sakes, you're not reading me at all."

"I think I am." And for a moment the sight of his face, the distress, gave her a small stirring of pleasure. It was she who was in command now.

"No, you're not. I just want us to be sure."

"Sure of what?"

He shrugged his shoulders, turned from her, and turned back. "I'm talking about marriage." His eyes were moving excitedly.

"And what about tomorrow?"

"That's what I mean, don't you see? I want us to be sure. Doesn't that make any sense? Any sense at all?"

Winky said nothing. Yes, she was in command, but she didn't want it now. She was thinking that her own feelings, now, this minute, could never change. Next September, the year after and the year after that, she would love this man who now moved about the room so anxiously. He was too tall for the small room and the sight of him, his long legs fit more for the out-of-doors than a small Parisian apartment, closed her further in this warmth. Yet, now, she must keep her distance.

"Don't you see?" he said again.

"I suppose."

He picked up both their drinks from the coffee table. "Will you have a drink with me, Charleston?"

Winky just looked at him.

"Drink?"

Her face burst into a smile.

He put the drinks back on the table, and took her in his arms, gently burying his face in her hair. "I've never loved anybody else. . . ."

After dinner they walked along the Champs-Élysées. The night was cool as they walked, and once Winky looked up to see if there were stars over Paris. There were. Strange, she had never thought there would be stars over Paris. The lamplights hazed the trees. The leaves were beginning to turn. In a few days they would begin to fall. In a few days they would be leaving. She counted the days in her mind. Two days more here, the flight to New York. One day in Pittsburgh. She had promised to go home with him, only for a day. And then— She didn't want to think about it. Then was then. Now was now, absent of a future, detail, worry. Perhaps that was all there was to happiness. It was enough.

They stopped once at a café. It was still warm enough to be outside, and they sat saying nothing, watching the people, lovers, girls alone. Indians in their elaborate robes, businessmen, young men with beards, the elderly, the mad. The people streamed before them, people they would never meet or know, all going somewhere. Impossible, they, these endless streams of people, would still be here. She wouldn't.

They walked leisurely back to the apartment. The rooms were home now, theirs; no longer possessed by the ghosts of strangers. The two half-filled glasses rested on the table where they had abandoned them earlier. The cigarette Winky had so impatiently put out lay torn now like an old passion. The rooms were warm, still, and totally theirs.

The moment seemed to stretch for hours. Walter carefully took up the two glasses, placed them on the bar and, not turning, stood there. Winky watched him with the heaviness inside her she knew he, too, possessed. It was intolerable, his standing there, not turning. She was afraid.

"Winky?"

She could not speak.

He came to her then and in his arms the night cloaked them, closing out fear, want and the terrible aloneness. Then as the forgetfulness came further nothing existed, ever would, save that they were here, together, and there was no other life outside the night.

"Can—can there be so much love?"

And even as she asked the well of sorrow was sweet within her.

O city, when you were young and the love so magnificently sad and we so very alive!

Part Three

Chapter 12 ❧

It was true, Winky thought later, that things never happen when you want them to, only when you least expect them. She had come home late that afternoon from the newspaper office. There had been no mail that morning, but then that was the usual and she treated it so, like an old ache one finally becomes accustomed to. She had stayed later than usual at the office, writing two features for the Sunday edition of the paper, one on the year's oyster yield from the Folly River (it was good) and the other on Castle Pinckney and its undetermined fate.

There was a current move to "do something" locally about the one-time castle. It was named after one of Charleston's most famous natives, Charles Cotesworth Pinckney, and was built in 1798 by the order of President George Washington. During the War Between the States it was used as a prison for federal troops. Now, however, no one seemed to want it, and it stood alone on Shute's Folly Island, lonely and tattered, like a ghost disturbing the city, isolated but always there. A government agency had said "that the history of Castle Pinckney does not justify its maintenance as a national monument," a statement that caused Aunt Pett to fire back: "Just because it's Southern! Don't you see? Haven't I told you all along? Those people don't know history when they see it—building all those monuments to Mr. Kennedy just because he got shot."

Whatever, Winky was tired and she thought of calling Tom and telling him she couldn't have dinner with him tonight. Tom had really been a bit of a savior these past weeks, trying to distract her from what he termed "your obsession," Walter. Besides, Faber Ruffin, the Negro indicted by the

181 ❧

grand jury for the so-called rape of the Forzier twin, was to go on trial soon. She was deeply interested in the case, not only because she was to be one of the reporters covering it, but she was convinced he was innocent and she didn't want to hear Tom's "bleeding heart" philosophy about it all again.

She parked her car, and when she entered the courtyard there was Leuvenia on the piazza, her right hand waving in the air and the other, even in her excitement, pushing her skirt down to keep the wind from blowing it too immodestly.

"Lawd, Miss Wanky, thanks to heaven you're heah! I been talking to that man for *fifteen* minutes just runnin' up the bill!"

Tom, no doubt. But she asked anyway: "Who is it?"

"Lawd, I don't know. It's long *distance!*"

Winky stopped.

"Hurry, he's just waitin' and the bill—"

Winky ran, picked up the telephone in the library. "Hello." She was out of breath.

"Who in the world is—Loo-venia?"

His voice, deep, the word *welhd.*

"Walter!"

"She's been telling me how to fry a chicken."

"Walter! Where *are* you?"

"New York. How *do* you fry a chicken and what is She-Crab soup?"

"Where have you been? Why haven't you written? Have you been sick?"

"I've been in New Hampshire."

"New *Hamp*shire?"

"Uh huh, holed up in a cabin, trying to be a writer."

"I've been—I thought you were back in the *hospital* or something—"

Winky sat down in her father's chair, leaned her head against the leather back.

"Have you missed me?" he asked.

"Missed you?"

"Uh huh."

"Not at all."

"Come now. Just because I don't know what She-Crab soup is."

"Did you get my letter?"

"Just got it. No telephone, no mail."

"In New Hampshire?"

"Nothing. I can cook a great omelet."

"Walter," her voice softened. "I've missed you terribly."

"You're awfully bad for writers."

"Bad?"

"Distracting."

"I'm glad, I'm terribly glad."

"You use that word too much, you know."

"What word?"

" 'Terribly.' "

"Well, I *have*."

"You shouldn't say things like that, don't you know?"

"What?"

"Be harder to get, play it cool."

"*When* am I going to see you?"

"How is your father?"

"Good days, bad days. It's awful to watch, especially for Mother."

"I'm so sorry."

"I know."

"Keeping the chin up?" His voice seemed to be fading.

"Trying to."

"Good girl."

"How is—how is the writing going?"

"So so."

"Novel?"

"Sort of."

"Walter, when will I get to see you? I was really planning on New York. But, *you* know. I can't leave now."

"Then it looks as if I'll just have to come down there." She sank back into the chair. "When?"

"Next week, the week after. I'll let you know."

"How simply— It's not the best time to see Charleston."

"I'm not coming to see Charleston."

"I know. The camellias are blooming and most of the gardens are green but—"

"I'm coming mostly to see Loo-venia."

"Oh, Walter. I can't *wait*. When? Tell me exactly."

"I have a few things to get out of the way here first. I've got a job."

"A job?"

"Uh huh. A magazine. Myself and a few other half-demented souls. A quarterly."

"But that's marvellous."

"We'll see. *Any*-way, I'll let you know when I can get away."

"Where are you now?"

"In New York. I told you."

"I mean where are you phoning from?"

"My apartment."

"What does it look like?"

"Terribly chic—furnished in Old Attic, you might say."

Was she mistaken? Didn't she hear other voices? "Is there someone there with you?"

"In the other room. A few friends, drinking up all my scotch."

A tinge of jealousy passed through her. "Who are—they?"

"Just some old friends."

"Oh."

"Your accent has gotten worse."

"What accent?"

He laughed.

"What will you be doing tonight?"

"Tonight?"

"Uh huh."

"Well, just about now I'm going to play some squash, then dinner—and, if the telephone will remain quiet long enough, get some writing done."

"I'll think of you."

"What will you be doing?"

"I have a date for dinner."

"A date?"

"Just a friend—I told you—Tom Gearhart. He knows you, but you don't know him. Remember?"

"Ohhhh, yes."

"Is it snowing up there?"

"Yesterday, not today. Slush."

She heard someone call his name again, a male voice.

"Who was that?"

"Just a drunk I know. Keep talking."

"I'll save it all for when I see you."

"All right, but watch out for that Gearhart."

"No danger."

"You're all right?"

"All right?"

"It's not too bad with your father."

"I'm better now."

"You're my girl?"

"Oh, yes. Yes, yes, yes."

"Good."

"Please come—soon."

"As soon as I can."

"*Everett, what in the name of—*" The same voice, closer now.

"I had better go now," Walter said.

No, don't, she wanted to say. *Stay. Just talk*. She said nothing.

"Winky?"

"Yes?"

"I thought we'd been cut off."

"No, I'm here."

"*Everett, if we're going—*"

"I'd better hang up, Charleston."

"Hurry here." Her voice was thin.

"I will."

She remained in the chair, her eyes closed. *Here. He'll be here in this room.* She rubbed her hand tenderly over the arm of the chair, then tossed her head back. *Here!* She sighed heavily and the release was like a healing. She didn't see the door open.

"Winky, what are you doing, just sitting there that way?"

It was Aunt Pett, dressed in a long-sleeved brown dress, her mother's cameo at the neck.

Winky quickly got up from the chair. "Pett, Pett. He's coming!"

"Who is coming?"

"Come sit down."

"I'm trying to find my sewing basket."

"Come, sit." Winky went over and stoked the logs in the fireplace, but the excitement was so high in her she turned immediately.

"Who is coming?" Aunt Pett said, sitting with some difficulty in the chair opposite.

"Walter. Walter Everett."

"Put that thing down," Aunt Pett said.

"What?"

"The stoker."

"Oh!" Winky put it back in the stand. "But he's coming."

Silence.

"You don't approve of the way he sounds or anything, but—darling, darling Pett. He's most marvellous. You'll adore him."

"What's the matter with you, Winky?"

Winky plopped into the leather chair again. "I'm happy, that's all."

"He's the one up there?"

"Yes."

Aunt Pett looked at her for some time, her eyes almost stern. "Then I approve of that."

"You *do?*"

"The young man should visit the young woman."

"Well, he *is*. Maybe next week, the week after."

"Is he a funny man?"

Winky gave a short laugh. "What do you mean?"

"You know what I think about funny men. Don't ever marry a funny man, they're always trying to be the life of everything, never succeed in anything."

"No, he's not that at all. He almost went into the ministry."

"Is he a Roman Catholic?"

"No. Presbyterian."

"Well, that's good anyway. There are some nice Scots Presbyterians in the Northern states, I understand."

"You'll like him. You really will."

Aunt Pett sighed. "Thank heaven he's not a Roman Catholic."

"What would be so wrong with that?"

"Odd people. You know, I've always thought they ought to worship Martha instead of Mary."

"Why?"

"Poor Martha always had to give all those luncheons and things, worked herself to the bone. Mary didn't do anything but have a baby."

"Don't you think you're slightly missing the point?"

Aunt Pett chuckled.

"But, really, Pett, you'll *adore* Walter."

"Hardly that, I'm sure. He's from Pittsburgh?"

Winky laughed. "Pittsburgh really isn't as bad as people think it is. I met some rather attractive people there. Walter's family lives in the country. It's quite beautiful—hills and meadows. But you just wait—you'll be taken with him. Everybody is."

A twinkle then came into the older woman's eyes. "Are you?"

"What?"

"Taken with him."

"Most heartily. He's everything, Pett. I'll never marry anyone else."

"Marry?"

Winky nodded.

"Well—" There was a sound of finality in the word.

"Yes," Winky said almost in argument.

"Well, well, well."

"Is that *all* you have to say?"

"No," and the word "*dear*" was hard come by. "I'm happy for you, if he's good enough for you."

Winky smiled. "Pett, I knew you would be this way. He *is* good enough for me, and better." She opened her eyes, and Pett was looking at her, a peculiar questioning look in her aging eyes. There were these moments when she looked old, the unaware moments.

"Don't let him trick you, Winky."

"Trick me?"

"You don't know him very well."

"I know him *very* well."

"I see."

"I don't think I've known anyone better."

Aunt Pett looked toward the burning logs. "Young women often think that."

"We were together a lot. It wasn't like being in college or something—having weekend dates—that sort of thing. You're—you're thinking about Aunt Etoile or something."

Aunt Pett turned to her, and then she gave a short laugh. "No, I wasn't thinking of her at all."

"What *did* happen about that, Pett?" Winky really didn't want to hear about all that again. She wanted to go to her room, be alone, think, imagine, wait. Still, now, she thought she could stand just about anything.

"Poor Etoile," said Aunt Pett, rather surprisingly. "She's had a very unhappy life."

"Oh?"

"Yes, very—unhappy."

Winky smiled, almost teasingly. "You really love her, don't you?"

"I worry about her."

"Was there actually a man?"

"Yes. But never serious—at least, from his viewpoint. She's talked about it for so long now she believes her own exaggerations."

"But you said she had to go away. Was she pregnant?"

"For goodness' sake *no!*"

"Then why are you always indicating it then?"

"She likes for us to think that, you know. Etoile—was a wallflower."

"Poor dear."

"Yes. But she's a fine woman."

"Then why do you two— Why are things always flying around the room when you two get together?"

"Etoile's a very high strung woman."

Winky considered the reasoning in that.

"No, she never got on with the young men."

"But you—you weren't a wallflower, I'll bet."

"No, I don't think I was. I had beaux, you know." She looked toward the fireplace again. "Etoile was just unfortunate that way."

"Still, I think she's happy. She has the shop and friends—that sort of thing."

"That's not enough, not enough for a woman. You must remember that."

For a moment Winky considered the possibility of living alone—years of nights and days—alone. She quickly dismissed the thought, so remote was the possibility now. "Oh, Pett. I just can't *wait* for you to meet Walter. You see, it's—oh, Pett—it's a magnificent wonder that he's come into my life."

The woman's eyes softened. Was there pity?

"I can't wait for you to meet him—and Mother—and, and—Father."

At the mention of the last Aunt Pett sat straighter, gathered herself together, and rose from the chair. "I shall look forward to meeting your young man. Now, *where* is my sewing basket?" She looked about. "Leuvenial Where is that girl?"

Winky watched her leave. For the first time Aunt Pett was beginning to walk like an old woman—hesitant, careful. For years she had looked the same, ageless, and now, almost suddenly, it seemed, she was shuffling, guardedly feeling her way into obsolescence. "What will I do without her?" In the distance Winky heard the faint ringing of St. Michael's bells. She turned her head and caught sight of the telephone. "But—" She hugged her arms to herself. He's coming! She put her hands to her face as if to push back the extraordinary excitement within her. A week. Two weeks. The days would drag so.

"I'll call Tom," she thought.

They went to the Yacht Club on East Bay for dinner. Tom's idea. Winky said he just wanted to show everybody how much weight he had lost. He had. And the painfully detailed descriptions of his butterless, breadless, yogurt days amused Winky, knowing his almost prayerful adoration for luxurious cooking. (He had actually memorized Escoffier's *Ma Cuisine*; he told her so.)

"And what about scotch and all that?" Winky asked as they sat in the parlor outside the dining room, waiting for a waiter to take their order for drinks.

"Given it up."

"What?"

"Nothing but vodka. Vodka has about twenty calories less and besides the hangovers aren't as bad."

"Tom, you're just too much."

"No. See." He put his thumbs into his pants top and, drawing in, pulled the belt together.

Winky laughed. "That was exactly what I was talking about."

"What?"

The waiter stood before them.

"Vodka martini here," Tom said. "Only a pinch of vermouth. And you?" he asked Winky.

"Scotch and water, please."

The waiter handed Tom the menu and he quickly put it aside.

"Are you going to have *another* one?" Winky asked.

"Of course. All I had today was yogurt."

"No martinis for lunch?"

"None."

"How did you stand the day? Wasn't it awfully long?"

"A bore. But I made it."

"Sell any cars?"

"No, but I did yesterday. Mrs. Radcliffe finally got rid of that ancient wreck of hers and bought a Mercedes. She said she liked them because they weren't 'showy.' " Tom laughed. "Dear girl."

"Success at last."

"She'll probably wreck it tomorrow. She wanted the whole gear shift changed."

Winky laughed.

Tom glanced at her. "You certainly are Miss Cheer tonight."

Winky looked at him over her glass.

"Coy, too."

"Walter called."

Tom hesitated for a moment, then put down his glass. "Well, hooray! Word from the deity."

"Don't be sacrilegious."

"And what did the prince of peace have to say?"

"He's coming down."

"Peachy."

"Is that all you have to say?"

"Shall I go to City Hall, arrange a parade down King Street?"

"Tom, you'll like him. Honestly. I'm counting on you anyway."

"What for?"

"To give one of your little do's, I want you to know him, and I want him to know you."

"I can scarcely wait. Besides, I know him."

"Not well."

"Well enough."

Winky sipped her drink. "What if I marry him—won't you like him then?"

Tom picked up his drink again, settled back on the settee. He was smiling.

"Won't you?"

"Why the long silence?"

"What silence?"

"Why hasn't the great lover been bombarding you with little billets-deux?"

"Because he's been writing."

"It sickens me."

"What?"

"Just the thought of the poor struggling poet, slaving away in his penthouse."

"He's been in New Hampshire—no telephone or anything."

"Imagine that."

"Don't be that way, Tom."

The waiter returned. Tom handed him his empty glass. "You?" he asked Winky.

"I'm all right."

When the waiter left Tom asked: "Just where will you live in this wedded bliss?"

"In New York, I guess. Maybe—" She smiled, "—even in Norway."

"How quaint."

"Walter loves Norway."

"You and the fisherfolk. You're not the type, daughter. I can see you now—standing over your hot stove frying whale blubber."

"Not amusing."

"Pity."

The waiter reappeared with Tom's drink. "I fear, dear girl, you belong here."

"Don't call me 'dear girl.' "

"But you do, you know?"

"Do what?"

"Belong right here—" he lifted his glass, "in sweet old aristocratic Charleston."

"You sound like Aunt Pett. Why all the loyalty all of a sudden?"

"Not loyalty. Just wisdom. If you knew you were moving away—I mean forever—it would really do something to you."

"Tom, do you know what?"

"No, what?"

"You don't know me at all. Just—not at all."

"We'll see. Just when is this exciting wedding to take place?"

"I'm not sure. I guess we'll decide something when he comes."

"I see."

Winky reached for his hand. "Tom, you *are* my friend, aren't you? I haven't told anyone this except Pett. I mean we're friends, good friends."

"Absolutely bonded in friendship."

Winky leaned back in the chair. "I don't know."

"Walter Everett is just not your dish. As a matter of fact, it would surprise me if he *ever* marries."

"And just why do you think that, Zarathustra?" She was becoming irritated now; the amused superiority, real or not, was grating.

"I just don't think he will, that's all."

"No," Winky said with an edge to her voice, "there's nothing wrong with him if that's what you're trying to say. He's perfectly normal—in every way."

Tom drained his glass. "Oh, I think he's all nicely heterosexual and all that."

Winky was angry. "Tom, you're just about impossible!" She put her glass down.

"Now don't go and get all dramatic. We're just having a peaceful little discussion."

"You are, I'm not."

He picked up the menu. "Besides, I've decided I'm going to have a huge sirloin steak with a baked potato, butter, sour cream, caviar and—"

"Go right ahead."

He glanced at her. "You mean you don't care? You don't care if I gorge myself with calories and pop off with a fatal stroke or— You'll miss me, you know. Who else would sit up and discuss your grand passions with you? Oh, you'll miss me, all right."

"All right. Well, let's order then."

They did not discuss Walter at dinner and over brandy Tom amused Winky, telling her about a man he had met that morning, a friend of his father who used to live next door to them in Ohio:

"You know what he said? He said he remembered me because I was the only boy on the block who had a football uniform from Abercrombie's and never played football. I just stood around in it."

Winky couldn't help but laugh, imagining Tom's round boy-adult face in a football helmet. "Tom, Tom. There'll never be another you."

"No, I suppose not," he said a little sadly.

After they left the club they drove along the battery. The night was unseasonably warm and out in the harbor she saw a buoy tossing in the water, a bobbing flash from the dark night of the sea.

"You know," she said. "I suppose I *will* miss Charleston."

"Of course. You'll never be happy anywhere else. Not really."

"Oh, I will. Besides, I'll come back—often."

"It will never be the same."

"Not *just* the same maybe, but I'll come back."

Later that night she wrote Walter, and at the end of the letter she added:

> . . . How strange it is. You know I always cry on New Year's Eve. When everyone else is gay, I want to cry. Did I ever tell you that—that I hated New Year's Eve? We'll never celebrate it. Will we?
>
> I don't know why I mention that now when it isn't even near New Year's, but I saw a buoy out in the water tonight. It bobbed so happily in the dark, and it made me sad. Just a small fact I wanted you to know. I'm so terribly (forgive me) happy. I count the days.
> W.

She hastily addressed the envelope and sealed it. The St. Michael's bells were striking midnight.

Chapter 13

"And all her sorrows turned to labor," Winky thought as she watched her mother move about the house, the garden scissors clicking nervously in her hand. Just where Winky had first heard the quotation she couldn't remember. Wherever, it was applicable.

A heaviness of mood had fallen upon her mother in the past weeks. In the mornings she busied herself determinedly with house details, her lips pinched, rarely speaking, preparing menus, arranging flowers, attending to the nagging disease of an old house: getting plumbers, seeing about sliding shingles, chipping paint, a leak. And when the frenzy was over, for frenzy it was, she disappeared, staying in her room with the blinds closed, doing what Winky did not know. She was unable to sleep, she said. At night she sat listlessly, her lids heavy as her father's talk droned on, endlessly detailing the past. There was an eschatological quality to these nights, and it was all Winky could do to witness them.

Her father had suddenly changed the habit of going into the library at night under the pretense of "writing the book." Instead, his creativity seemed to take the form of verbosity, the same stories and histories repeated over and over, night after night, and his occasional interjection: "You're not listening, Ann."

"Yes, I'm listening," always came the weary reply.

And the more he talked the more removed her mother seemed to become as if all light had gone from her days. She took to her bed for days at a time, the doctor diagnosing "touches" of things: bronchitis, neuritis, intestinal upsets. He prescribed sleeping pills. The seasonal flowers beside her bedside disappeared, and it was Winky who each morning continued the rite by rising early and cutting the leaves and blossoms, asking Leuvenia to place them by her bedside.

"Your mother'll be dead long before your father," Miss Boggs helpfully told Winky one night.

It was frightening. Ann Carr had always been the spirit of the house. She loved Christmas and celebrations and from her innate artistry the household moved and caught her love of the beautiful. It sang with it. And now there was drabness, heaviness. Even the garden suffered.

"I've lost all interest in it," Winky heard her telling Aunt Pett one night. "Beauvoir seems to know what to do."

Yet she made her attempts as if she were saying back to them: "I'm doing my duty, am I not? What are you complaining about? It's what I'm here for. It's all being done." The strained hysteria of the mornings was almost worse than the silences and the illnesses and the nervous nightly sighs and twisting of the ring. All of it hit Winky like a doubled fist jabbed into her stomach.

She stood now by the newel post in the hall and watched her mother place a vase of cherry laurel leaves on the table.

"Greens are so lovely in the late fall," Winky said.

"Don't you have to be at work?" asked her mother. "It's late."

"I'm going in just a minute."

A few drops of water had spilled on the table, and her mother picked up the large vase, holding it in one arm, trying to wipe the damp table. Ordinarily, she would have asked Winky to aid in the process. But she asked no one to do anything.

"Here," Winky said, taking the vase from her. "Let me."

The process done, her mother stood back and glanced at

the arrangement. A strand of gray hair fell over her left eye. She pushed it back with her fist, rubbing her forehead, indicating another headache.

"Well, don't just *stand* there!" she said irritably. "I can't stand to have people staring at me."

Truly surprised by the bite of the words, Winky gave a short laugh. "I'm not staring at you."

"Then *do* something. Don't just stand there." The dark eyes, usually so soft, full, were slits and the pupils as small as two pinpoints.

"Mother, don't you think you should go back to bed? Why don't you just stay in bed today?"

"That's all any of you ever say. That's your father's cure for everything—just stay in bed."

"It used to help when you got all keyed up."

"Who else is going to see that things get done?"

"Leuvenia. She can do some of it, and Miss Boggs."

"They can't do anything."

"Of course they can."

"Someone has to be with your father."

"Miss Boggs sees after him."

"Your father doesn't like Miss Boggs."

Winky sighed in half frustration. "At least they can do some of this house detail."

"They don't have time. Pett calls for one thing, and your father—"

Winky shrugged in resignation. "All right, then. Have your own way. I'm just trying to help."

"You're gone all day."

"Do you want me to quit my job?"

"No." Her lips pinched further.

"Well, I don't know what to do," Winky said, exasper-

ated, turning from her. "But you've just got to care for yourself."

"Is that all you have to say this morning?"

"No, I was just going to tell you—" Winky chose her
words carefully. But it didn't matter. "Walter is coming—
here."

"Oh, dear," her mother sighed.

"But he's coming," Winky said, turning around. "Isn't
that rather good news?"

"Well, he can't stay *here!*"

Anger rose. It was the way her mother bit the words,
the expression on her face, her mouth turned downward in
sour reproach. "You said if he should come he could stay
here with us. Don't you remember?"

"No, I don't remember. How can you ask me to have
house guests *now*—of all times?"

The contrast of the bright green leaves, so fresh, shining,
against the distorted face stunned Winky. Was her mother
acting, or was she truly ill? "Then, he'll just have to stay at a
hotel or something."

"I guess he will," her mother said. "We've just got too
much to contend with now."

"All right. I'll make reservations somewhere."

"Very well."

"Don't you even want to meet him?"

Her mother then tossed the kitchen towel on the table.
"Can't you see the situation we're in? I don't want to meet
*any*body, not *any*body!"

The anger did come. "All right!" Winky shouted and
slammed the front door as she went out. She regretted the action as soon as she was outside. She really hadn't been as
much help as she should have been; gone all day and at night,
she was either with Tom or out somewhere. Charleston had

overdone itself with entertaining this fall. She had purposely kept herself busy, trying not to think. But tonight, she vowed, she would make it up. She should and wanted to be with her father anyway.

She told her mother that when she returned from work.

"I'm sorry we quarreled this morning," her mother said, still tight-lipped.

"I'm afraid I haven't been much help to you. I meant to."

"Well, you're young," her mother said by way of admitting the lack—admitting, too, the stupidity of youth, as if the years, the very paucity of numbers, excused all. Youth was self-gilded. Had her mother forgotten so much?

"But you will meet him when he comes, won't you?"

"Your Walter?"

Winky nodded.

"Yes, of course. But I'm so tired. I really can't have him here."

"I understand." If only, Winky thought, we had met a year ago, if Walter could have come two years ago when life sang in the house and charm was so complete. "Now, why don't you try to get some sleep? I'll be with Daddy. Everything will be all right."

"It's my responsibility."

"Not entirely. Now, run upstairs, take one of your pills and just forget everything."

"I'm taking too many of those things."

"They won't hurt you."

"I guess not." The sigh was heavy.

"Upstairs."

"Very well."

Winky watched her go, holding onto the railing, her usually straight back curved slightly.

Winky went into the upstairs parlor. Her father was

sitting in the round-back captain's chair, an odd smile on his lips, the newspaper, unread Winky was sure, in his lap. It had startled Winky more than anything else when she discovered her father was unable to read. Reading was so much a part of his life. It wasn't so much his eyes, the doctor had told them, it was just an inability to bring the words to the brain in any logical form. Yet he pretended to read, as if he were absorbing every detail of the day's events. It was that, the pretending, that led Winky to believe he knew something of his condition and she wondered to what depths his suffering went. He never complained, only an occasional mention of "forgetfulness," "age." Still, most of the time he seemed completely unaware of the ridiculousness of some of the things he said.

"Ah, Winky!" he said as she entered the room. "I'm glad to see you. Bless your heart. I've been waiting for your mother."

"I sent her to bed," Winky said casually.

"To bed? So early?"

"She's not feeling too well."

A frown came to his face. "She hasn't been well at all this year." He filled his cheeks with air and slowly exhaled it, a characteristic gesture when he was in thought or concern. He put his hands on the arms of the chair in an attempt to rise.

"Where are you going?"

"I must look in on her."

"No, no," Winky said. "I think she wants to be quiet."

"But if she's ill—"

"She's not really ill—just tired. There've been so many things around the house to do lately. That's all. I just told her to try to get some early sleep."

This was the difficult part of all his sickness. The doctor had told them never to cross him, never to stop him from anything he wanted to do—*within reason.*

202

"Yes," said her father, sinking back into the chair, his face troubled, his mouth hanging slightly loose.

"Well," Winky said cheerily. "What have you been doing?"

His face brightened then. He had always had a sweet response to people, their moods. "Ohhh, I've been sitting here. I was waiting for your mother—to tell her an idea that came to me this afternoon."

"An idea?"

"Yes. Very exciting."

"Well, what is it?" Winky sat in Aunt Pett's chair, the Chippendale with its wood-worn arms, a chair that as a child she sometimes felt was Aunt Pett herself. She was never allowed to sit in it:

When young girls come into drawing rooms we always put our hands behind our backs, just so, don't we? We never touch anything, do we?

"I do wish your mother were here. I think she would find my ideas as exciting as I do."

"Won't I do?"

"What?" He looked at Winky with bright blue eyes.

"I like ideas, too, you know, especially if they're exciting."

Her father smiled, a kind of inner self-satisfaction.

"Leigh," he said slowly, trying to hold back his smile.

There was only a small thrust of surprise. Winky had become used to the interchange of names now.

"I have been thinking of moving back to Southerland House."

The shock did show.

"No, don't look so surprised."

"But, Southerland House, Daddy. Festus is there." She was speaking of Festus Mayhew, their cousin.

"Yes, but Festus is getting on now and the place needs care. Besides, the house will be yours some day—yours and your children's—when you marry."

Southerland House. Mine. Would Walter like it? When he comes I'll show it to him. For a moment she tried to picture the old place through Walter's eyes, seeing it for the first time. One of the oldest houses in South Carolina, it was a single house, not large, but it looked over the Cooper River, surrounded by dogwood and a drive of old oaks. They said Southerland House was "haunted."

"Festus, you know, has started with the Black Angus," her father said. "But not enough. Cattle is becoming a major industry in the low country now."

"But what would Festus think of such a thing?"

"You know," her father leaned forward, "I think Festus would welcome the idea. He's alone now, no children, and the place is a care."

"But what about Mother and Pett and— What about *this* house?"

"I've thought of that, too," he said proudly.

"There's young Stoney coming along. He's doing well, married to a fine girl."

Stoney Mayhew, another cousin. Winky wanted to smile at the words "fine girl," which simply meant a Charleston girl with passable connections. Perhaps Charleston was changing, but, with some, it would never change. Just as a few years ago when the St. Cecilia Ball was cancelled, not for the public reasons (if there was anything *public* about the St. Cecilia), but because of the tinges of "poor blood" which were slowly creeping into Hibernian Hall.

"I think Stoney would like to live in this house."

"I'm sure he would, but don't you think Pett would have something to say about that? After all, this really is her house."

"Pett has a great feeling for Southerland House. But if she wants to stay here she certainly can. She admires young Stoney. But, you see, there is money in cattle now. Amazing, isn't it?"

"What?"

"How the world changes."

Winky said nothing.

"I mean, take Southerland House—how it's been able to care for itself—first rice, then indigo, rice again, cotton, timber, now cattle." He chuckled. "Even those Yankees that lived in it for a while helped it along. Have I ever told you about the history of the old plantations? Do you know about them?"

Winky mentally sighed. She had heard it all a thousand times and more, knew by heart every inch of low-country life. She had been brought up on it, schooled; everyone had: the monied years, the near death during Reconstruction and now prosperity coming again to some of the more enterprising old families. "No," she said. "Tell me."

Her father talked for two hours, piling detail upon detail. It was remarkable how he could remember so much of the past, his grandfather's days, his father's, his own days as a boy. Then why couldn't he remember the simplest facts of three days ago? What current had been clipped from him?

He talked as if she were not there, never demanding of her response. Yet she knew now what wearied her mother so. It was not so much the physical act of sitting, listening, watching the facial expressions change and diminish. Rather, there was guilt, guilt for the boredom one felt, the unwanted, unasked boredom, almost to exasperation, and all the while his sitting there so innocently unaware.

Tomorrow he would repeat the same stories, the same detailed histories. No doubt he would have forgot about

Southerland House and his sumptuous plan. At least there was hope he would; there was always hope. The doctor was correct. He became irritable when he was crossed and irritability was a foreign quality with him. At least the show of it. Depression was his nature, aloofness, the quieter personality, the quieter charm.

Winky's only relief during his recital was to somehow close her mind and think of Walter. They would spend a day in Old Town, and then she would show him "her church," Saint Andrew's Parish, as he had done in Lillehammer. Maybe it would be a good day, and they would go sailing. Planning this way made the talk bearable. But then occasionally there would be the words "you know?" and the daydreams, plans, were broken. Walter gone.

At eleven-thirty she suggested they make an end to the evening.

"A lovely night, Winky," he said. "We've had a very pleasant evening, haven't we?"

And his words, his face so pleased, brought the guilt further and she wanted to cry for the pity she felt. It had taken so little from her, really, the sitting and listening, and it had meant so much to him. His golden plan.

She turned out the lamp by the door and when she turned he was still sitting in his chair.

"Aren't you coming?"

His mouth hung loose again.

"You need sleep, too," she said, trying to erase the look of him.

"Oh, Winky," he said quietly. "I'm good for nothing."

"Now, what sort of talk is that?"

He just shook his head and then with horror she saw the tears gathering in his eyes and his terrible strain to keep them back.

"Daddy, Daddy, what is it?"

He just shook his head.

Winky had never seen her father cry, and the sight was almost more than she could bear. She wanted to go to him, put her arms about him. But there had never been a physical show of caring between them.

He rose from the chair, and with his head bent walked from the room. She heard the door to his bedroom close, and she stood rigid in the room, her body aching with grief.

Unseasonably warm weather came to the low country and with it a thick blanket of fog which rolled in from the sea. The Cooper River bridges looked ghostly in the early morning hours and the fog horns wailed like lost people. It was an eerie sight with the water veiled by the fog and the bridge standing like an abandoned structure in a lost cloud. Winky drove carefully, the headlights on her car finding a dim path. But she was glad for the morning and its release. Today she was to interview the Negro, Faber Ruffin, and though she dreaded it as much for the man as for the Forzier family there was nothing else to do. The case had got national attention since the Civil Liberties Union had shown their interest. The paper, therefore, decided to give full coverage, though they had tried to keep publicity at a minimum.

It had taken some doing getting permission for the interview, and it was still in doubt whether the paper would use such a piece. But the city editor told Winky to go ahead with it "in case." The question that had interested most of the press who had come into Charleston, as well as the self-styled sociologists, was just why a Harvard-educated Negro would return to his native city and commit such a crime. Most of the press was convinced the man was innocent and Winky concurred. But, to her, one of the more tragic aspects of the case was the lost potential should the man be found guilty. Why would someone throw everything away in one single act of passion? Was it an act of "revenge" as one of the "sociologists" put it? Or, was Faber Ruffin just another "smart-ass nigger" who had gone up North and "gotten ideas," as several of the less original Charlestonians put it? Winky listened to all the talk and held her own ideas.

As she drove she was thinking she would be glad when all the hue and cry over Civil Rights was finished. For decades it had been so much a part of the city, not only Charleston, but the whole South. It hung over the land, an issue, entering into every phase of work-a-day life. She was tired now of the pundits, the writers, the words, the singers, the politicians and all those who attached themselves to the cause for whatever reason. It seemed to her that many of the people, especially the whites, who so frantically followed the cause applauded themselves, their own "virtue," without true thought for the human being whose dignity they claimed to espouse. The talk, the writing, humiliated rather than uplifted.

Winky had been to the county jail many times before, interviewing, writing features. She knew most of the jailers and was on easy terms with them, especially Joe Breck. Once he had carved a wooden letter-holder for her, a rather large container with bright paints which stood on short legs. She had been touched by the gesture and kept it in her room by her desk, an ugly eyesore that her eyes always saw with special warmth.

It was Joe now who met her as she entered the jail. There was an odd courtliness about Joe Breck in spite of his missing teeth, graying dark hair and pallor. He would rather have been a sea captain than a jailer, and the switch, so hopelessly opposed, was his own quiet desperation.

"What's Tom Waring up to now?" he asked, speaking of

the editor of the paper. "Don't say Tom's become a liberal!" He laughed at his own joke, though Winky's attention was more on how he said his words rather than what he said. Joe Breck had the thickest accent Winky had ever heard, almost Gullah.

"Bill Izzard called you, didn't he?" Winky asked, speaking of the defense attorney.

"Yes, he called, but I can't see why the peyupuh wants *you* locked up in theah with that darkie."

Winky cocked her head. "I'm not exactly looking forward to it," not explaining she had asked for the assignment, that she was there because she wanted to be.

"Aw, Ruffin's all right," said Joe. "Been quiet as a mouse in theah. Probably scared to death."

"And with good reason, I guess."

Winky followed Joe into the elevator. There was the odor of new oil as the elevator ascended smoothly. The silence was broken only by the clinking of the keys in Joe's hands. Joe was proud of his world, Winky saw in his face; it was his ship. How easily the great doors opened and clanged shut behind them. The modern factory. A feeling of claustrophobia wrapped her. Her hands were damp and with the closing of each door a further sense of smothering came over her.

"This won't take too long," Winky said. "Will you wait?"

Joe Breck laughed, a kind of sucking-in laugh. "You don't like our jail?"

"I don't think I'd want to be in it for very long."

"Don't worry, Miss Winky, I'll be near."

"Thanks," she said as she glanced into the cells as they walked, their footsteps echoing along the floor. Young men, old men, huddled creatures staring emptily into space met her glance. One middle-aged prisoner whistled as he caught sight of her, and she heard his empty, half-crazed laugh as they continued down the hall. They seemed fixtures, the men, just like the cots, the urinals, the doors, yet all different in their way, like specimens in a zoo, she thought horribly.

Faber Ruffin sat on his cot, his face buried in his hands, posed like an actor waiting for an audience. He was not what Winky had supposed. She had expected a larger man. But he looked almost fragile, his dark flesh wasted from his body. He glanced up with reddened eyes, and the eyes, so large, dominated the flat nose with its flaring nostrils, thick upper lip and the beginnings of a beard. She was frightened.

"All right, Faber, you talk to this lady," said Joe in a surprisingly softened voice. The door opened and she entered conscious of the door shutting behind her. She smoothed out the rolled piece of copy paper in her hand, not looking at the man. He was rising from the cot, an instinctive gesture of manners. The paper shook slightly in her hand. She looked at him then.

"You're a friend of Leuvenia's," Winky said, smiling at him. "Leuvenia Lucas."

"Yes, I know Mrs. Lucas."

The timbre of the voice, the accent, decidedly not Southern, was surprising. It was an accent that had been worked upon, leaving only the rhythm of the Charlestonian.

"You're Sister's son?"

"Yes."

"Well, Faber," Winky sat down on the cot. "I'm from the paper. Mr. Izzard, your attorney, said you wouldn't mind answering a few questions."

"Anything you want to know."

"All right," Winky breathed heavily and gazed at him. "Why are you here?"

"Because I am a Negro."

Winky put the copy paper aside. "And you think that is the only reason?"

"There's no other reason."

"You were identified, I believe, by Miss Forzier as the person who committed the assault?"

A tight smile appeared on his thick lips, and he shook his head. "I've never seen the young woman before in my entire life. It's incredible." He looked at her steadily.

"Then why? Why would she identify you so positively?"

"I just told you."

Winky imagined Carolyn Forzier, her straight dark hair, blue eyes, fragile features, the curved forehead, tilted nose, the small mouth. The last time Winky had seen her she was with her twin sister, hurrying into the back entrance at Ashley Hall. They were wearing polo coats, young, eager. Was there any reason for her to lie?

"Do you think she could have been so emotionally upset she was unable to identify you correctly?"

"Any Negro would have done. All Negroes look alike here; they're Negroes, that's all that matters."

"Do you think there is that much indifference in Charleston?"

"I do."

"I shouldn't think so."

"You are not a Negro."

"No, but I'm a human being."

The man said nothing.

Winky looked down at her paper. "You were a student at Harvard?"

"Yes. I was there on a scholarship."

"What were you studying?"

"Political science—and other things."

Winky scribbled on the paper, more for composure's sake than for memory's.

"And what were you doing here in Charleston? How old are you, Faber?"

"Twenty-three. I came home because Mama was sick again." *Mama.* He was forgetting his other accent.

"Was she in the hospital? Your mother?"

"No."

"Then what were you doing at the hospital? I mean why were you on the grounds?"

"There were some bills there. Mama had been in the hospital last spring, and I went to see about her bill."

"I see."

He leaned against the wall, his arms folded in front of him. Was the look on his face one of amusement, or was it scorn? He didn't trust her. Did Negroes ever trust white people? She thought not.

"Do you mind these questions? Just say so, if you mind."

"Go right ahead."

"Your sweater was found near Miss Forzier's car door. It was your sweater, wasn't it?"

"It was mine, but I hadn't been wearing it."

"Then how do you suppose it got there?"

"I don't know." He shook his head. "I've been sitting here for days thinking of little else."

"Do you think somebody else could have been wearing it?"

"Definitely." He licked his upper lip.

Winky met his dark gaze; it was her own eyes that shifted first. "Then, this is terrible, isn't it? Your being here, innocent of a crime you didn't commit? Are you being treated well?"

"As well as can be expected, I suppose." He yawned. And somehow the yawn was irritating.

"Faber, you did *not* commit the assault?"

"No, I did not." The voice was edged with anger.

Winky regarded him with level eyes.

"I did *not!*" He began to shake his head. "I did not." And then with no warning whatsoever he crouched to the floor, put his hands to his face. "They tricked me."

When he looked up at Winky, tears were beginning in his eyes. "They got me heah—" he wiped his nose with the back of his hand— "they tricked me." He was shaking. "I've never done anything wrong in my whole life."

All at once Winky thought of her father last night, his the more gentle tears, yet each crying out for the pain of living, or dying. She heard herself saying: "I believe you, Faber. I believe you."

He wiped his nose again. "I *never* attacked that girl. Can't you tell 'em?"

His accent was changing slightly. Winky had noticed this before in both whites and Negroes who had been exposed to other regional accents, no matter how long; when the person became excited or forgetful there was reversion.

"Tell whom?" she asked.

"The folks that read the newspaper."

"I wish that I could," she said quietly.

"Why can't you?"

"Prejudicial. The Courts would say so. A jury will have to tell the people."

He looked up, his face distorted and his eyes full with tears. "Juries don't 'mount to anything. They don't care about the colored."

"There'll be other colored people on the jury, and if you didn't do it—"

He brought his hands slowly down his face, making his

wide eyes and mouth slant downward grotesquely. "The Lord knows I didn't do it. *He* knows."

"There'll be a way." Winky was almost whispering.

"There won't be any way."

"You don't know that. You have a very good lawyer, really the best."

"Yes."

"Juries here for the most part have been fair."

He was shaking his head slowly.

"Tell me, Faber, what did you plan to do with your life? I mean why did you take political science, for instance?" She wanted to divert his thoughts.

"I wanted to help my people. Teach, I think."

"Would you have come back here? To Charleston?"

"I was planning to."

There was something in the look of his eyes—a momentary dream, and then he hung his head.

"Was Harvard better—than here?"

"Yes, I guess it was. Now, I *know* it was."

"You liked it better?"

"In some ways."

"How did you do? You were a bright student. I've seen your grades here and at Tuskegee. Was it more difficult for you at Harvard? Your grades, I mean?"

"I don't know." He shook his head again. "I don't know anything now."

"I'm very sorry," Winky said, not knowing exactly what she meant. Sorry for the whole thing, she supposed, his hope, his life, the loss if it was to be.

She kept looking at him, the crouching, frightened figure. Could he possibly be lying? She was positive he was not. She rose and said: "Thank you. I appreciate your letting me talk to you, ask you these questions. Is there anything I can do for you? Do you want anything?"

"Tell Mama to bring me some cigarettes—and some writing paper."

Winky looked into her pocketbook. "I thought I had—no—no cigarettes. I'll tell Leuvenia when I get home. She'll call your mother."

He stood up slowly, avoiding her eyes. "Tell Miss Leuvenia hello for me."

"I will."

Winky went to the door. "Joe," she called softly.

Behind her, behind the bars, she glanced back once and saw the frail figure plunge face downward onto the cot, a fleeting glance, a dark figure seeking the only solace he could find—a dumb white cot.

She was visibly shaken by the interview. She said an abrupt good-bye to Joe Breck as if he himself had played a part in bringing the man to his lowly state. She was convinced more than ever of his innocence. How could anyone, if he were guilty, show such emotion? The tears were real, so very real. But if he were guilty, the lost spirit, the lost mind—bitter ground.

She drove straight home. She wanted to tell Leuvenia about the interview and give her the message for Sister. But there was a letter waiting for her on the hall table:

> . . . Will see you on the twenty-sixth. Am practicing my accent now. Plane should arrive four-ten in the afternoon from New York.

Five days! Only five—

She forgot about Faber Ruffin until later that afternoon. By that time it didn't matter; his mother had already been to visit.

It was Suzan Ribaut on the telephone, her high, child-like voice another world, another time:

"Bob and I just thought we *had* to do something. I haven't given a party in so long I've almost forgotten how. It's just going to be a *sup*-pah thing."

Winky had got the invitation several days ago; she thought of declining but then she thought it would be amusing for Walter to see Suzan's corner of Charleston, too.

"Sounds fun," Winky said. "But, Suzan, the reason I haven't called—would it be all right if I brought someone?"

"Tom's already accepted. Don't worry. I had the most hysterical R.S.V.—"

"Not Tom."

"Oh?"

"A friend. From New York."

"Man or woman?"

"Man."

"Oahhh? Win-ky, what are you up to? Tom will be absolutely crushed."

"Will it be all right?"

"Certainly. Bill will be here, too."

"Bill Ashe?"

"Uh huh. The more bachelors the better. Who is this man?"

"Just a friend. I met him this summer."

"Over there where you were, wherever it was?"

"Yes."

"Win-ky, have you got something to tell me?"

Winky laughed. "No, just a friend. I think you'll like him."

"When is he coming?"

"This afternoon."

"I can hardly wait."

"We'll see you about that time, then."

"Fine."

"Good-bye."

" 'Bye now."

Winky was amused, wondering what Walter would think of Suzan. No doubt she would play up the innocent little girl bit—"Charleston's little Lolita," as Tom called her. Winky had seen Suzan out riding not too long ago, sitting the mount pristinely, a picture in tweeds with her long dark hair braided at the back, her black eyes, petulant mouth. She was an excellent rider, and she knew it. She gave a passing wave to Winky and then turned to the other riders, their more curved backs, their rounder faces. Winky did wonder what Walter would think of her. As a matter of fact she wondered what he would think of everybody.

She looked at her watch. An hour and a half. "He'll be here. In Charleston!" Why should she be so nervous? The idle waiting.

Behind her was the interview with Faber Ruffin. A watered-down version of it had appeared in the paper. Still, the city editor had said it was one of the better pieces she had done. She had heard nothing from Charleston as a whole, except from Aunt Pett who was voluble on the subject:

"Why can't you do what the other young women on the paper do—write about receipts and houses and things? It's unbecoming, Winky, a young lady in a cell with somebody like that—especially when he's committed something so disgusting and to one of your family's friends, too."

"The jury hasn't said he's committed anything so disgusting—a man is innocent until—"

"Bosh! I never heard of such a thing. I wouldn't be a bit surprised if Charleston didn't just out and out ostracize you. It's—it's peculiar, Winky. You don't want to be known as a *peculiar* young woman."

"You will be pleased to know that Suzan Ribaut has just invited me to a party."

"She probably wants you there just to create excitement or something."

"Like a freak, you mean? A conversation piece?" Winky was determined to keep the talk on as easy terms as possible. Actually, she had expected more of a clamour from Aunt Pett. But in recent weeks some of the sting had even gone from her, reflecting again the sickness of the house.

She had heard from Tom about the interview, however. He said it was "touching. I nearly wept."

She didn't care. Walter was coming. She didn't care what anybody said. Charleston was Charleston; she was she. There was not the slightest meeting between the two now, and she liked it that way, not a part, not having to act. Walter was all that mattered, and soon they would be as removed from the city as two stars, loving it but without its bothers.

The main thing now was to look her best. She had lost all of the summer's tan, and the last two months had taken its toll. The circles beneath her eyes were dark, and she had lost weight, too much really, in spite of Leuvenia's constant warning about "eating proper" and "menfolks don't like no po'-lookin' gehls."

Leuvenia was not very clever either in guarding her secret suspicion that Winky's sure-fire fate was that of an "old maid." There were frequent references to Aunt Etoile and Miss Boggs: "You take womenfolks like that, they gets *mean,* just gets to thankin' single, and they stay that way." Leuvenia herself was married when she was sixteen. She *knew* "menfolks."

"But I'll tell you, if mah mama had been living I wouldna married *no*body. Couldn't *no*body take me away from mah mama."

"Then you'd have ended up an old maid and when you got sick and old there wouldn't be anybody to care for you or bring you oranges in the old peoples' home."

"Ain't got nobody now. John, Jr. don't care. Last time I heard from him was on Mother's Day and then it wasn't nothin' but asking for money."

Leuvenia was oddly pleased about Walter's arrival. She kept giving Winky shy, knowing looks, smiling cunningly as if she, and she alone, were in on some cute and embarrassing scheme. Love, such as it was, the man-woman variety, was embarrassing to Leuvenia. Even the word was embarrassing. Men were creatures to growl about and complain about, never to speak tenderly of. Her second husband was a drinker who made and sold "white lightning" whisky and finally died of the "T.Bs." He died right there in Leuvenia's house and at night sometimes Leuvenia could see Edward's eyes, round and large, still looking at her. Winky once asked her if she had loved Edward.

"No'm."

Edward was just a kind of "somebody—come along during Hoover days when old lady Mattee at the Welfare wouldn't give you nothing but a handful of yellah meal and it with bugs in it."

But the coming of Walter was another thing entirely, exciting and embarrassing all at once.

"He says he wants to meet you more than anybody else," Winky told her.

"What for?"

"I don't know. He just said so."

"You isn't going to look like *that*, is you?"

Winky had on an old skirt and sweater, the sweater a left-over from college, baggy and thinning at the elbows.

"Of course."

"That's downright shameful. Who ever heard tell of such? Can't nobody look any better'n you when you dresses yourself up some. But you been going 'round here lately lookin' like po' folks."

Winky laughed. "Should I wear my crown and evening dress?"

"No, just fix yourself up some now. Don't wear those run-down shoes. Dress yourself up and fix your hair nice. Put it like I likes it. You don't want stringy-lookin' hair— all comin' down round your face."

Winky sometimes wore her hair with a bun in the back. Leuvenia was a great admirer of that because "it looks right neat theah behind."

"I guess I'll have to do something," Winky said.

"Why, yes. You don't wanta be going to no airport looking like that. Wear that nice suit, that gray one. That makes you look very nice, I thank."

"The tweed one?"

"Yes. That's how you oughta look."

"You're awfully interested in all this, aren't you?"

Leuvenia smiled her shy smile.

"All right, I'll do what you say."

"Yes, you go meet that man lookin' like some*body*."

Somebody or not, when she was dressed she came downstairs for Leuvenia's approval.

Leuvenia posed her hand on the stove and stood back

inspecting. "Now theah," she said proudly. "You looks right pretty."

"*Right* pretty. Is that all?"

"No'm. You looks *ve*-ry nice. You're a pretty-lookin' woman nohow, I thank."

"Why, Leuvenia, that's the nicest thing you've ever said about me."

"But you ain't got your mama's legs," she said, inspecting her shoes.

"What's wrong with my legs?"

"Ain't nobody in the world got legs like your mama's."

"I said what is wrong with mine?"

"Nothin'." She started giggling. "They just awful long-like."

"Well, I can't help that."

"Naw, I was just teasin'. Your legs look all right. But your mama's—"

"I know. I know," Winky said, leaving the kitchen. "I've got to go. I'll bring him back here first thing." She paused for a moment, put her hand to her stomach. "I don't know why I'm so nervous."

"That ain't nothin' to be nuuvous about. He ain't nothin' but a man."

"I know."

"Now you just get gone and act like you're *proud*."

"Okay, Vinnie. Remember, I'll bring him back here first."

"Lawd, what he wanta see po' old me for?"

The day was perfect, golden and blue, only a slight breeze coming from the sea. The small airport was crowded. Winky went immediately to the Eastern Airline counter. The flight from New York was on schedule. She looked at her watch. Five minutes. Her stomach was still turning over with nerves. She decided to go outside and wait. She put on her dark glasses more for confidence than for glare. There was a wind blowing across the empty field and it cooled her heated face. Relaxing somewhat she looked about. The Charleston airport was the least attractive place for a stranger to meet the city in spite of the azaleas, now green, planted here and there. The people, too, looked rather dowdy, but then they did in most airports now. How different it was from Scandinavia. What would he think?

In the distance she heard the far sound of the plane, and a small girl said: "Look! Thar hit iz!" Winky's throat tightened. It, he, came with such a roar, such force. The excitement mounted, and the plane landed, a silver creature on sparrow legs. She went to the gate, smiling, wondering if he could see her by now. She pictured him inside, glancing out the window, amused by the small airport, searching for her, gathering his coat, lining up now, waiting.

She watched as the people streamed from the mouth of the plane: navy officers, a woman with a child, young men, an elderly woman she thought she knew. Of course Walter would be the last one. So like him. Her body tingled with excitement, and she touched the wire fence. *Walter—Walter. For heavensakes!*

But there was suddenly no one.

She stared at the dark door of the plane and the stewardess was not smiling now. Only that dark door. She kept standing. *Why doesn't he come? What is he waiting for?*

But there was nothing, and the wind came again, then the cart piled high with luggage. She stood there watching it, other people's luggage. *Another plane. There must be another.* She rushed back to the ticket counter.

"Another plane from New York? Today?"

"What is it, please?" asked the young man behind the counter.

"Is there another flight from New York? A later one?"

"We have a morning flight."

"But—"

"May I help you?" The man's face blurred before her.

"I was expecting someone. He said he would be here on the four-ten flight. Is there any flight at all today?"

"No, not from New York."

She hated the impersonal smugness of the man, and she stood staring at him. Then as if he had pushed her away he looked beyond her for the next person.

Winky drove home in a daze. Automatically she stopped at traffic signals, turned corners. It was as if she were being borne along, senseless. *Maybe. Maybe he's coming some other way*. Did she have the date wrong?

At home she got out of the car. Leuvenia was sweeping the piazza. She didn't look up as Winky approached.

"Has anybody called, Leuvenia?"

"There's a telegram inside," Leuvenia mumbled, still not looking up. "I tried to call after you."

"When did it come?"

"Just right after you left." She kept sweeping.

Winky knew what was in the message before she opened it, and she stood there by the hall clock, half-hearing its ticking in the silence, an accustomed thing like the table where the telegram lay, the mirror above it, the cherry laurel leaves. Tick. Tick. Tick . . .

DELAYED. SORRY. WILL WRITE.
WALTER

"Why?" she said aloud to the dark afternoon of the house, and when she looked up Leuvenia was coming through the French doors, the broom in her hand, her expression aloof.

"He's not coming," Winky said, seeing Leuvenia's dark solemn face and hating her face then because it was the same old face like the same old house and the same ticking and the same everything.

"How come?" Leuvenia asked, her mouth now hanging loose, her eyes showing pity.

"I don't know."

"Well, I declare," Leuvenia said, shaking her head.

Winky kept gazing at Leuvenia, regarding her heavy-lidded eyes. "What could have happened?"

"Maybe he took sick."

"He would have said so."

"Thangs like that happens. Somethin' just gets in your way and you ain't able to move."

Winky looked beyond her, crumbled the telegram in her hand. "I hate him, Vinnie. I hate him. I really do."

"Now, that ain't no way to talk. He couldn't hep it probably. He'll letcha know." Leuvenia was talking as if she were talking to a sick child.

"Well, I can't stay here. I just can't stay here."

"Then, why don't you just go out to visit for a while? Go by and see Miss Anne or Miss Beverly. You ain't been by to visit them in a long spell. That would be very nice for you to do, I thank."

"Very nice." Winky wanted to scream. "What time is it?"

Leuvenia looked up at the hall clock. "Now on to five."

"I'm going to that party, Vinnie. I'm going, and I'm going to get drunk. I'm going to throw the biggest drunk Charleston's ever seen. You just watch."

"That ain't gone hep nothing," mumbled Leuvenia. "That ain't gone hep *no*-thin'. Sho," she kept mumbling all the way back to the kitchen.

Winky ran up the stairs.

By seven o'clock some of her anger and disappointment had subsided and in its place came hope again. She was sure he would call. Maybe he would even come—tomorrow. Just arrive as he did sometimes. Or the next weekend. But what could have happened? What? Who? And her imagination stretched itself, teased. Illness? The magazine? Writing? Someone? Who?

Whatever, she was part of the city again, for the time anyway, not a watcher, not distant. She was a part, here to succeed or fail, to judge and be judged, Petrie Carr's daughter "going on twenty-seven, going on . . ."

Suzan and Bob Ribaut lived in the old Ribaut house on lower Meeting Street. It was a "double" house. Winky had shown it once a few years ago during tourist season. She had learned its features well. Built by the Huguenot family shortly before 1740, it was impressive in scale with stone quoins at the corners of the walls. Inside, the house was a collage of artifact: George III silver, rugs, Hepplewhite, Louis XV furniture, paintings, portraits, moldings, fretwork, pilasters.

"The house, of course, lends itself for charming entertaining," Winky always said on the guided tours.

In the hall standing before a pier mirror was Suzan Ribaut herself, as much a part of the collage as the two small Federal chairs placed beside the mirror. Suzan was wearing a long white dress, simple, with her hair piled high on the back of her head, a flaming red camellia placed just so. And Bob, land-line disputes aside for the evening, stood by her in black tie acting the host, an unnatural aura of congeniality about him.

From the upstairs drawing room came the buzz of Charleston voices, some recognizable, older couples, young, all gay, genuinely so. If nothing else Charleston loved and held its gaiety.

"Where is he? Where is he?" asked Suzan, receiving Winky's handshake.

"He couldn't make it," Winky said. "Last minute change."

"Awwww, how mean."

"He'll be here later. I do want you to meet him."

Suzan's eyes brightened. "Anyway, Tom's here, and Bill. You just forget that old Yankee and have a good time. Hear?"

Winky smiled. "You've forgotten—Tom's an old Yankee, too."

Suzan giggled. "I know, but he's gotten to be sucha fixture I forget." She wrinkled her nose. "He's kinda half Charleston. Don't you think?"

"You look lovely, Suzan."

"Oh, thank you. So do you. But, Winky, you've lost so much weigh-ut."

"Does it show that much?"

"No, not really. How's your darling daddy?"

"Good days, bad days."

"I read your whatever-it-was in the peyupuh," said Bob Ribaut, relaxing his fixed grin.

"My interview?" Winky smiled mockingly at him. "I thought you would."

"That jig is guilty as hell."

"Seems as if you're being—"

"Now, Bob, don't go into all that sordid stuff at the *pah*-ty," said Suzan, her small mouth puckered in a rosebud pout. "I want Winky to be hap-pi."

"You heard her, Bob," Winky said. "I wanta be hap-pi —and a good beginning would be a drink."

"Of course," said Suzan. "Matthew and Adam are swirling around with trays somewhere. Just go on upstairs."

"See you later," Winky said and slowly walked up the stairway.

Adam, Winky's favorite of the Negro bartenders who served most Charleston parties, met her at the entrance to the drawing room. He had gained weight through the years; his stiff white coat tight, almost creaking, pushed the flesh on the back of his neck upward. The legend of Adam was "the better the family the stiffer the drink."

"Your scotch, Miss Winky," he said, extending the silver tray.

"Thank you, Adam. Is this guaranteed to make me have a good time?"

"Yes ma'am. 'Specially for *you*." The emphasis on the *you*— Winky wondered if Adam had read her interview with Faber Ruffin. Subterfuge, a message of thanks. There was a kind of subterfuge in these matters between the Negro and the white in the South, an unwritten language.

She took the glass and paused at the entrance for a moment. The room was beautiful—camellias here and there, picking up the colors from the Aubusson rug, contrasting against the blues in the fabrics and the porcelains. And they were all there, the familiar faces, moving easily about the room, as accustomed to the surroundings as the very clothes they wore.

"How is your father, Winky?"

It was Judge Hargood, shorter than most men, his hair whiter and somehow more startling now in his tuxedo. His third wife, dark-haired and greatly girdled, was wearing a flowing white gown, and a white feather decorated her piled hair, resting there, a salute to the occasion.

"Oh, good evening, Judge," Winky said.

"I do want to know how your father is."

"Yes," said Mrs. Hargood.

"He's a very ill man, I'm afraid."

"Oh, my dear, we are so concerned," said the third wife.

"Why that should happen to Petrie I'll never understand," said the Judge, shaking his head.

"I suppose we never understand these things," Winky said.

"Such a sweet man," said the Judge. "I guess you don't say that about men. But there's no other word for Petrie. He was a *sweet* man."

Was. Winky caught the word immediately. Is that the way Charleston saw him now, in the past? She had not come to that, not even now.

"And *such* charm," said Mrs. Hargood. "Oh, when I was a gehl—to have a deyut with Petrie Carr was just pure heaven —pure heaven. How is your mothah?"

"I think she's a little tired."

"Of course, poor dear. You know, I do think she should get out more. I wish you could have talked her into coming tonight. It would have been good for her."

"She doesn't like to leave him alone, I guess."

"No, I can see—"

"Good eve-en-ing, Winky."

It was Bill Ashe. "Evening, Judge, Mrs. Hargood."

"Well, Ashe," said the Judge, shaking hands. "Are you still travelling about?"

"Afraid I am," said Bill tiredly, so tiredly. He sighed, and took his stance, the weight on his left foot and the right heel lifted slightly. "The Near East this time."

"Oh, how exciting!" said Mrs. Hargood in the forced enthusiasm third wives seem to have.

"Very interesting just now," said Bill.

"I *know* it is. I just know it is."

"Well," drawled the Judge, "tell you the truth—I don't want to go anywhere."

"You know, Bill, I just can't get Hughley to go any-where," said Mrs. Hargood. "He just wants to stay right here in Charleston."

"Why go anywhere else?" objected the Judge. "We've got everything right here. Good hunting, the sea, beauty, the most attractive people you'll find anywhere." He looked at Winky. "Why bother yourself with anybody else. Isn't that right, Winky?"

"Oh deah," sighed Mrs. Hargood. "I'll be glad when the hunting season is over. Every weekend."

"Say, Ashe, how long will you be here?" asked the Judge.

"Only a few days, then *back* to Washington."

"Too bad. I thought you'd like to join us next weekend out at my place. Hunting's good this year."

"Afraid not. It's good of you to ask."

Bill Ashe's new accent seemed to puzzle the Judge. He examined Bill's face for a moment. He seemed to be saying "peculiar fellow, really—not like his father at all."

"Hughley, dear, I think we should speak to Matilda." Mrs. Hargood looked at Winky. "You will excuse us. Matilda Manning, you know. She's Angus Forzier's cousin," she said in a voice almost confidential, "here for a while because of—" And Winky saw the recognition of error come to the woman's face—the newspaper interview with Faber Ruffin. Obviously, she and Judge Hargood had been discussing it. "Uh, do excuse us, please. Bill, nice to see *you*." She smiled and patted Bill's hand as if he were in mourning.

Winky looked down at her glass and was surprised to see it empty.

"Here," said Bill Ashe, taking her glass. "We'll get Adam." He lifted the glass tiredly.

Winky took another drink from the tray, wondering momentarily if Adam took note of the speed and quantity of guests' drinking habits.

"What is all this about your being in the cell with that Negro rapist?" Bill Ashe asked, not tiredly, his eyes shining.

"Interview."

"Whose side are you on?"

"Nobody's."

"You created a bit of a—uh, uh, here he comes."

Winky turned. Tom was making his way toward them.

"I'll leave you two to your own devices," Bill said with a sigh and left, heading straight for the hallway, and, no doubt, Suzan.

"Where's the lover?" asked Tom.

"Last minute change."

"How churlish."

"Why?" Winky stared straight at him.

"What's his excuse this time?"

"The magazine," Winky lied.

"What magazine?"

"Didn't I tell you? He and some others have started a magazine—a quarterly."

"How acid, how precious."

"Tom, can't you ever say anything without beginning with the word *how?*"

He laughed. "What are you going to do now? Stay locked up in your room like a brooding mare?"

"Hardly."

"There's scotch in that drink, isn't there? You're drinking it like the good, late Liz."

Winky looked down at the drink. "I just feel like getting skunko."

"Good!"

"I— Oh, Tom—" (*Dear God, was she going to cry here?*) She turned her head slowly.

"If you're going to get dramatic let's go somewhere else —in the library."

Winky nodded.

On the way Tom took Winky's glass, put it aside and picked up two more from Adam's tray.

The library was empty.

Tom sat on the sofa and Winky sat beside him. "I thought you had given up scotch," she said, trying to get command of herself.

"Not on the weekends. Now what is all this about?"

She looked at him. "Tom?" And then she knew she was going to cry. She was crying. "Everything's so awful."

She heard his voice: "I know." The gentleness of the tone surprised her, stopped the tears. She regarded him, his face completely relaxed, the blue eyes averting her own.

"There's Daddy and Mother is—"

"*And* Walter Everett."

"Why didn't he come, Tom?"

"You don't know?"

Winky shook her head. "I went to the airport. He just wasn't— He wasn't there. When I got home there was a telegram. He said he would write."

"Favorite expression of his."

"What?"

"That he'll write."

They sat in silence and over the mantel Suzan's great great grandfather, John Ribaut, with his lean face, dark brooding eyes and high collar smiled gently down at them.

"There are people like Walter Everett," Tom said. "They get so absorbed with living their own lives they forget about everybody else. The old-fashioned word is *selfish*, I suppose. There's not much room for anybody else in those lives."

Winky slowly put her handkerchief back in her purse. "You surprise me."

"Why so?"

"Walter *is* that way. He has a love affair with life. He once told me I had never learned the art of living. His own words."

"And I suppose he has?"

"I think so."

"An affair with life," Tom smiled to himself. "Is that all?"

Winky looked at him sharply.

"Well?"

"No, I don't think there's anybody else."

Tom said nothing.

"Tom? He is in love with me, isn't he?"

"I don't know."

"It wasn't just a summer thing. Honestly. Not with him, not with me. I'm not that much of a fool. He asked me to marry him. We were—" There was a loose thread on the skirt of her dress and she toyed with it. "You see, it was so perfect. This summer, I mean. I was so happy."

Tom was gazing at her, his arms folded in front of him.

"Tom?" she asked softly.

"You'll probably hear from him. He'll let you know." He was mumbling.

"Oh, Tom. I'm the one who's being selfish. I'm sorry."

He smiled at her. "Don't worry. I got over you a long time ago."

"You're lonely, Tom, aren't you?"

"Isn't everybody?"

"No."

"I got used to that by the time I was ten—always the one left out of the game. They never chose me, daughter. Good old, good-hearted Tom."

Winky touched his arm. "I adore you. You know that."

He drank from his glass. "Come, queen, let's get drunk."

"All right."

Tom poised his drink in the air. "Just a good, old-fashioned crying drunk for all the lonely, torn-up creatures who got lost."

"Oh, Tom."

"You've said that before, too."

"Anyway, here's to you." Winky lifted her glass.

Tom saluted Suzan's great great grandfather. "And here's to you, too, you sweet bastard! You old snob, you, you Hugue-not!"

They went back into the drawing room. The party was at its peak:

"Golf Saturday?"—"The reason his camellias always win is because he"—"And it's really a good buy, built sometime in the 1840's"—"She's been dying to show her garden. Just ask her. She's been waiting for yeahs, simply yeahs and nobody"—"Thank you, Adam."—"She's actually making a Chinese rug. Has the loom and everything"—"Remarkable. Remarkable."—"Thank you, Adam."—"The Fort Sumter Hotel at one?"—"All day at Middleton Gardens and I was simply"—"The Carolina Hunt"—"Just got through with a house full of guests, and Peter took the men hunting but"—"There just aren't any democrats any more. You know what I mean?"—"Thank you, Adam."—"He just left her and she's"—"Thank you, Adam."—"He's mean, he's—"

"Telephone, Winky."

"For me?"

"Yes, try the one in the back hall."

". . . Hello."

"Winky?"

"Yes, Mother?"

"Petrie has fallen! He's—hurry. Is there a doctor there? Is Williams there?"

"Yes, he's here."

"Hurry!"

Chapter 15

He lay there eagle-spread, face down on the hall floor, neatly dressed in a dark suit as if he might be dressed for morning. No sound or motion came from the body, and Winky's first thought was death. Miss Boggs and her mother knelt beside him and Aunt Pett was seated in a chair, her stern gaze fastened to the prone figure.

Winky turned away, and she heard her mother: "Petrie, Petrie," calmly, methodically.

A slight groan came then. Winky turned, and Williams, no longer the cousin but the professional man, the doctor, was bending over the body.

"He fell from the upstairs landing," her mother said. "Not down the stairs. He fell over the railing."

"Petrie," Williams was saying, "now does that hurt?"

"No."

"That?" He touched his hip.

"No."

"I didn't want to move him," her mother said.

Williams moved her father's arm, slowly, tenderly. There was no sound of pain.

"He was just going upstairs to show me some drawings and—"

Williams stood up. "I'd like to take some X-rays, Ann." He turned to Winky. "Would you call an ambulance?"

"Is he all right?" Winky asked.

"I think so."

Winky called the ambulance, and then came to kneel beside her father.

"Is that you, Winky?"

"Yes, Daddy." She was Winky; not Leigh. His mind was clear.

"Wasn't that a crazy thing for me to do?"

"No, now, don't move."

"I feel like such a fool, lying—" He groaned again.

"Now, just be calm, Petrie," her mother said. "You mustn't move until the ambulance gets here."

"I feel like such a fool."

Winky reached out, started to touch the side of his face, brought her hand back. "You're going to be all right, Daddy."

"Yes."

Winky rose and in impatience went to the front door, stood outside waiting to hear some sign of the ambulance. There was none. "Ah, God." She went back into the house. Her mother was kneeling beside him again. Miss Boggs, Aunt Pett and Williams were standing watching.

Winky went over to Williams. "Is he all right?"

"I think so," Williams said. He looked up to the second floor. "But, my god, what a fall! A miracle he wasn't—"

"I heard it," said Miss Boggs. "I was just sitting in my room listening to the story on television and it sounded like an airplane had hit somewhere. I said 'Mercy' and run out here, and your mother, of course, was already here and—"

Winky wasn't listening. She kept staring at the figure of her father, the foolishness, the indignity. She could not look away. But why didn't the ambulance come? She closed her eyes. "*Why* doesn't it come?"

He lay in his hospital bed, unfamiliar in his hospital gown, his neck and chest naked of collar and coat. He looked older, defenseless, stripped of identity, only a body to be healed.

The good news was there were no broken bones. "Remarkable. Remarkable," they all said. His entire right side was greatly bruised, but that would heal, they said. He lay troubled, turning, trying in his way for comfort.

"Do we need a special nurse?" her mother asked Williams.

"No, I don't think so. But let's keep him here tonight. Just for observation."

"Wasn't that a crazy thing for me to do?" her father kept asking. "Crazy. Crazy."

"You're all right, Petrie," her mother said. "You're just all right."

It surprised Winky what command her mother had. There were no tears, she seemed perfectly calm. But then she had always been that way, taking crises as they came, rising to them, accepting them. It was the small things, the nagging tag-ends that brought her low.

"You'll give him something to ease him, make him rest?" her mother asked Williams, her eyes darting nervously.

"Oh, yes," he said easily, but Winky saw in his eyes, eyes she knew from the blood line of his mother, a darkness which belied his casual manner.

"Then, we'll leave now." Her mother went over to the bed. "We're going home now, Petrie. You're all right. We will be here in the morning."

"Wasn't that a crazy thing for me to do?" The voice was a rasping whisper.

"No, you try to rest."

He looked up at her with full blue eyes. "Good night, Ann."

"Good night."

Winky smiled down at him from the other side of the bed. "Good night, Daddy. We'll be here first thing in the morning."

And surprisingly he took her hand: "My girl," he said slowly. "My girl."

Those were the last rational words her father ever spoke to her. For during the night the terrible raging began. It was two o'clock in the morning when Winky answered the phone.

"Perhaps just your presence here will help," said the nurse stiffly. Winky and her mother left the house immediately, and as they entered the corridor where Petrie lay in his hospital bed the sounds of fury reached their ears. Winky held back for a moment. It was her father's voice but crazed: "No! No! No!"—cries of horror.

"Oh," came the small voice from her mother.

They hurried. A Negro orderly and a nurse were holding him. Her father, his face distorted and red, was struggling to get up. The sides of the bed had been lifted and he lay, raging, as if he were pinned inside a crib.

"Have you called the doctor?" her mother asked the nurse. "Dr. Williams Lagare?" Her mother glanced at Winky. "I think I'll call Williams."

"He's already been here, Mrs. Carr," said the nurse. She was an older woman whose look of impersonality was one which must have deepened through the years of dealing with pain, death and the intrusion of grieving families. "Dr. Lagare gave him medication an hour ago. But they don't want to give him too much because of his other condition."

"I see," said Ann Carr. She went over to the bed. "Petrie? Now, Petrie. We're here. It's all right."

"Pett! Pett!" he shouted. "Help me!" He cried as he must have done as a small boy, as another boy under different circumstances would have called for his mother. He began to struggle with the orderly. The Negro man's hands were strong as he held him down.

Winky tried to find her own voice. "Daddy." He momentarily stopped the struggle, and then it began again.

"He doesn't know what he's doing," said the nurse.

"Is he in pain?" asked her mother.

"I don't think so," said the nurse stiffly. "My other patients are unable to sleep."

The remark infuriated Winky. "Other patients! Have you been here with him all this while?"

"I have other patients, too."

"Then he's been alone like this?"

"We've tried to do our best," said the nurse. Her tone was decidedly defensive.

"I'm going to call Dr. Lagare," said her mother.

"As you like," said the nurse and disappeared from the room.

The shoutings grew louder and Winky, alone in the room with the orderly, said: "Do you have to hold him so firmly? He seems to want to get up or something." Her father kept lifting his head methodically from the pillow. Up, down. Up— He groaned. "Pett! Auntie!" The Negro's arms clamped down harder.

"Quit it!" Winky cried to the man. "Quit it!"

The Negro looked up at her with wild eyes. "He may hurt hisself. He isn't got his mind together."

"He was all right when we left him earlier."

"Yes'm."

Her mother returned. "Williams is coming." She went

over to the bed: "Petrie, now Petrie." She placed her hand on his forehead. He bellowed, an animal's cry, and the struggling went on.

"Oh dear— Oh." Her mother turned to Winky in desperation.

Winky stood there as if all her will had been drained from her.

"Auntie!" came the cry again.

"Let him up," Winky shouted to the orderly.

"He's liable to do most anything, ma'm."

And the raging cries went on.

"Williams will help him," her mother said. "Williams will—" . . .

At dawn, exhausted and worn, Winky and her mother left the hospital. Her father was sleeping, his face fixed in a hurt frown and his mouth set like a whimpering boy's.

The news that Petrie Carr had suffered an irreparable stroke found its curious way through the circuits of Charleston, and by noon the flowers began to arrive: to the house, to the hospital, azalea plants, white, pink, red, specimen camellias; flowers were everywhere, bringing to the medicinal room the kindness of human hands and the aura of death.

And so, it was all over, all save the long waiting. Miss Boggs took over the nursing by day and another nurse, a young nurse with a starched rural prettiness, came by night. The raging had quit; the voice had gone. Ann Carr was adamant: "I won't have any of that feeding with tubes or any of that. It's too cruel." So Winky watched as the great machinery of her father began its starving, his chest rising and falling with great breathing, his head still lifting up and down. A gauze was finally placed over his open mouth, and they sat in turns—her mother, Aunt Pett, Aunt Etoile, watching, waiting. Friends came, a few of her father's hunting friends with mortality clinging so firmly to them, yet in their eyes was the vision of their own deaths, and they shook their heads at the sight of their old friend. For Winky, as she watched, it was her own death. It was she who was dying, blood of her blood, marrow of her marrow. *Oh, my father, you who were so good, so kind, so honorable, will you not always be with me? Will I not be with you?*

Winky had sometimes imagined her father's death, thought of him lying in his own bed at home, letting go of the world in dignity. Even that had been too dreadful to contemplate for long. But this, the powerful breathing, his strong body wasting by hours was an end she could never have fathomed. His face had not been greatly changed by the stroke, only the deep frown, the hurt.

All the years, she thought, the simple things, the going away in the mornings and the returnings in the evenings, his small grandeur, the way he sat at the table, the head of the house, the undisputed head—his strong hands, the gentleness of him—going.

Each morning Winky went to the hospital, came home in the late afternoon and returned again at night, a terrible urgency driving her. She could not stay away. She had a letter from Walter, and she read it coldly, unemotionally. He wasn't able to come last week because he had got bogged down in magazine work. He was sorry. And then the letter took a political vein: He was "disgusted as hell" with the small band of literati, critics, writers, editors, who were trying to ruin the country with half-baked leftist theories, shouting about issues they knew absolutely nothing about. Issues. Winky smiled wearily at the word. How little one knew. The world of the healthy was too pathetically small. Success and failure. What did it all matter? She read the letter, not caring; not caring even that he was coming: ". . . just when I can't say just yet, but soon." She did not answer the letter.

Daily she saw her father's arms become wasted, the color of his face fade to sallow. And all the while the terrible breathing as if with an iron will he must cling to life. At the end of the third week Winky sat in a daze, automatically watching Miss Boggs as she turned him first on one side, then the other, moistening his lips, smoothing his brow with a damp cloth.

Once Winky protested: "Let's do feed him. Let's do. Maybe he'll—"

"You wouldn't want him that way, Winky. He'll never be able to swallow again; he'd just be a vegetable."

"Can't he swallow?"

"No."

"Oh." And she heard her voice, a plaint. *Ah, God,* she called to the faith of her childhood.

The Episcopal rector, John Laird, came and went. He was a young man, his clerical collar uneasy somehow with his youthful, unlined face. He had replaced an older, much respected rector whose vestment and face seemed easily one. But Winky liked John Laird because her father had. He, too, had been a Rhodes Scholar, and there was that as well as the deep convictions of both their faiths. John liked to play golf and last spring he often came by the house to pick up her father, his cheerful, easy personality then so in contrast to his vested Sunday self.

Once when Winky was alone in the room John said prayers for her father, and her father began to cry as if he could hear the familiarity of the voice and hearing knew his death to be and, hating death, wept. Winky ran for Miss Boggs. She found her in the corridor.

"He's crying, Miss Boggs!"

"Crying?" asked Miss Boggs, and she returned to the room. "Now, now," she said to her father as she might to a child. And then she turned him on his side again. He seemed easier, and Miss Boggs left again.

"Patients like this do cry," said John Laird.

Other patients? But Daddy is different.

"It means very little really."

"Is there a heaven?" Winky blurted out to him. "Is there really a life after death?"

"Yes."

"Someone told me once that we should always think Eternity. I find it—difficult."

"Yes, but there is a life beyond this one."

"How do you know? How are you so sure?"

"Because it was written."

"Many things are written."

"Yes."

"I can't believe."

"You will." Hadn't someone else said that to her? Who? She looked up into the hazel eyes of the man, probing, trying to seize from him his own belief but seeing only the unlined face, answering nothing.

She turned her gaze back to her father, his chest rising and falling with his powerful breathing. How could one believe that this man, mortal now, would die, live again, journey to the far Christ? "How possible?" she asked aloud.

"Winky?"

"Yes?"

"Why don't you go home now? I think you need rest."

"Rest?"

"Yes."

She closed her eyes.

"Come, I'll walk out with you."

"I'll have to wait for Miss Boggs. She'll be back in a minute."

And they sat in silence, the breathing from the bed, even, labored, the hurt frown never changing. Winky wondered if in all the days to come she would ever be able to erase this memory, if she would ever be able to see her father as he was, the eyes, the slight smile, the charm; and then she remembered the night not too long ago when he was dressed for the party and how proud he was standing there in the hall in his tuxedo. Two large tears rolled down her cheeks.

Miss Boggs returned, and Winky and John Laird left the hospital together with the promise Winky would be back that night: "But if anything should happen—call me, *please* call me."

In the main entrance to the hospital Winky saw the headlines:

NEGRO ADMITS GUILT IN RAPE CASE

She took up the newspaper and read fitfully:

> Faber Ruffin, accused here of the assault of a seventeen-year-old white Charleston girl, yesterday admitted . . . through his attorney . . . In Judge Hughley C. Hargood's Circuit Court the Harvard-educated Negro entered a plea . . .

"What's the matter?" asked John Laird.

Winky sat on the bench near the newsstand. "I don't believe it. I just can not believe it."

"What?"

"Faber Ruffin. He's guilty!" She looked up at the rector with wide eyes.

"Yes, I read that."

"But—"

"A tragedy all the way around, isn't it?"

"He told me—he told me with tears *streaming* down his face he was innocent. I *believed* him!"

"A terrible thing. Such a waste."

"But—he *told* me." She crumbled the paper. "Who *can* you believe? Truth. Where *is* it? Where is it?" She was sobbing. "People are always looking for the truth. What is it? You can't believe any . . ."

She remembered John Laird leading her to the car. She remembered the doctor giving her a shot and voices, far, ever so far: ". . . Too much of a strain. Anxiety. Too great a strain . . ."

And did she dream? Her mother and Aunt Pett—black gloves, veils and something about triumph and victory. A pall; green grass. Hands and a work done.

When she came to herself they were a house of women.

Chapter 16

February teased the city—spring-like days, then bitter cold which killed the shoots of green already birthed by warmer days. It seemed an endless month, the low country's worst with the Battery winds stubbornly edged in winter.

Winky had quit her job under doctor's orders and, idle, had worked out a schedule for herself, rising in the morning after ten, wandering about the house, then two o'clock dinner with Aunt Pett and her mother, then bed again, reading, trying to sleep, waiting for night.

There were occasional breaks in the routine. She went to the Dock Street Theatre to see Aunt Etoile in *Pride and Prejudice*. Etoile had only a small speaking part, but she did it with a certain air, her Charleston accent emerging only occasionally to define the amateur against the two professionals from New York.

Aunt Pett did not attend the performance, not for disapproving reasons, but since the death of Petrie something, too, had died in her, even the fire of protest. For the first time she looked a very old woman. She had lost a great deal of weight and the wrinkled skin clung to her bony face giving a glazed look to her watering, yellowed eyes.

"It won't be too long before your aunt goes, too," Miss Boggs said to Winky one day. "She's slipping fast. I can't help but wonder where I'll be next."

Winky tried to avoid Miss Boggs as much as possible. She irritated Winky more than ever now, her confidences, complaints, the very ordinariness of her. All during her father's illness and eventual death there had been an aura of excitement about the woman: her face flushed, endless chatter, up each morning, eyes bright. She tasted death, and it excited her into action, usefulness, even kindness.

She dwelt on the technical side of death:

"When the skin gets sticky like this you know it won't be long . . ."

Yes, there had been a decided lift to the woman. Her routine with Aunt Pett, trays and pills, the afternoon walks, had been broken and she herself flourished, even grew better looking. Winky watched it and loathed every inch of her. After the funeral it was Miss Boggs who said rather grandly:

"I declare, the best of the South went with your father. Now all we've got is trash with money—not many left like your father . . ."

But as the days turned, Miss Boggs' spirits sank with them, only occasionally finding something to comment on such as the condition of Aunt Pett and with it her own future:

"Of course, I know your mother will recommend me to some nice people. I never have worked for just *any*body, you know."

"I'm sure Mother will give you a good recommendation, Miss Boggs," Winky said testily.

"Your mother—now she's a brave one," pronounced Miss Boggs.

True. It was her mother, and only she, who worked to keep the spirit of the house alive. She worked with Beauvoir in the garden, helped Leuvenia with the cooking and drugged herself into work for the Historic Charleston Foundation. She wrote countless letters to individuals and foundations asking for aid in the "revolving fund" for the preservation of Ansonborough, one of Charleston's finest concentrations of early architecture.

She even began entertaining again, having friends in for small dinners. Winky was usually present at these, taking them as they came and then bed again, trying to lose her thoughts with the aid of sleeping pills, trying to forget.

She had finally written Walter about her father's death, and he had answered immediately: ". . . Wouldn't it do you good to get away for a while now, come to New York?"

She didn't write again. Between the lines she read something forced. The letter was very short. She had accustomed herself to the gradual losing of him, and the pain of realization was not as great as she had thought it might be. Still, she remembered Paris, she remembered him, and when her imagination began to stretch itself, divine the impossible, she pushed the thoughts away. She could not think of any of it; she could not afford the luxury of even dreams. She *must* heal.

Tom was her one relief. He was moving into a house, a diminutive structure near Price's Alley, white clapboard with long dark shutters, a wall and a garden. Sometime during the year he had caught the fever of Charleston. Out went the pop art, "The Madonna with the Lollipop," the Bahamian bar, his mother's reproductions, and, obsessed, he haunted shops and country houses for antiques, pictures, "the real thing." He had even found a painting of Commodore Perry, artist unknown, and he placed it over the brick mantel with swords and antique pistols.

Winky joined him on some of his buying excursions, actually delighting in his enthusiasm over some particular discovery.

"You remember that table," he said one afternoon when Winky was helping him place furniture, "the one we found in that country woman's house, the one with the sewing machine on it—well, it's worth a *fortune*, ancient, made by one of Charleston's oldest cabinetmakers, the same man who did some of the things in the Pringney house."

"Just think, Tom, one of these days they'll probably ask you to show your house on tour," Winky said.

"Never."

"They might, you know."

"I don't want a bunch of women from Indiana snooping around in my liquor closet."

Actually the little house was charming. Winky told him so.

"Yes, but where do you think *this* chair should go?"

It was a wing chair with Queen Anne legs he had just had repaired and upholstered. His mother had "found" it for him.

"Put it by the fireplace. But, Tom, the main thing is you've got to get rid of this wall-to-wall carpeting. It's ghastly."

"I don't think it's so bad. Gray, inoffensive."

"Now, look," Winky said, pulling some of the rug away. "See, you've got this wonderful floor, wide boards. It would be better not to have any rugs at all."

"I'm trying to talk the Dragon out of one of hers, a Tabriz, really an old one."

"Doesn't she need it?"

"She doesn't even know what it is."

"Tom, really. Your mother isn't that dumb."

"No, she's just retarded. Pity."

"Have you two been at it again?"

"Again? We never stopped. Want a drink?"

Winky looked at her watch. "I'm supposed to be at a meeting, Ashley Hall alumnae."

"At the *drinking* hour? How uncivilized."

"Maybe I can skip it."

"Good! And the stove came today, so we'll christen it with dinner."

"And ruin all those gorgeous copper pans?"

Tom laughed. "You know, for a minute there you almost sounded like your old quaint self again."

Winky sat in the wing chair. "Maybe. But I'm not."

"Well, before you go into your vapors again come and chop up the shallots."

"I thought we were going to drink."

"We are—in the kitchen."

Dinner was served in the living room on the table that once held the sewing machine. The small dining room with the long windows was empty waiting for future "discoveries." Pewter candlesticks lighted the table and a yellow jasmine branch, grabbed by Winky at the last moment near the kitchen door, was the lone centerpiece.

Tom sat at the head of the table, obviously pleased with his creation.

"You're really getting a bang out of this, aren't you?" Winky asked.

"Just old Mr. Bang himself."

"You are, really."

"Have some more wine." He took up the bottle, poured some into Winky's glass and more into his.

"You know, a host is never supposed to say *more* wine." She looked at his glass. "You're sure you have enough for yourself, though?"

"That reminds me. That's what the Dragon took her text from the other day."

"Drinking?"

"No. Obesity. She actually called me obese."

"You've lost a lot of weight."

"She sat right there where you are and said I looked like an obese clown—her way of expressing things."

He leaned back in his chair. "But, now, I have a great announcement to make."

Winky looked at him. "All right. I think I can take it."

He crossed his arms. "My dear, I am now the assistant head salesman at Green Motor Company."

Winky must have shown her surprise.

"Yes," he nodded solemnly. "I, Thomas Gearhart, the turd, am coming up in the world."

Winky didn't know whether the look of pride was real or not.

"Yes, all women are alike, I see."

"Just what do you mean by that?"

"When I told the Dragon about it she wept."

"*I'm* not weeping. I'm—"

"The Dragon always thought a son of hers would *be* somebody, president and king of Soap Suds, Incorporated or something."

Winky put her napkin to her mouth.

"That was when the obese clown bit came up."

"But—Tom—that's—that's marvellous."

"You should have seen that crook Green when he told me. He's got a white office—white desk, white telephone, white rug, white curtains, and green teeth. That bastard! He went into all this spiel about America and how salesmen had made it what it is today, then he told me about my great promotion, and we both stood up and sang 'God Bless America.' My salary has now been increased thirty-seven dollars and eighty-two cents."

Winky placed her napkin back in her lap.

"Of course I'm on a commission—the old ear of corn. But I'm loyal. I'm loyal, all right. Every night before I go to bed I stand in front of the mirror and sing the Green Motor Company song." He was referring to a particularly irritating commercial on the local television station in which the owner, Mr.

Green, introduced his rather effeminate twelve-year-old son, who sang the song in a cracker Carolina accent.

"Why don't you quit?" Winky asked.

"*Quit?* Why, how speak you! That little glass and brick place down there on Broad Street is my *life*. I breathe it, sleep it, live it, and you dare mention *quit?*"

"You should be in something more creative."

"Such as?"

"I don't know. Interior design maybe?"

Tom placed his napkin on the table. "I'm not a flit, you know, even though I think my father has his ghastly suspicions."

"Tom, quit it."

"I mean, if that's what you were trying to suggest."

"I wasn't trying to suggest anything. Perfectly virile men do that sort of thing."

"Not many."

"Why is it that any man who shows the least artistic sense is supposed to be some sort of perverted beast or something?"

Tom laughed then. "It's the American way, doll. Like the Fourth of July and Mother's Day. When I die, dear, I want you to put the Green Motor Company song on my tombstone. Perhaps little Horace Green can sing it at my funeral. Will you have that done for me?" He got up from the table. "Come, I'll dry and you wash."

"Tom, I can't. I really have to get home."

"You mean you let me go to all this trouble and you're going to leave me with all this *grit?*"

Winky giggled. "I'm sorry. But it's Miss Boggs' night off, and I can't leave Pett alone any longer. Mother's gone out."

"That bat Miss Boggs. What does she need a night off

for? She doesn't do anything anyway except snoop around like an old witch."

"I've really got to go. Sorry about the grit."

Tom saw her to the car.

"Now don't just leave the dishes on the table like you usually do," Winky admonished him. "Actually *wash* them." She started the car.

"I'll leave them so you can wash them tomorrow."

Winky stepped on the accelerator, then stopped. "Hey, Tom," she called as he was going back inside the house, "that's a beautifully-shaped dogwood in front. It'll be divine this spring."

"That's why I bought the house," he called back, not turning.

Winky drove off. She felt really quite good. Tom, with all his faults, was a badly needed tonic. "The Green Motor Company song." She was smiling. "Tom, Tom, if you just weren't so— But I do like you. I like you very much."

She parked the car and began to hum as she walked up the sidewalk to the gate of the house. And then halfway she stopped. A figure was leaning against the brick gatepost, a man in shadow. The sight frightened her momentarily. There had been more than a few incidents of crime in Charleston during the past months. The figure did not move. She thought of going into the Traywicks' house, asking Mr. Traywick to see her through the gate. The man tossed a cigarette out into the street and began coming toward her, a tall, slender . . . no!

"Walter!"

"Don't you ever stay at home?"

Her mind spun. She looked up into his face, half-hidden by his raincoat collar and the shadows.

"Is that all the greeting I get?"

She hesitated, then went to him uneasily.

"When did you get here? How long?" She was chattering, trying to cover up her awkwardness. "I was just having dinner with a friend. There's nobody at home."

"Cool down. Just simmer a bit."

She saw his face for the first time in the lamplight. She had forgotten the half-amused look in his dark eyes.

"I've been ringing the bell on this gate for one solid hour."

"Everybody's out, except Aunt Pett, and she can't hear too well. But why didn't you let me know you were coming?" She put her fingers to her cheeks. "I look awful."

"I didn't know I was coming myself until yesterday."

"Did you fly?"

"No, drove."

"Where's your car?"

"At a place called the Fort Sumter Hotel."

"The Fort Sumter?"

"The plumbing's great."

Winky laughed then. "Well, come. Let me give you a drink or something."

"That's why I'm here."

Her hands were shaking as she unlatched the gate.

"Incidentally, you were correct. Charleston's great!"

"How do you know?"

"I've been wandering around, walking, waiting for you to come home."

Winky closed the gate behind them. She put her hand to her breast and took a large breath.

"And you've been keeping all this from me."

"What?"

"This house. It's a masterpiece."

The simple lines of the Georgian house stood veiled in

shadows and Winky found herself seeing it in pride. "Yes, it's beautiful."

They walked the distance to the door, the excitement so high in her she felt almost dazed. "Have you had dinner?"

"Yes, Henry's. I had She-Crab soup. The taxi driver told me to go there."

"Why didn't you call me when you got to the hotel?"

"I did. Leuvenia told me where she *thought* you were, but she couldn't remember 'Mr. Tawm's' last name. Who is 'Mr. Tawm'?"

"Tom Gearhart. I told you." She laughed up at him. "Walter. I can't believe it! You're actually *here*." She opened the door.

"Hey, let me look at you."

Winky raised her face slowly, smiling at him. "I must look awful."

"You've lost weight."

"I know," she said, quickly turning her face, trying to bring herself to ease.

"We'll have to do something about that."

Winky opened the door and paused inside the hallway. The arches, the full sweep of the staircase, the door beyond with its carved honeysuckle across the architrave were in half shadow, yet it greeted them with a reclusive haughtiness even Winky felt.

"So this is Charleston," Walter said, pausing, too.

"Yes."

"It is beautiful," he said simply, and Winky looked at him. Whenever she had remembered him she had seen him darkly tanned, his hair, eyebrows, slightly lightened from the sun. His face now was ruddy, and there were circles beneath his eyes. Even the way he stood seemed different, strange. He had gained weight, not much, some.

"Very, very beautiful."

"That is where my father fell," Winky said, pointing to the upper landing, "over the railing to the floor."

"He didn't die instantly, did he?"

She had written him, written in detail what had happened. "No."

She kept standing there, regarding the hall, the stairway, trying to see it as he must be seeing it, following his eyes as he gazed in the distance from the landing to the floor. Hadn't he read her letters?

"Now for that drink," he said.

"Of course."

His eyes were teasing.

"I'll fix it for you. Go into the library. I won't be a minute."

"I'll go with you."

Their eyes met. She laughed and instantly felt easier. The excitement of the summer began to fill her. "Oh, Walter. I've missed you. How long can you stay?"

"Not very long, I'm afraid."

"How long?"

"Now, about that drink?"

"It won't take a second. Just browse a bit."

In the kitchen she leaned against the refrigerator. ". . . I still love him." She closed her eyes for a moment as the warm glow gathered into her. "We have all night. He still loves me. God, thank you. Thank you for this . . ."

She heard the front door close, recognized her mother's footsteps, then Walter's, his voice:

"No, I'm not a burglar."

Silence.

"Mrs. Carr, I'm Walter Everett."

Silence again, then: "Oh, Walter! How lovely."

"Your daughter is fixing me a drink. Did I startle you?"

"A bit, I think. But how delightful to meet you. Did you just arrive?"

"This afternoon."

"I had no idea you were coming. Winky didn't tell me."

"She didn't know either. I infuriate all my friends by popping in this way, messing up everybody's schedules."

Her mother gave a short laugh. "You're not interrupting anything here. We're leading very quiet lives just now."

"You've had a difficult time."

"Yes, but do come, let's sit in the library."

"Shall I tell Winky to fix you a drink?"

"No, I'm really a little tired, and I'm afraid a drink is not the thing just now."

Faintly Winky could hear Walter's voice from the library: "The portrait? Is that Mr. Carr?"

"Yes."

"He had a remarkable face. I would have liked him."

"I wish you could have known him and—he, you."

Winky placed the two drinks and napkins on a small silver tray. Her hands were shaking. She laughed to herself, placed the tray back down and lifted it again with more assurance.

Her mother and Walter were still standing before the portrait of her father, and in her father's eyes, wistfully gazing, she seemed to read approval.

Her mother was still wearing her glasses, the horn-rimmed ones, "the Historic Charleston Foundation ones," as she called them. The tweed suit, the glasses, gave her an official look, but the gentleness of her gaze and voice belied the former.

"Your drink," Winky said, extending the tray to Walter

and trying to hold back a smile. "And you two have already met, I see."

"We're old friends," Walter said.

"Yes," said her mother and from the twinkle in her eyes Winky could see she liked Walter. But then Winky knew she would.

Walter sat in her father's red leather chair and his sitting there, his presence, a man, seemed to bring back the life of the house.

"I wouldn't have missed this," he said. "Charleston is an extraordinary place."

Her mother smiled softly. "I shouldn't think you would have seen very much of it."

"Oh yes. While your daughter was galavanting, locking me out in the cold—"

"I did no such thing," Winky said.

"I"—he ignored Winky—"went on a one man's tour. I don't believe people realize what you have here."

"You're very kind," said her mother.

"No, as a matter of fact, I'm not. Highly critical, they say."

"And he's a very poor correspondent, too," Winky said.

"Let's not go into that." He sipped his drink. "Charleston's been in the news recently, hasn't it? I read something in *The Times*—about a Negro."

Neither Winky nor her mother said anything.

"Am I stepping on sensitive ground?"

"No," her mother said. "It was a tragic thing. The young woman, the victim, was a friend of ours."

"Yes, that's it. It was an assault case. The Negro was at Harvard or something?"

"He had been," her mother said, "only a few months, it

turned out. He was there on a scholarship and left before the year was out. Winky became rather involved in the case."

"You?" Walter glanced at Winky.

"I did an interview with him, that's all. I believed he was innocent."

"And do you still?"

"I guess not—now." She didn't want to go into that.

"Winky," her mother said as if she sensed the uneasiness, "you must show Walter the gardens—Middleton is nice just now."

"I'm afraid," Walter cocked his head, "I won't have time tomorrow."

"Oh?" said her mother, her eyes widening. "You won't be with us for very long then?"

Walter looked at Winky. "I'm meeting some friends in Florida."

"Friends?" Winky asked.

"Julie and George. You remember." He looked back at her mother. "They have a place at Hobe Sound, rather her parents do."

Winky slowly put down her drink. She felt the color coming to her face.

"They say Hobe Sound is a lovely place to stay," her mother was saying.

"I like it. It's quiet and just far enough from Palm Beach to be civilized."

"How are Julie and George?" Winky asked, and she heard the iciness in her voice.

"The same. Julie's gone on an art kick, rather an artists' kick, sponsoring any poor bearded devil she can pluck out of the Village. It's driving poor George half mad."

Her mother rose from the sofa. "I do hope you will excuse me, Walter. I seem to have had a busy day, and I find the older I get the earlier the night. But you will stay here with us tonight, won't you?"

Walter rose. "Thank you, but I'm at the Fort Sumter." He took her hand. "You're everything Winky said you were and more."

"Oh? Winky thinks well of me?"

"I don't know about her, but—"

"Thank you, Walter. You're a very kind young man." She smiled at him slightly. "Good night."

"Good night, Mrs. Carr."

"Good night. Winky, dear, why don't you light a fire? It's rather chilly."

"She's a lovely woman," Walter said after her mother had gone.

"Yes, she's been wonderful."

Walter glanced up at the portrait of her father again. "Who did the portrait?"

"A man from Boston. Do you like it?"

"Very much. A scholar and a gentleman. The artist also caught a certain strength, didn't he?"

"I wish you had known him."

He turned to her then. "God, I'm sorry."

Winky kept gazing at the picture. She was able to take kindness now, words like "I'm sorry." For a while she wanted to cry whenever anyone was kind. Rudeness, indifference she could take. "It was a very bad time," she said.

"I'm sure."

She didn't avert her gaze from the portrait. "You know, during all that time—when he was—dying—I tried to find your God."

"My *what?*"

She looked at him. "Your God," she said softly.

"Oh, oh yes."

The drink was soothing her, easing her. "All that time there was such a noise inside me, that terrible tolling as if the world would end. I would look at other people. They seemed so calm, so sane. I thought when my father was dying the whole world would weep. It didn't." She turned to him again. "Most people, women, have a God. They go from childhood to death with the same belief. It's all so simple for them. Do you still wish you had gone into the ministry?"

He avoided her eyes. "Look, Winky—" He gave a short laugh, almost embarrassed.

Had she embarrassed him? There was no sympathy in his face, only preoccupation. She wanted his sympathy. Sympathy would keep him here perhaps, away from Julie and George. She imagined his planning: *And I might as well stop off in Charleston.* All at once he was a stranger.

She knelt to light the fire.

"Here, let me," he said.

She stood, watching him, wanting to kneel beside him, wanting to touch him, find in him the rest, the peace, bring back the summer again.

"You're pretty good at this sort of thing, aren't you?" She forced the gaiety in her voice.

"Boy Scouts." He grinned up at her.

"*You* were a Boy Scout?"

"No, afraid not."

The fire caught, and he stood. "Tell me about this mantel."

The glow from the fire heightened the carved scrolls and collared eagle's head, a particular favorite of her father's.

"It's pre-Revolutionary. That's about all I know about it. We don't know who the craftsman was."

"You've grown up with beauty, haven't you?" he said, not turning from the fire and touching the eagle's head.

"I suppose. I never really thought about it that way."

"Never touched by ugliness. How remarkable. Your father's death is the only thing that has ever touched you—I mean truly."

She felt very tired, her throat burned from too many cigarettes. The fire caught with a tremendous blaze.

He looked at her for a moment, his face in half shadow, serious, and then as casual as a toss of a pebble his expression changed. He glanced about the room. "You know I thought Charleston would be something like New Orleans or restored Williamsburg. It's neither. Far, far more interesting."

"I thought you would like it. But I wasn't sure." She sat on the sofa.

He did not join her there. He sat in her father's chair, silent, his feet placed on the footstool, his eyes fixed toward the blazing fire.

"You still have your silences, I see," she said at last.

He glanced at her. "What? What did you say?"

"Nothing."

"Winky?"

"Yes."

"I've something to say to you. I guess that's why I'm here, partially at least."

"You don't have to."

"You know then?" He looked at her with half disbelief.

She wanted to say, "No. No, I don't know anything. Speak to me, tell me." But the corners of her lips ached from the forced smile. "Yes," she said aloud.

She saw the relief ease to his face, and, seeing, she felt a constriction inside her and she wanted to cry out.

". . . I don't know when or why it began to fade. In New Hampshire I thought I'd go crazy if I didn't see you. The Great Father Hemingway said love was good for writers, that you wrote your best when you were in love." He moved slightly in the chair. "He was wrong as rain. All I could think of was you. There was no other direction. And then—"

"Why didn't you write when you were in New Hampshire?"

"I did, a thousand times, but I tore them up."

"Why?"

"I wanted to get you out of my mind—while I was writing the book at least. Every time I'd try to write something—all I saw was your face."

"I see."

He looked away. "Then New York and I got so god-awful busy with the magazine and there was one thing after another. I can't begin to tell you."

"What is she like?"

He looked startled, his tongue slid across his upper lip. "Just a girl."

"Just a girl," Winky repeated.

"And you? You've changed, too, haven't you?"

"I think so," she lied. "Perhaps we didn't really have anything after all. It seems so impossible in a way."

"Perhaps we didn't."

She put her hand to her throat and sat up straighter.

"Tell me something about her."

"She's from Pittsburgh."

"Pittsburgh? That surprises me."

"Surprises me more."

"Have you known her for a long time?"

"Yes. Our families have houses near each other in Maine."

"How nice for you, Walter. Someone you've always known. That's very nice." Her throat was throbbing.

"Of course, she's grown up now." He was smiling to himself.

"What does she look like?"

"Not like very much. But you would like her. She would like you. She works on the magazine."

Winky heard the last only faintly. There was a roaring in her head. *Where do I go now? Where do I go now?* For a moment she thought of abandoning all pride, going to him, crying out her love, making one last desperate try. She held back.

". . . More energy than any female I've ever known, filled with half-cocked ideas. How she got in that family I'll never know—conservative, rock-ribbed Presbyterians, pillars of the community . . ."

Her glass was empty. He had scarcely touched his.

"But enough about me. Tell me about you, about this Tom Whatever-his-name-is."

"Tom?"

"I know he's a bachelor, has a house of his own, and you go there for quiet little dinners. Tell me about him."

"Who told you all that?"

"Leuvenia. We had quite a talk this afternoon."

In her mind's eye she saw Tom's face, the large sad blue eyes, his large body. She put her hand to her stomach. She felt ill. "Tom is just a friend, a very good friend."

"Friendships like that often grow into much more."

"Not this one." She tried to laugh. "No, I've never found anyone I could live with, not for the rest of my life, I guess. But, then, as they say, loneliness isn't the worst thing."

"Are you lonely?"

"No, not really. Charleston is very gay, keeps you busy."

"You belong here. I see that now. You, the city, this house—they're all a part of you. Certain people like certain flowers never transplant very well."

"Will you live in Lillehammer—you and—"

"You remember that, do you?"

"Yes."

He leaned back in the chair. "Oh, some day. Did I tell you? Mrs. Baarli died. You remember her? I took you by her house one day. She was blind."

Winky suddenly smelled the pines, the spices of the North, felt the wind in her hair, and remembered the painting of the eager young girl with the lilies of the valley. Love and spices and cool nights; they were all one. "How wonderful she was."

"Yes."

"Did she die alone as we feared?"

"I don't know. A lawyer there sent me a silver thimble and the pearls I gave her. There were no details."

"She left you her thimble?"

"Yes." He turned toward the fire again.

"How touching. You were very sweet to her."

"It wasn't very difficult."

Winky looked down at her glass again. "I seem to have finished my drink. Would you like another?"

"No, no. I really have to get back to the hotel. It was a long drive, and up and early tomorrow morning."

Winky put the tips of her fingernails to her lips, watched him get up from the chair. *Don't go. Not yet. Give me a little more time.*

He was standing before her, his head cocked. "You know, Charleston, you're a very beautiful girl. You won't be lonely very long." He put his hand to his forehead, over his brow, and then stood back viewing her as if through an imaginary lens. "Here in the firelight you look like a Gainsborough."

"Oh, Walter."

He dropped his hand. "I haven't hurt you, have I, Winky?"

"Why, no." She looked away.

"I couldn't write you this. I had to come. You're the first person to know about our plans."

"That was very nice of you." She sighed heavily. "I know you'll be very happy. I wish that for you."

"Thank you." He stood looking at her and for a moment Winky thought she saw a flicker of regret on his face. But then he took her hand. "Come, see me to the door like a good hostess." He helped her up from the sofa.

"I hate good-byes."

"Good-*bye?* Are you crazy? I'm going to see you often. Peg and I'll have an apartment right in town, and *you're* going to be our most royal guest."

"Is her name Peg?"

"Peg, Peggy, Margaret."

"Does she look like a Peggy?"

"A little, I guess."

He picked up his raincoat in the hallway. Winky watched him put it on, her heart pounding so her vision was blurred.

At the door he took both her hands and kissed her on the forehead. "So long, Charleston." He tightened his hold on her hands.

"Good-bye, Walter."

He turned to go and then she heard herself speak his name.

He looked back.

"We had a lovely time. I shall never forget it. It was the loveliest time I've ever had." She fought the break in her voice.

"I won't forget you, Winky." He placed two fingers on her forehead. "Maybe some day I'll even be back. Who knows?"

"Good-bye."

He was gone, and Winky stood looking at the white panels of the closed door. She fingered them timidly, still trying to smile.

Chapter 17

Spring came to Charleston.

The gray dreariness of February gave way to sun, and by the middle of March the city sparkled with color. Behind the gates the lawns lay clipped and green; the azaleas branched like plumes from old-time hats and over the walls peeked the yellow Lady Banksias telling the forbidden there was a wink somewhere in the tall stateliness of the houses. Tourists were everywhere: in buses, ambling, idling by a gate.

On Palm Sunday the Bishop spoke from the pulpit of St. Philip's Protestant Episcopal Church. He spoke on Nicodemus, and he brought Nicodemus to terms the congregation might readily understand: Nicodemus, said the Bishop, was from an old, *old* family; he had all the gifts the Lord Thy God might bestow upon a man. Whether he had *inherited* wealth, the Bishop was not sure. But he had riches, position, family, and he sought righteousness. "Yet," said the Bishop in his accent, clearly Carolinian, "Nic-o-de-mus worries me . . ."

After the sermon the male chorus heartily sang "The Palms" and for a Benediction "Father in Heaven," followed by the full-robed choir singing "Crown Him with Many Crowns!" Even Amasus Manning, the gentleman's gentleman standing solitary, tall and elegant on the white pristine balcony above the congregation, smiled a bit. Clearly, it was a joyous day, and after the service a cocktail party followed somewhere in the city.

Spring had truly come.

Winky and Tom decided not to go to the Bennets' cocktail party. With the tourists and visitors in the city they had been somewhere practically every night for the past three weeks. Besides, it was Tom's mother's birthday.

"Strange, isn't it?" Tom said as he and Winky got in the car after the service. "People waving palms and carrying on for the Dragon and J.C. all on the same day."

"No comment," Winky said. She felt marvellous today. No particular reason. So marvellous, in fact, she even believed she could face Tom's parents. Mrs. Gearhart had invited Winky to come for a "little drink" the day before. "After church. You can come with Tom."

"Pops is having another couple over, too."

"Oh, who?"

"I don't know. An engineer and his wife, new at the plant."

"Joy," Winky said.

"It won't be too bad. We'll kick out early."

"I have to be home anyway." (After-church drinks at the Gearharts' residence usually carried over to the five o'clock hour and on.)

They were approaching the drive to the house, and each time Winky glimpsed the drive with its thick arch of live oaks and moss she thought of Aunt Etoile:

"I never want to see it," said Etoile. "I haven't seen it since John Chesney died, and the idea of those people living in it sickens me."

The rest of Charleston, however, tolerated the idea. The house had been in ill repair for years, and the Gearharts had spent a great deal of money preserving it. It was one of the plantation homes pointed out during tourist season.

"And what have we here?" Tom asked, slowing the car. "Tourists."

The middle-aged couple standing by the tall gates had the unmistakable look that tourists in Charleston uniquely seemed to have: well-dressed, politely smiling, uneasy that they had been caught snooping.

Tom stopped the car. "Good morning," he called.

The wife was wearing a Liberty cotton blouse, gray cardigan, matching skirt, "invisible" hair net and had the lined-tanned skin imported from Florida or the Bahamas. She wore her gray hair short and behind her smile her teeth were white against the tan.

"We were just admiring the *trees*," she said in a lilting voice.

"They've been here an awfully long time," Tom said.

"I say," said the tweeded man coming toward the car, "could you tell us something about the Spanish *mo-us?*"

Tom glanced at Winky. "*She* can. She knows everything about mo-us."

Winky got out of the car, introduced herself.

"Bob Orr," said the man, extending his hand. "Rye. Rye, New Yohk." He had a stocky build which somehow seemed wrong with his rather over-done politeness—shy smile, the slight bowing. "And this is Mrs. Orr."

"I hope we aren't bothering you," said Mrs. Orr, a slight slur to her speech.

"Not at all. Can I help you with anything?" asked Winky.

"You're from Charleston?" asked the man.

"Yes, I am."

The man smiled sheepishly.

"It's really stunning," said Mrs. Orr, slowly regarding the drive.

"The moss?" Winky asked.

"Is it a parasite?" asked Mr. Orr.

"No, actually it's an air plant. It feeds on air-borne particles, will even live on a wire fence."

"How *fascinating*," said Mrs. Orr. "Those are live oaks, aren't they? Green throughout the year?"

"Yes."

"Stunning," said the man.

"And what is the plant there?" asked Mrs. Orr.

"That's pittosporum."

"I've never seen it before. It has such a lovely leaf and form."

"Wouldn't you like to walk about the grounds?" Winky turned back to the car. "This is Tom Gearhart, the son of the house."

Tom got out of the car, shook hands. "Just wander about anywhere."

"*You're* not from Charleston," said Mr. Orr.

"Only halfway," said Tom.

"That must be a mighty big half," said the man taking in Tom's height and size. He laughed at his cleverness.

Tom was not amused.

"I could tell from your accent. I'm pretty good at accents. Philadelphia! You're from Philadelphia. Right?"

"Wrong," said Tom. "Cleveland."

Mrs. Orr placed her tanned hand to the side of her neck. "See, Bawb, you're not as clever as you thought you were."

"But do, wander around," Tom said.

"I think you'll find the house lovely," Winky added. "It was built rather early, 1808, typically Charleston. The double portico, pediment and columns there on the front are really worth seeing."

"Thank you, thank you very much," said Mrs. Orr. "You're sure we're not intruding?"

"We would show you around ourselves," Tom said, "but it happens to be my mother's birthday and—"

"Oh, of course," said Mrs. Orr.

Winky shook hands with them again. "I hope you like Charleston."

"We adore it," said Mrs. Orr.

"Good," Winky said. "Well, we'll leave you now.".

" 'Bye now," said Mrs. Orr. She waved them off.

"They were nice," Winky said as they drove on.

"He was a grinning bastard."

"You're just hacked off because they didn't think you were from Charleston."

"How regional you are. That was the nicest compliment I've ever had."

"Not regional. Just knowledgeable."

"In a few days it will become my greatest pleasure to say I'm not even half from here."

"What *are* you talking about?"

"Tell you later."

Tom's mother was standing on the front portico waving at them. That son bore resemblance to mother was brought out not only in their rather distinct tendency toward fat. But whereas Tom was big-boned, tall and dark-haired, his mother, now dressed in knitted blouse and skirt (yellow) was short, top-heavy, girdled, and her hair was streaked with hairdresser gray and black. Both looked through the same startling blue eyes, though the mother's were more piercing, examining the world over a slightly beaked nose. What could have passed for attractiveness in younger days now had become tired, puffed, overwrought in spite of her feminine effervescence and generally well-groomed attire.

"Hellew, hellew!" she called to Winky and Tom.

"Happy Dragon's Day," Tom said as he kissed her on the cheek.

"Oh, son," whined Mrs. Gearhart.

"I agree," said Winky. "Tom, why don't you take that name and bury it somewhere?"

"I think it's kind of cheery."

"Happy birthday, Mrs. Gearhart," said Winky. She handed her a small box of Peach Leather candy bought at Aunt Etoile's shop.

"Peach Leather! Big Tom is just wild for it."

"Well, done, then," Winky said.

"Oh, children," said Mrs. Gearhart in a conspiratorial voice. "Before we go in—Big Tom has asked a couple by from the plant. He's an engineer, and she's not very attractive, but she's a marvel at flower arranging. She even lectures on the subject."

"Peachy," said Tom. "Is she going to lecture to us?"

Mrs. Gearhart giggled. "Winky, you can imagine how I felt when she told me, and all I've got in the house are a few branches of dogwood Ernestine arranged last week." Ernestine was the Gearharts' Negro maid.

"Oh, well." Winky shrugged her shoulders.

"They're dying to meet *you*, Winky. I do hope you can see them sometime. Big Tom wants them to be happy here, meet some nice *young* people. He's a brilliant engineer."

Faintly from inside Winky could hear the bongo-bongo of the Caribbean.

"That's Big Tom again. Ever since the cruise he's been driving me in-*sane* with that music. Let's go in the side way."

The "side way" meant the new room, "the family room," as Mrs. Gearhart curiously referred to it. It was built as an addition to the house two years ago, an unnecessary addition, as far as Charleston was concerned, since it ruined the lines of the house. It was a "life-saver" to the Gearharts, however: "This is where we *really* live," Mrs. Gearhart told everyone. There was a place to put the bar, the record player and Big Tom's hunting trophies. And the glassed-in section was just right for Mrs. Gearhart's myriad pots of plants, ferns, orange trees, African violets.

It wasn't an unattractive room, such as it was. Hunting prints lined one wall, bookcases were intermittently filled with shiny jacketed books, pieces of glass and figurines. Wicker furniture was mixed with mahogany tables holding magazines and kidney-shaped ashtrays. It was pleasant, colorful, air-conditioned, expensive, and in the winter Big Tom could actually barbecue in the huge brick fireplace "right inside."

Big Tom also liked to cook. Barbecuing was his specialty, winter and summer. Draped in an apron, a shorter man than his son, Big Tom would stand over his gas-jet pit outside and, fuming and frowning, would baste the night's chickens, steaks or whatever his appetite called for. He was an awesome man, large-boned, an executive of the old style whose wrath came down upon the junior executives like the hand of God. Junior executives would line up in turns for his drinking bouts, they said, and marvelled at the fact that in all his thirty-five years with the company he had never been late to his office nor shown the slightest sign of a hangover.

Some of this spilled over into his social life. One did what Big Tom wanted to do. If he wanted to listen to Caribbean music one listened; if he wanted to have a showing of his guns one looked and listened. If he wanted to sulk, which he often did, one respected the mood, waited for it to pass, did not cross.

Young Tom, Winky knew, revered and feared his father.

He was proud of the man's business skill, proud of his money, position in the world of business. He still kept a 1956 copy of *Fortune* in which Big Tom, nattily groomed in a dark pin-striped suit, looked out from the page a pink-cheeked master of industry. Had the slow climb upward been different perhaps young Tom would have been more like his father. The pity was that his mother had been more a part of Tom's life than his father. Still, Tom really loved his mother; Winky was sure of that, too. It was her approval he sought above all others. That he should ever have been the cause of her distress, "her nerves," was a desolate thought.

He had told Winky much about the past: his mother taking him to the circus when he was small, his mother when they were living in the New Jersey flat before Big Tom had his first success. She was sweeter in those days. Later, there were just the two of them when Big Tom was travelling so much. And they had good times together, he and his mother, listening to television, watching the "Amateur Hour" and laughing at the losers. They had tea parties in which they pretended guests were invited; they went to movies, cooked. Sometimes they would cook great heaping pans of fudge. Those were nostalgic times for Tom.

And then Tom went to college and all that changed; at least outwardly. Tom knew his mother was lonely.

"And here comes Mr. Fatso!" called out Mr. Gearhart as Tom and Winky entered the room. He was standing behind the bar flourishing a glass.

Tom's shoulders drooped instantly. "Hi, Pops," he said in the voice he always used at home. Tom was a different personality when he was at home: respectful, even shy. This had somewhat surprised Winky when she first saw it.

Mrs. Gearhart giggled nervously. "Big Tom loves to

tease son," she said to the couple who were sitting side by side on the wicker sofa like two pieces of unrisen dough.

It was to be a difficult hour, Winky saw immediately. The couple Mary and Bill Rickert were irritating, fused together for just that purpose, it seemed. Both had the same self-satisfied expression some couples in their mid-forties grow to have who have spent their youth in day-to-day plugging "to get ahead" and finally do.

They looked alike: average height, bland, blue-eyed, sturdy, unimaginative and satisfied. Bill Rickert wore glasses and behind them his weak gaze darted to and fro, the one signal that all the numerals and fractions were there, correct, years of calculating, ever alert.

Mary Rickert was more irritating than her husband somehow. There was something stubborn, even depressing about her, a true blue club woman, everything in its place, no nonsense, forthright. Everything she was wearing matched: dark blue dress, dark blue shoes, pocketbook and, a little pathetically, blue eye shadow, an effort for the occasion, totally wrong with her solid look of sturdy efficiency.

"Winky is from Churrrleston," said Mrs. Gearhart.

Both acknowledged the fact with blankness.

"And where are you from?" Winky asked.

They both looked at each other as if they were sharing an old, tired joke.

"Everywhere," said Mary Rickert, addressing her statement to Mrs. Gearhart. "I guess you could say we're just from everywhere."

"I know," said Mrs. Gearhart, "when you're an engineer there's no telling where you'll be next."

"We've lived in Ohio, Canada, Illinois, and we've just left St. Louissss."

"Oh?" Winky said.

"Have you ever been there?" asked Mary Rickert. It was like a dare, the question.

"Yes. I loved it."

"I liked it, too, but Bill didn't. It gets so durn hot there."

"Bloody, witch?" Tom asked Winky.

"What *are* you saying, son?" asked Mrs. Gearhart.

"I am asking Miss Carr if she wants a Bloody Mary. Any Objections?"

"Yes, thank you," Winky said, "but don't put too much of that hot stuff in it."

Mary and Bill Rickert were drinking sherry.

Winky went over to the bar.

"Hello, gal," said Mr. Gearhart. "Been to church?"

"Yes."

"Preacher lay 'em in the aisles?"

"No, the Bishop was there."

"What can I fix you?"

"Tom was going to fix a Bloody Mary, I believe."

"*He* doesn't know how to fix anything."

Winky gave a short laugh. "He's pretty good sometimes."

"Aaaah, he can't make a Bloody Mary."

"Pops really can make a good Bloody," Tom said. "What is it you put in there, Pops?"

Winky watched the older man laboring over the procedure. "Now, you see, it's just the *right* amount of celery salt. Just the right— That's what makes a really good Bloody Mary." He carefully sliced a lime, topped the drink with it and handed the glass to Winky. "Now, taste that! See if you don't like *that*."

It was a command. Winky sipped as Mr. Gearhart stared. She didn't taste the great difference. "Marvellous," she said. "Absolutely marvellous." She smiled at him. "Really, you're awfully good."

No comment. Big Tom was sulking again. He went over to the record player and began going through the stack of records. Winky sat in the chair by Bill and Mary Rickert.

"You must have been from somewhere originally," Winky said to Mary Rickert.

"We're both from Pennsylvania. Just little towns. Bill lived about twenty miles from me."

"And did you know each other in high school and all that?"

"I had *heard* about Mary," said Bill Rickert. Huge grin.

"But I never heard of *you*," said Mary.

"Hah, hah, hah," laughed Tom pointedly.

"Then where did you meet?" Winky asked.

"At Washington and Jefferson College."

"How interesting."

"I was in Home Ec. and Bill was—"

"We've just gotten back from a cruise," interrupted Mrs. Gearhart. "That's why Big Tom's so fascinated with those records. A Caribbean cruise, you know."

They all knew but Winky relaxed as Mrs. Gearhart began telling about the costume party they had had aboard ship: "Big Tom wore . . . and I . . . I . . ."

It was two-thirty, and they had been drinking since one. The room was filled with smoke and across the way the hi-fi continued to spin the bongo-bongo of the Caribbean.

Winky, without success, had tried once to get Tom to take her home, but the spell of his father and the protest of Mrs. Gearhart won, and Winky resigned herself.

Tom was dancing with his mother.

"Cha, cha, *CHA*."

Mrs. Gearhart, glass in hand, was finding serious satisfaction in the fact she had at last conquered the rhythmic shoulder movement of the dance:

"You're just not getting the beat, son," she whined. "Now, look, pay attention! Da, dah, DAH! See!" she exaggerated the thrusting-forward of her left shoulder. "Cha, cha, CHA!"

Winky, curled up on the sofa, began idly tracing her forefinger over one of the red-coated huntsmen on her glass. Over by the bar Big Tom was talking to Bill and Mary Rickert. He was holding a swizzle stick in his hand, one with a happy little Haitian head on it.

"How interesting," she heard Mary Rickert say.

For no reason she could possibly think of Winky began to think of Walter. Perhaps it was the sensual beat of the music or maybe it was the couple from New York they had met earlier. Whatever, she was suddenly and hopelessly sick for him. Every day she had bought a copy of *The Times*, turning immediately to the women's section, searching the endless engagement announcements.

"You're only torturing yourself," her mother had told her.

"He was really so right for me."

"No, I don't think he was. He was a charming young man, of course, but a little brash, I thought. I shouldn't have liked you to marry him."

"I'm so terribly unhappy."

"What's done is done, Winky. Why don't you think seriously of going to New York now, find a position that will absorb you. You're really quite a talented young woman."

"New York," Winky had said, knowing full well that that time was over. Charleston had become a cloak she could hide in, warm, easy, safe. She was afraid of New York, afraid of most things now, especially change. There was a time in one's life when the roots were easily taken up. That time had passed. She said none of this to her mother.

She rested her head on the back of the sofa. Outside, through the glassed-in doors, she could see the live oaks, the moss. It was a windless day and the tall branches were still against the sky. Above, a flock of birds passed by. The last bird passed, and she watched until it was out of sight. Where were they going?

"Drink, Wink?" Tom was grinning down at her, his face damp with sweat.

Winky looked at his glass. He had switched to bourbon, dark amber, his fourth or fifth.

"No more, thanks."

"Listen to her, listen to her," Mrs. Gearhart said. "Nooah," she said working her mouth in an attempt to catch the Charleston accent. Mrs. Gearhart had made the attempt before, an absurd failure mixed as it was with her own nasality.

"At least she doesn't make two syllables out of the word 'it,' " said Mary Rickert overhearing. "There was a girl from Tennessee in St. Louis in our garden club and she said 'ee-yit.' "

Tom laughed, a kind of low chortle. "Sow-yuth in the mow-yuth. Charlestonians don't have that accent, thank god." He reached for Winky's glass.

"All right, one more. Very small, Tom," Winky said. She looked at her watch. "Heavens! It's almost three. We've been—"

"Re-lax," Tom said.

"Me, too, son," said Mrs. Gearhart, handing her glass rather unsteadily to Tom. "If nobody else wants to celebrate my birthday, *I* will." She smiled sheepishly, slumping her shoulders like a shy ten-year-old, a highly unbecoming gesture.

"Goddam, Bill, you're an engineer!" shouted Mr. Gearhart from across the room. He was sitting cross-legged on the floor. "Come here and fix this thing!"

Bill Rickert fairly bounced to his feet.

"Big Tom's cameras again," whined Mrs. Gearhart. "By now you'd think—"

Cameras had played a part in other after-church drink sessions with the Gearharts. There were cameras from Germany, Japan, Italy and God knows where else. They were like the Bongo drum and the Haitian head. Toys. Big Tom had many toys. Yet with it all Winky rather liked the man. Somehow through all the homemade exterior there was an instinctive kindness, almost a sweetness. Even with his roaring, sulking personality at least one could not say he was a bore. The men in Charleston rather liked him.

"Does he actually take *pictures* with them?" asked Mary Rickert, turning to see if her husband had obeyed the command from on high.

"Oh, yes. Big Tom's a fine photographer," said Mrs. Gearhart. She had a habit, when drinking, of stretching her mouth widthwise and one never knew whether she was smiling or experiencing pain.

Tom returned with the drinks.

". . . There was a lee-tul gull from Ahm-sta-dahm," sang Jamaica Joe or whoever from the record player.

"Let's dance, Mary," said Tom.

"Me?" asked Mary, putting her hand to her bosom. "I can't do any of that sort of thing."

Tom attempted to reach for her hand and as he did he knocked against the coffee table, spilling his mother's drink.

"Oh, son." Mrs. Gearhart dabbed at the table with a paper napkin and left the magazines drenched.

Tom ignored the accident. "Come, I'll show you how it goes," he said to Mary Rickert.

"Do you think son is drinking too much?" Mrs. Gearhart asked Winky when the two had left them.

"Tom?"

"Uh huh. Sometimes I think—"

"No, not really. Not any more than the rest of us."

"He does everything too much. If he could only lose weight. If he could only learn some con-*trol*."

"Tom's all right."

"I know," Mrs. Gearhart said. "I know."

They turned to the dancers. Tom, his eyes red and half closed, was shoving the stalwart Mary Rickert about the room.

"That girl is *so* talented," said Mrs. Gearhart. "If people in Churrrleston only knew what she could do with flowers they'd—" She didn't finish. She didn't have to. Charleston and its sometimes diffident ways was a favorite topic with Mrs. Gearhart.

"She seems to be a very nice person," Winky said.

Mrs. Gearhart took up her half-empty glass. "Impossible," she said.

Winky looked at her quizzically.

"This town."

"Charleston just has its ways, that's all. I suppose every place is a little like it, really."

"And how lone-ly it is for son." She looked almost defiantly at Winky.

"For Tom?"

"Ohh, yes. In Cleveland the house was literally running over with young people. I had a special room built and Tom was always having his little friends over. All the time.”

“Everyone here *likes* Tom. He’s always invited places.”

“Tom was a sweet child,” Mrs. Gearhart said. “I can see him now, as a little thing, coming up to me and saying ‘I love you, Muttee.’ ” She glanced at Winky. “He used to call me that. He still does sometimes, you know.” She looked into space, blinking. “It’s hard on a girl like Mary Rickert, too.”

“Oh?”

“Moving to a place like this after having been around, you know.”

“Charleston is changing in some ways.”

“No, they’ll never take to her. I know this place. The people are so—” She stopped short. “But I keep forgetting you’ve always lived here. How rude of me. How absolutely *ruuu*de!”

“No, I don’t think it would be very pleasant living in Charleston if—”

“Family!” said Mrs. Gearhart. She fairly gulped the last of her drink. “All family. Don’t they know that’s passé in this world now? That’s all these ridiculous people think of.” She looked down at her glass. “I never say anything about it, of course, but if people here knew my great great grandfather was a general in the Revolutionary War they’d—” She sat up straighter. “My family goes way back, you know—*waaay* back.”

Winky couldn’t take her eyes from the woman—the constant blinking. “It’s interesting to know the history of your family, I guess,” she said. But she was remembering what Tom had told her once: On a trip to Ohio his mother had found a photograph of some vague relative and had an artist paint him in all his contrived splendor. It, along with other “ancestors,” now hung in splendidly gilt frames in the drawing room. Winky had never been able to look at the portraits again after Tom had told her that.

"Do you know your Aunt Pett has never spoken to me?" said Mrs. Gearhart. The corners of her mouth were turned down. "Not in church, not anywhere, and I've met her, I know, a thousand times."

Winky laughed then. "It's only because she doesn't see you. She's not really like that." It was true. Aunt Pett had her ideas, of course, but she was never deliberately rude, a virtue she particularly prided herself on.

"Churrrleston!" said Mrs. Gearhart. "Oh, they're not too proud to let Big Tom give money to the church or the Historic Foundation Society. Ohhh, no."

Winky ignored the error in the foundation's name. "Mr. Gearhart has been more than generous."

"I'd just like to see them—just *once*, just one of them, in Cleveland! They wouldn't have a friend to their names. They'd know then. They'd know—" Her voice seemed to go away.

"They don't mean anything by it, Mrs. Gearhart. It's sort of a hold-over when the townspeople felt they had to protect themselves, cling together. Besides, much of all that is exaggerated anyway, and, too, Charleston's changing, really it is. The older people are fighting it, but it's changing all the same."

Mrs. Gearhart looked away and sat looking into space with her head wagging from side to side. In a moment's panic Winky thought she saw tears in the woman's eyes, but she was mistaken.

"You know, Winky, son is terribly interested in you." She placed her hand on Winky's knee.

Winky looked from the speckled hand with its tremendous emerald and diamond ring on her finger back to the woman's face. She had that same stretched smile.

"I mean he's *very interested* in you."

Winky started tracing her finger over her glass again. She said nothing.

"Do you know how sensitive he is?"

"I think so."

"Son's a very, *ve*-ry sensitive child. He told me all about it, you know."

"Told you? What, Mrs. Gearhart?"

Mrs. Gearhart nodded. "He came over that very next day, and we both cried."

"About *what?*" Winky lit a cigarette and abruptly blew out the match.

"You laughed at son when he asked you to marry him. You laughed! It hurt. It hurt right here." She jabbed a finger into her diaphragm.

Winky stared at the finger. "Tom misunderstood, Mrs. Gearhart."

"How could he have misunderstood a thing like that? A young man asks a young woman to marry him, and she laughs in his face."

"I didn't think he was serious. There had never been anything—I mean serious—between Tom and me. We were just friends. He's just a friend. I'm terribly fond of him."

Mrs. Gearhart leaned forward. "How old are you now, Winky?"

"Twenty-six." She looked straight into the narrowed eyes. "I'm twenty-six years old—soon will be twenty-seven."

"Yes, well." Mrs. Gearhart picked up the damp magazine from the coffee table, turned it over and slapped it down again. "I'm not like a lot of mothers," she said. "I want my son to marry. I can't understand why he doesn't. Thirty-three years old and nothing but a car salesman." She looked across the room. "It grieves Big Tom so. Grieves him to death. He thinks Tom should start showing some responsibility. He's never shown any responsibility."

Winky sighed heavily. "He'll marry some day."

"Son's going to have a great deal of money some day. You know that, don't you?"

"I have supposed he would."

"And he needs a level-headed woman for a wife. I married when I was eighteen, just a slip of a girl."

"Some people seem to prefer that."

Mrs. Gearhart brought her glass unsteadily to her lips. "It must be unhappy for you."

"What, Mrs. Gearhart?"

"Being in a place like Churrrleston. I shouldn't think there'd be many eligibles left by now."

"Most of my friends are married."

"You and Tom see so much of each other I should think—"

"I enjoy Tom."

"Yes, I'm sure. But don't you worry. You're an attractive enough girl. If I were you I wouldn't worry at all."

"Oh, I'm not." The anger was beginning to rise.

Mrs. Gearhart patted her on the knee. "You and son will get together in time. Just wait and see." With a look of almost peace she was gazing into space, smiling approval of her dream. She turned slowly to Winky. "In time."

"I'm afraid not," Winky said after a pause.

Mrs. Gearhart shot a glance at Winky. "Then you ought not to see so much of him then! You're just *using* him, and I don't like anybody to do that to *my* son."

Winky started to get up from the sofa.

". . . birthday to you. Happy birthday to—you. Happy

birthday, dear Dra-gon. Hap-py birthday to you." Tom, Mr. Gearhart, Mary and Bill Rickert were all singing. Tom was singing louder than the rest and holding a pink birthday cake, and Mr. Gearhart was holding up his Japanese camera.

Winky looked up into the faces of the father and son, similar in their half-closed eyes, not smiling, their bodies unsteady, and then Tom said: "Dragon, what *is* the matter?"

Winky turned to Mrs. Gearhart. Her face was hideously distorted, and then horribly she burst into a flood of tears. "I'm so lone-ly. I'm so *lone*-ly," she blurted out to them.

Winky insisted she drive home. It was six o'clock. They had finished dinner, one of Big Tom's barbecued chickens. Eating had somewhat sobered Tom. Nevertheless, Winky wanted to drive.

"Sorry about that," Tom said as they turned out the gates.

"What?"

"The Dragon's bid for attention."

"She doesn't want me to see you anymore. She thinks I'm *using* you."

"The loyal Dragon. How perceptive she is."

Winky stepped on the accelerator. "I don't know what she thinks I'm using you for."

"Someone to take you to the local do's, your ever-faithful sheep dog."

"I've had just about enough of all that for today. I think your mother's right. You'd better stay in your corner, and I'll stay in mine."

"Don't worry. I will—beginning just about—Thursday."

Winky kept driving at the same high speed. "Why Thursday? Why not Monday?"

"Because I won't be leaving until Thursday."

"Oh? Where are you going?"

"New York."

"For a visit?" Winky bit the words.

"No, to stay."

Winky slowed the car.

"And what a happy day that will be."

"Tom, what *are* you talking about?"

He didn't look at her. "Nothing in particular."

"You're still drunk."

"No, I would say my mind is clearer than it ever has been."

"Are you serious?"

"Yes."

"Are you really leaving? For good?"

"I am."

"Tom, you're not. Your mother didn't say anything about it."

"She doesn't know. You're the first. Doesn't that flatter you a bit?"

"Do you have a job or something?"

"Do you think that's so impossible?"

"No, but—" Her voice was thin, breathy.

"I have a job in advertising, with Latham and White— beginning May one."

Winky said nothing. Her mind was confused, spinning.

"Why, I see you have no belief in me. My ability."

"It's just a bit of a shock, that's all."

"I can't see why."

"It's—it's just a shock, that's all. You're serious, you're really serious?"

"Absolutely. Thursday I shall take off and ye shall see me no more."

"Tom!"

"I didn't know you cared so much."

"Of course I do. I'll miss you—terribly."

"Pity."

"No, I *will*."

"Maybe you can work on Bill Ashe now. I understand he's coming back here to live, and Suzan Ribaut's pregnant—by her husband, I presume."

"Don't be silly."

"Bill Ashe isn't a bad guy. A bit light on his feet, but what's that in a world torn apart anyway?"

"I just can't believe it."

"You'd better. I'll look up the Golden Calf for you in New York, give him your regards. Walter Everett is the name, I believe?"

Winky said nothing. They drove the rest of the way in silence. When she parked the car in front of her house she put her hands on the wheel again and rested her face.

"Do you weep, child?"

Winky raised her head. "No, but I feel a little like it, I guess."

"You'll recover."

On the sidewalk an abandoned newspaper page blew against the wall.

"This has been in my mind for a long time now," Tom was saying. "A roommate of mine's father worked the magic. But the greatest pleasure is going to be telling dear Mr. Green: 'Boss, I quit, leave you with your jingles, your white office and your damn cars!' Hallelujah, play it again, Sam!"

A curious jealousy was growing in Winky. The hot summer would be here soon; no doubt she would be writing for the paper again, the same routine. And at the end of the day? Yes, at the end of the day— What? She watched the newspaper page as it was blown further along the wall.

"I take it back. You're not the first to know. Pops knows about it. He's footing the bill for an apartment, sudden generosity."

"What are you going to do with your house?"

"Sell it."

"That shouldn't be too difficult, I suppose."

"I'm going to sell it, furniture and all."

"You don't plan to come back, do you?"

"Hell, no."

"You don't have to be so adamant."

"Yes, I do."

She looked at him. "Well."

"Aren't you going to say some touching good-bye or something?"

"Certainly. I'll see you before you go?"

"I'll try to drop by. I've got a million things to do. If I don't, tell you mother and Aunt Pett good-bye for me." His eyes brightened. "For some reason I always liked that aunt of yours. She hated my guts, but I liked her."

"She never hated you. Pett never hated anyone."

"No. I guess not." Tom sat up straighter. "Well, dear, *arrivederci* and all that."

It was a decided invitation to leave. Winky got out of the car, and Tom immediately slid over to the driver's seat.

"So long, angel." He drove off.

"Good-bye." Winky started to wave, but she stood there with her hand slightly lifted watching the car until it turned the corner. She stood that way for a long time.

Chapter 18 ～

"How come all that sighin'?" asked Leuvenia.

Winky was in the kitchen preparing the sherry tray, and Leuvenia was reigning over the myriad pots and pans which were steaming away for the two o'clock dinner.

"I don't know," Winky said, "these family things sort of get me down, I guess."

"That ain't nothing to sigh about. All we got in this world's family."

"I know. But the dinners go on so long, and I'm supposed to be at the Russell House at three-thirty."

"You sure is doing a lotta house showing round here lately."

"Nothing else to do."

Leuvenia was looking through the spice rack. "Foots! Where is that mace? Your Aunt Pett'll have a fit if I don't—Heah it is."

"I don't think Pett notices too much nowadays."

"Don't say nothin'. That's how come I tries to fix thangs nice. She don't eat enough to keep a beyud alive."

Winky poured the wine in the decanter.

"Better you put out a glass for Miss Bawgs."

"Is *she* going to have dinner with us? I thought this was her day off."

"Your mother say she is." Leuvenia's mouth turned down in disgust.

"Oh me." Winky sighed again.

Leuvenia began to hum, a recognizable tune, once

Winky had heard often, something about peace in the valley. ". . . Thah will be *peeeece* in the val-ley for me-ee—some deyyy . . ."

"Do you suppose there will be?" Winky asked.

"Ma'am?"

"Peace in the valley."

Leuvenia looked at Winky slow-eyed and haughtily tossed her head. "Sure will."

"Who's going to give it to you?"

"Jeeeezus, that's who." She went right on washing the casserole dish.

"Did He tell you so?"

Leuvenia looked back at her. "Who tell of Jeeeezus telling anybody anythang?"

"Some people say so. 'He walks with me and He talks with me.' All that."

Leuvenia turned back to the sink. "Lawd, Miss Wank—." She turned her head sideways, and then with her hand to her mouth tried to stifle the giggles. "Them's just—" wheeeze —"sanctified folks." She plopped into the rocking chair. Wheeeeeze.

Winky couldn't help but laugh. Leuvenia, without a doubt, was the one truly bright spot in the house. Undoubtedly she would be an anathema to the young Negro generation. But she was herself; probably would never change, and Winky sometimes thought her cheerfulness was a planned thing, an innate kindness, trying in her way to bring sanity once more to a rocking household. Whatever, she was greatly welcomed. Winky told her as much.

"But you can just kiyill me sometimes, talkin' 'bout—"

"I'd rather kill myself." Winky took down the extra glass for Miss Boggs.

"That ain't no way to talk now."

"Maybe not."

"Talking 'bout *killin*' yourself. Who ever heard tell of such?"

"I'm not exactly serious."

"No'm, course you ain't," said Leuvenia in her exaggeratedly sweet tone which usually indicated suspicion.

"I don't have to. I'm already half dead anyway."

"Donchu be talking that way round heah now." Her mouth was pursed for argument. But her eyes shone with the eyes of the curious.

"All right."

"You know what you needs?"

"No, what?"

"You needs some kinda *comp'ny* keeper."

"And who would you suggest?"

"Mr. Bill, he ain't no baaad looking man. I thank he's right handsome."

"Bill Ashe? Hah!"

"Now don't go acting like that about folks. Ever since Mr. Tawm gone up the road you don't never get outta the house, just *draggin*' round. You oughtta dress yourself up some, get out with the peoples, go to the beer garden."

"Beer garden" was a term Leuvenia used for any place, private or public, that served alcoholic beverages.

"Too dull," Winky said. "Besides, I do get out. Just like this afternoon. I'm going to show the Russell House and soon I'm going to take my job back."

"You been saying you gone do that for the past five months."

"Saying what?"

"You was gone take your job back. I don't see you

gettin' it back. Just like I says—if you got out more maybe you'd *find* yourself some nice comp'ny keeper—like Mr. Walter or somebody."

Leuvenia was trying to ease Walter into the conversation again. The subject intrigued her. Weekly she would nonchalantly ask if Winky had heard anything about his marriage. The answer was always an ungarnished *no*.

"We don't mention that name, do we?" Winky said, looking around at her. Leuvenia was rocking in the chair, her head lifted, gazing out toward the back garden.

"No'm," said Leuvenia. "But I sure do wish I'd had a look at that man. I wouldn't waste my time of day on no man like that. I'd send him runnin' so fast he wouldn't no wheah he was comin'."

"We still don't mention the name, do we?" Winky took down the cocktail napkins and began folding them.

Leuvenia yawned. "Lawd, lemme get up from here 'fore I forgets this dinner. We gets to talking and nothing comes out right."

Winky lifted the silver tray with the glasses, decanter and napkins. "Here goes nothing."

"You be nice to them folks, now heah."

"I always am, I thought."

"Like you *means* it. Don't just set around *sighing* and *yawning*."

Winky carried the tray into the drawing room. They were all there: her mother, Aunt Pett, Aunt Etoile, Miss Boggs—all arranged like actresses in a play.

"I'm sorry, I didn't know you had come, Aunt Etoile," Winky said. She glanced at her mother. "Have you been waiting? I was talking to Leuvenia and the time just went by."

"Etoile just came in," her mother said. "Would you mind serving the sherry, dear?"

Winky served the glasses, took one for herself and sat on the settee beside Aunt Etoile. "I hope the tourists won't smell this," she said holding up her glass.

"Oh? Are you going to show a house this afternoon?" asked her mother.

"The Russell House. I'm taking Suzan Ribaut's place. She's not feeling well or something."

"She's pregnant!" said Aunt Etoile. "I wonder just who is the—"

"Now, Etoile," said her mother. "There's nothing to that talk, not at all."

Etoile lifted her chin, a tight smile on her face.

"Well," said her mother, lifting her glass slightly. "How lovely it is for us all to be together. So nice to have *you* with us, Miss Boggs."

Miss Boggs, not in uniform, was dressed for the occasion, yellow suit, black patent leather shoes. She smiled timidly as if she were among strangers.

"I think it's so pleasant when we can be together like this," her mother said as if she were speaking to herself. "We haven't been together since—well, since Winky's birthday."

Winky looked about the room: Aunt Pett sitting with her mouth slightly open, her eyes dulled, glazed; Aunt Etoile nervously tossing her head from side to side; her mother with the aura of widowhood which seemed to grow more fixed day by day, trying but never adjusting to her gradually lowering status; and Miss Boggs, sweetly smiling with her two-tone red and gray hair cut shorter now.

"And I am one of you," Winky thought, "fitting as neatly as a glove."

"How old are you now, Winky?" asked Etoile.

"Twenty-seven."

"How the time does go by," said Etoile.

"Yes, it goes by," Winky said.

"Oh," said her mother, "did I tell you the Whitfields are coming? Sarah and young Felicia?"

"You didn't tell me that, Mother," Winky said. She liked her Aunt Sarah, her mother's sister now living in Ashton, Georgia. And she was amused by her cousin, Felicia, seventeen now and going through one adolescent stage after another.

"Are you up to that now, Ann?" Aunt Etoile asked.

"Of course, Sarah is my only sister, really my only family now."

"I guess we don't count then," said Aunt Etoile.

"Of course you do. What I meant was on *my* side of the family. I'm really looking forward to having them, and young Felicia is no bother at all."

"She was kicked out of that school, wasn't she?" said Aunt Etoile. (Just why her mother's family had been a trial to Etoile, Winky had never quite understood.) "What was the name of it?"

"Chesney. Chesney Hall. But I still think they were harsh with the child."

"It was for cheating, wasn't it?" asked Aunt Etoile.

"No, no, for *heaven* sakes!" said Ann Carr. "She was only trying to help that other girl. I guess she was in the wrong, but I do think the school was too harsh. She's at Westover now. Sarah says she's talking just like a little Yankee."

"I hope she isn't marching about the streets with all that rabble."

"I hardly think so, but Sarah says she's much improved, even quite nice looking."

"I always thought she was nice looking," Winky said.

"And such a funny child," her mother said. "Oh dear." She smiled and Winky was thinking about the book Felicia had written about the family, *The Last of the Whitfields*. She had let everyone read it. "Even perfect strangers," had been Aunt Pett's cry.

"I'm giving up the shop," said Aunt Etoile.

Everyone looked at her startled, even Miss Boggs stopped smoothing out her dress.

"Why, Etoile!" said Ann Carr. "Whatever for?"

"Gussie and I talked it over yesterday." Gussie was her helper at the shop. "We're both getting on, and it's just getting too much. The tourists don't want to take things with them any more. You have to *send* the things in the mail and all those zip codes. People never know their zip codes, and you have to look them up at the post office."

"What will you do with it, then?" asked Ann Carr.

"I know exactly." She tossed her head and turned to Winky. "I've talked to Owen Ebaugh at the bank, and I'm going to turn it over to you, Winky."

Winky stared at the woman and for a moment was speechless.

"Yes, to you."

"To *me?*" Winky looked about the room and back to Etoile. "Aunt Etoile. What do you mean?"

"Just that exactly. You're mature now and can handle a business. Of course Gussie and I will help you until you feel easy with it."

Winky looked at her mother for help; her mother immediately lowered her head.

"Why I—I just don't know what to say," Winky said to the room at large.

Her mother then met Winky's eyes and then turned her

gaze to Etoile. "What a lovely thought, Etoile. Don't you think so, Winky? Etoile thinking of you in such a way."

"Yes, yes it is." Winky slowly placed her glass on the side table. "But—"

"I have it in my will," Etoile said. "But I've changed it now. I thought it would be nicer for you, Winky, to start with it now while I can help you with it." She tossed her head. "You can change the name, of course. 'Miss Etoile's' wouldn't be right for you."

"You can name it 'Miss Winky's,' " suggested Miss Boggs, crossing her hands in her lap and smiling benignly. "That would be cute, I think."

"Gracious me," said Ann Carr.

Winky was seeing the shop, a tiny cubbyhole with boxes and boxes of Peach Leather candy, greeting cards, prints of Charleston . . .

"Forty-two years," said Etoile. "I started the shop forty-two years ago when I was just about your age, Winky. Went through two wars, the depression. I've never asked anybody for anything, made my own way without a bit of help from anyone."

"You've been very brave, Etoile," said Ann Carr. "Just think, Winky, Etoile is giving you her life's work. How truly fine."

"Yes, yes it is," Winky said. A slow sense of claustrophobia was coming to her, the slight feeling of suffocation. She put her hand to her forehead; it was damp.

"You will have a much higher clientele than the average place," said Etoile proudly. "Goodness, the interesting people I've met through the shop. Once an English Lord came into the shop. A very pleasant man. He asked me to tea, and we corresponded for some years. I wonder what ever became of him. An interesting man. He liked the theatre. Would you fill my glass again, Winky?"

Winky took the glass, placed it unsteadily on the tray. The shortness of breath and the tingling in her arms were worse. "Oh, Mother," she said, "I just forgot." She put her fingers to her lips. "I can't be here for dinner."

"Oh?"

"I com-*pletely* forgot. A friend of mine, I knew her in school. She called yesterday. I promised her I'd come by to see her and her husband. They're staying at the hotel, the Fort Sumter." She glanced at her watch. "I've just time to run by there and then be at the Russell House. You will forgive me. I completely forgot."

"But, dear, you haven't had a thing to eat all day."

"I know. I'll pick up something." She turned to Aunt Etoile. "Please, I'm sorry." She began to back out of the room.

In the hall she picked up the car keys. She heard Aunt Etoile: "She certainly didn't sound very appreciative."

"Oh, I'm sure she is," her mother said. "Winky is very much like Petrie. You know he never really showed his feelings very much. But they ran very deep. Etoile, truly, how really lovely of you. How truly . . ."

Outside, Winky put her hand to her diaphragm and pressed it as if in this way she could force the fresh air into her lungs. She got in the car, placed the keys.

"But where shall I go? Who will I go to?"

In the house she had automatically thought of Tom. She would go to him, tell him everything:

"They're handing out Aunt Etoile's life for me, Tom. Miss Boggs wanted me to name it 'Miss Winky's' . . ."

And Tom would roar with laughter, in his own way

build her back again. For a little while. But Tom, too, was gone.

Ah God. For a moment, sitting there, she saw the days before her and she knew they would be so: She would take over Aunt Etoile's shop; she knew it. And the days would go by, year after year; the adjustment would slowly ease into her, and just as slowly the spirit would wither with it.

Oh, Walter, why? Why? Why was I not good enough?

She stepped on the accelerator, not knowing where she was going.

Her father's grave was enclosed in a black wrought-iron fence alongside the graves of other and older family members she had never known, small iron crosses marking their graves. Winky stood by the fence, staring down at her father's grave:

Why Art Thou Cast Down, O My Soul? She read the words, and it was almost as if she were hearing her father's voice so many times had she heard him read them. She stopped with the one line, then sat on the bench near the graves, noticing little things: the grass beginning to take hold now over the space where her father's body lay, the branches of the pink dogwood tipping the fence, and the leaning, weather-rusted cross at the head of her great great grandmother's grave.

She looked back at her father's grave. "You are there?" What a lonely place, a grave. Sometimes she felt closer to her father now that he was dead than she ever had when he was living. She sensed an omniscience as if he, dead, saw all the folly and wounds of the living and sensing she could cry out to him; whereas she was never able to do this while he lived, the barrier of pride having been between them then.

I'm afraid, father. I'm afraid of loneliness.

I know. I understand.

What shall I do? I'm so afraid, even of little things.
You must have courage.
But I shall be so alone, even the target for mockery, a withered maiden lady. Daddy, Daddy, can I bear it?
One can bear exclusion.
Can one? Oh, Daddy, can one? . . .
Winky sat on the bench near the graves. How long she sat there she did not know. It was so still. Only in the slow movement of the dogwood branch did there seem to be movement, and as she watched its lazy sweeping to and fro it lulled her, and, lulling, finally wearied. The fever so high in her earlier had taken its strength. She sat a while longer, wondering, calming, and then she rose and walked away.

The third group of tourists to come to the Nathaniel Russell House was a group of middle-aged women from a small town in Georgia somewhere. Winky saw them arriving by bus obviously in high spirits, on vacation from whatever life offered in their confined world. They were coifed in rainbow colors, following without fault the latest in magazine fashion, whether structure or bulge rebelled or not. Undoubtedly they were the town's "society"—competitive, jealous, yet oddly needing one another. Today they were all together, a strength in numbers. "We're having fun," they seemed to be saying.

Chatter. Chatter. Chatter. The woman named Sue seemed to be the leader of the group: "Oh, Sue, there's your lowboy. *Exactly!*" ". . . I knew you would adore this, Sue. Sue . . . Sue . . . Sue . . ." And Sue, the one in dark blue, the tallest, the thinnest, rarely responded. Adored Sue, envied Sue. Assured Sue. The village queen.

Winky took it all in. There had been many such groups

during the year. They were well-intentioned women, Winky was sure, and she often thought should she know them well, see them wholly, singly, perhaps she would discover even moments of nobility. But in group they were exasperating: their high-pitched voices, their aura of aging belles, their utter self-absorption grated.

Winky met them in the hall and began the same speech she had already given twice that afternoon:

"This is the Nathaniel Russell House. Mr. Russell was the son of a Chief Justice of Rhode Island, and he came to Charleston in the late seventeen hundreds. Charlestonians named him 'The King of the Yankees.' Whether this was meant as a compliment or not is not recorded." (Ripples of girlish laughter.) "Mr. Russell first lived on East Bay Street and later, in or about 1809, he built this house in the Adam style which was so popular in Charleston during . . ."

Winky moved closer to the staircase. "This is a free-flying stairway which curves upward to the third floor. As you can see, it never touches the wall." (Blankness from the women.) "Now, if you would join me in the dining room . . ."

Winky waited calmly for the women to gather. She had never felt so tired, exhausted, as if her whole body were weighted by some invisible object.

"Sue, there's your *screen! Exactly!*"

". . . You will notice the Hepplewhite table and sideboard. The chairs—"

"This room has been added onto, hasn't it?" said the woman in the yellow linen suit, almost defiance in her voice. "I can tell a new thing when I see it!"

"Yes," Winky said, hearing the weariness in her voice. "The room was made longer in the early nineteen hundreds, but it was almost identically copied from the original."

Buzz of chatter. "But it isn't like Williamsburg, Sue. *Every*thing there is new. I hated Williamsburg."

". . . Visitors are often interested in the matched chandeliers," Winky went on.

"I just knew that Mr. Russell didn't have that screen in his house," said yellow suit.

". . . Now, if you would like to join me upstairs, there are many interesting rooms to see."

"I knew I shouldn't have had that martini at lunch," said the woman with the gray bangs. "Imagine, wouldn't Bill just *dieeee*—me drinking at lunch."

Winky led the group up the stairway, paused, waited in the upstairs drawing room.

"Oh, the windows! I just luuuuve long windows."

"You could do that easily to your own house, Charlotte. Easy as pie."

"The mantel is classic Adam style," Winky started again.

"My *feet!* They're killing me."

". . . The mold was quite popular in Charleston at the time. This room was used for formal entertaining. The details were originally gold leafed."

Sigh. "Those days are gawne with the wind. It just makes me sayad."

". . . The painting over the mantel is by Angelica Kauffmann. The windows lead to balconies which look over the garden. The stucco-work on the door and window frames makes one of the more interesting Adam interiors in Charleston. You can see on this door the iris and . . ."

Methodically Winky continued through the rooms, pointing out details, pausing for remarks. When she had finished she thanked the ladies, suggested they might want to wander through the garden outside.

Two of the women came up to her smiling timidly. One was yellow suit, the other Sue.

"You're from Charleston, aren't you?" It was Sue, the leader, the admired.

"Yes. Yes, I am."

"What is your name?"

Winky hesitated. "Antoinette Carr."

"Carr? I don't believe I know that name."

Winky smiled at her.

"I'm related to the Pringney family here, way back, of course."

"How interesting."

"Did you go to Ashley Hall?" asked the woman in the yellow suit.

"In the lower school. Yes, I did." She gazed at the woman questioningly.

"I'm thinking of sending my daughter there."

"It's a very good school."

"I want her—," and she looked at Sue, "—to gather some of this atmosphere, you know. Charleston—," her voice heightened as if she were finishing a speech, "—is the last of the *real* thing. I mean the truly *real* thing."

Winky smiled at the woman again.

"But aren't you lucky?"

Winky must have shown her surprise.

"I mean to actually live in Charleston. You must be just the happiest person in the world. I'd just give anything to live in Charleston—the old-world charm, and people say it's so *gay*, parties all the time."

Winky gave a half laugh. "Charlestonians do have a nice time."

"Course if I lived here I'd want to be a part of it. You know what I mean. Is Charleston," the woman slumped her shoulders and gave Winky a teasing look, "as snooty as every-one thinks?"

"No, much of that is exaggerated."

"Oh, noooo it isn't," said Sue. "Mayhew and I came for a weekend last fall, and not one soul—not *one* spoke to Mayhew at the cocktail party our friends took us to."

"That must not have been very pleasant," Winky said, eyeing the stairway.

"Are you a member of the Junior League?" asked yellow suit.

"Yes."

"Are all you gulls who show the houses from the Junior League?"

"Many of us are, I guess."

"I have your cookbook, use it religiously."

"It's a good book," Winky said.

"Well, we just wanted to thank you for the tour," said yellow suit, "and tell you how *lucky* you are."

"Thank you," Winky said.

"I do hope you'll look up my child if she comes to Ashley Hall. I'm not being presumptuous, I hope."

"What is her name?"

"Mary Lee. Mary Lee Crowe."

"I'll remember the name."

"You're just a darling, and you lecture so *weye*ll."

"Thank you."

"Do you do this sort of thing all day?" asked Sue looking straight through Winky.

"No, just on occasions."

"What else do you do?"

Irritation was mounting. She must have shown it.

"Don't mind Sue," said yellow suit. "She's just trying to

gather material for her speech to our club. Aren't you, Sue? She's going to give a little talk on Charleston and Charlestonians—historical Charleston and modern-day Charleston—because of her connections here, you know."

"I don't do very much of anything just now. I plan to open a shop quite soon."

"Oh, how *fas*-cinating," said yellow suit. "We'll be on the lookout for it. Our club plans to come back next year. What will you name it?"

"I really haven't thought that far yet. My aunt has it now, 'Miss Etoile's.' "

"Oh, thayat place!" said yellow suit. "It's dahling. And that precious little old lady is your aunt!"

"Yes, she is."

Both women then glanced at Winky's hand, her finger. She recognized the look that followed: superiority, pride, pity and dismissal all combined, no threat, no threat anywhere.

"Well, you've certainly been nice."

"I hope you enjoyed the house." Winky began to back away.

"We *did*, and I hope we'll see you again next year. Remember how lucky you are. Remember, heah!"

The word rang in Winky's ears as she descended the stairway. Lucky. *Lucky*. LUCKY!

Downstairs Margaret Ritchie had begun her spiel to a new group:

"This is the Nathaniel . . ."

Winky fairly ran from the house.

Lucky. *Lucky*. LUCKY!!

Summer's end. September. And with it the beginning of cooler days. Charleston had been fortunate so far; no storms, no hurricanes, just the remembrance of summer, a long lazy hot season that seemed loath to go.

Now there were returnings once more. And the city eased itself into the coming season: The Dock Street Theatre would present its first play of the season September twentieth; schools and colleges were reopening; committees were reforming; sails were more spare on the water; and the Pringneys were entertaining with a large party in honor of their cousin, Charles Pringney, who with his "beautiful Frenchborn wife" would be visiting before returning to Paris.

Winky had always thought of September as a time for departure rather than returnings. But, as in most things, Charleston reversed itself in this. She said as much to her mother. It was twilight and the two of them were sitting on the piazza watching the curious shadows fade from the garden as night began to present itself.

"I remember packing," Winky said, "getting ready to go away to school, the excitement of seeing everyone again. Happy days."

"And busy," her mother said. "Oh dear."

"I thought I would always be going somewhere in September—if not school, New York, Paris, London. September always smelled like new clothes, airports and pieces of luggage. Everything seemed so possible." Winky leaned back in the chair. "It's sad to be left home in September."

"Not always," her mother said. "I'm just as content to be right here. It's so peaceful."

The oak tree far in the corner of the garden stood spreading before them like a tired old ghost. Winky said nothing. Yes, just to be going *some*where.

"How was the shop today?" her mother asked.

"The same."

"Many people in?"

"A few."

"Do you think you're getting more used to it now? Are you enjoying it more?"

"I guess. Charles Pringney's wife was in today looking very Parisian."

"Oh? Manette? Is she still as lovely as she was?"

"Yes, she's a beautiful woman."

"Charles always liked the pretty ladies."

"She was with Mary Pringney. I'm afraid Manette made a bit of a *faux pas*."

"Oh?"

"When they left Manette said, 'I vill see you tonight, Vinky.' "

"Oh dear. What did Mary say?"

"Nothing. But I know she heard."

"I still think it's strange."

"What?"

"That Mary didn't include us for tonight. It's really quite a large party, I hear."

"Oh, I don't know."

Her mother sighed. "That's the way it is when your husband dies. People tend to forget you. But I do think they should have included you."

"That's the way it is when you don't have a husband."

"Oh, Winky. Now don't."

"Don't what?"

"Don't get that attitude about things. Really, when you think of it, Mary Pringney doesn't owe you anything. You really should do a little entertaining yourself."

"I'm too tired. After all day at the shop I just don't feel like it. Maybe I just don't feel like it anyway."

"Etoile wasn't that way. Just think—she entertained, went to theatre practice, was very active in the city. She made a place for herself."

"Yes, she did."

"Well, honestly, Winky." There was irritation in her mother's voice. "If you don't like your life you ought to do something about it."

"Such as?"

"I don't know. Go somewhere else, find something you want to do."

Winky kept gazing at the oak tree. It was the same old argument. *Do something with your life. Do something.* "You know what I'd *like* to do?"

"What?"

"I'd like to go back to Scandinavia."

"What ever would you do there?"

Winky sat up. "I'd get a job—maybe with an embassy. I think I'd live in Copenhagen; no, Oslo. I liked Oslo. I'd have a little apartment, have friends in. I wouldn't mind the winters at all. I'd like them really."

She heard her mother sigh again.

"No, I'd adore that. I know people in Oslo. They're marvellous. I could sell the shop, get enough money to get me there anyway."

"And what would Etoile say?"

"I don't think she would mind too much. She understands, I think."

"Would—would young Everett be there?" There was caution in her mother's voice.

"I don't know. I don't know where Walter is. As far as I know he never married. Maybe he's in Lillehammer."

"Where?"

"Lillehammer, Norway. He said he wanted to live there. That's probably where he is."

The thought of Norway, going back there, had never really occurred to Winky before, not seriously. But now, talking about it, the longing to be there was so strong it was almost a hurt. She could feel the clean air, smell the aura of the small cafés, hear the sounds, all so different from the heaviness of Charleston's summer. Even if she could be there for a week that would be all she would ask.

"Oh dear, Winky. Dreams. I wish you could get your life settled. Just one dream after another."

"It isn't as much a dream as you may think," Winky said aloud, though she knew the impossibility of her words. The little barriers: money, practicality, the path that had already begun to be too fixed to seek another.

"Oh dear," her mother said again. Winky recognized the tone—the hurt, the worry. Her mother hadn't been well during the summer, nothing serious, just the same nagging complaints one after another.

"I'm sorry," Winky said then. "I guess I do like to dream."

"But aren't you at all happy with the shop? At first I thought you seemed to be enjoying it."

"Oh yes, I like it. I see people and that's good for me."

"But, dear, you *seem* so unhappy."

"Do I? I'm not, really."

"I just wish there were more young people here for you."

"They're here, but they're all tied up with babies and husbands and supper clubs." The dream of Norway vanished instantly.

"There's not much here for you, is there?"

"It isn't so bad."

Her mother was silent for a moment, and then, as if from a distance so quiet and still was her voice, she said: "Something will come along for you, Winky."

Winky turned to her. There was something in the look on her face. A wanting. That was it. A wanting to turn the world about so that the spring and loveliness could come to this daughter of hers. The wanting was so fierce.

"Oh, Mother. How dear you are. How truly dear. I don't mean to worry you with my little dreams. Really."

"Winky," the voice almost broke, "you make me want to cry. You were such an enthusiastic young girl."

"I still am!" Winky tried to laugh. "My life isn't over. I have years and years and—"

Her mother said nothing.

"Let's change the subject," Winky said. "What do you suppose they're doing at the Pringneys' just now? I hear they're having dancing. On the terrace." Winky glanced at her mother. "Don't you think it must be lovely?"

"What?"

"The Pringneys' party."

"Oh, yes."

"I remember the debut party they gave for me. Do you remember? There was— Isn't that where you and Daddy met? At the Pringneys'?"

"Yes."

"That always seems strange. I had always thought you two had sort of grown up together."

"Petrie was a few years older than I. I admired him from a distance only."

"You had a wonderful girlhood here in Charleston, didn't you?"

"Oh yes. I never knew an unhappy day, not really. But you had a happy childhood, too, Winky." Her mother was always saying that as if it were a proof of something.

"Yes, I did." It was true.

The shadows were deepening in the garden. The white chrysanthemums looked whiter. In a few minutes it would be totally dark.

"How changed everything is," her mother said. "I was just thinking—this house, just a few years ago how active everything was. Even though Petrie wasn't well his friends were always coming by, and Pett was her old self and— There was *such* a bustling."

"It does seem quiet," Winky said.

They listened to the night.

"Things have such a way of just dwindling away, don't they?" her mother said. "Just dwindling away." She sighed heavily and then rose. "I suppose I must go to see how Pett is. Are you coming?"

"Not just yet," Winky said. "I'll be in later."

Winky could hear her mother inside, opening the door to the library. During the summer they had made a bedroom there for Aunt Pett in order to avoid the stairs.

"Pett, Pett dear, are you all right?"

"Is that you, Ann?"

It was completely dark outside now. The tree with its

branches almost touching the ground was darker than the night. Winky wondered what the hour was in Oslo, if the long winter had come to the city yet. And all at once she remembered that night when she and Walter had first had dinner together at the restaurant on the water and how the lights shone from the ships further out and how she had said: "Look! If you lean just far enough you can almost touch the water!" There had been all the magic and excitement of beginning discovery as if the world, too, were beginning.

Couldn't, wouldn't that one night come again?

Things have such a way of just dwindling away, don't they?

And then for no particular reason she burst into a flood of tears. "Ah God! God! Give me your light."

But out there in the dark only the city, the Dowager, heard. And hearing, smiled. For once more she had claimed her own. Sly old woman, counting her jewels. This one, she thought, the one weeping, she would hold forever until, of course, it grew too old, lost, and finally went its way into earthly dust.

The wind blew the moss, and the twin rivers ran fast: Old Ashley. Old Cooper. The Dowager howled. Winter was coming.